Second Thoughts

Book Two of the Sententia

Cara Bertrand

LUMINIS BOOKS

www.carabertrand.com
www.thesententia.com

Hardcover ISBN: 978-1-935462-07-1
Paperback ISBN: 978-1-935462-12-5

Cover Design by Brit Godish
Images courtesy PhotoXpress.com

LUMINIS BOOKS

Meaningful Books That Entertain

This one is for Kristine, who's always an inspiration.

Praise for *Lost In Thought*
Amazon/Penguin Breakthrough Novel Award Finalist

"...my pick for the winner, a fantastic novel trying to break free...The boarding school setting is a lot of fun, and the chemistry with Carter snaps...Lainey and Carter begin exploring the provenance of Lainey's Legacy, the true extent of her powers, and just how those powers might be manipulated, the book starts to pick up momentum, leading to an action-packed ending with a twist that will leave readers clamoring for the next installment." – Gayle Forman, *New York Times* Bestselling Author of *If I Stay*

"...the novel is full of characters teen readers will enjoy spending time with, especially Lainey's vivacious roommate, Amy, and Carter, the mysterious and swoon-worthy love interest...a nice dose of romance, mystery, and supernatural thrills keeps the pages turning." – Jennifer Besser, Vice President and Publisher of G.P. Putnam's Sons Books for Young Readers

"The tale of Lainey Young's journey from being a seemingly normal girl with a secret to an extraordinary girl with many secrets will draw readers in and leave them wanting more! Cara Bertrand's sharp writing makes the unbelievable utterly believable, and the well-drawn characters likeable and equally despicable and, in Carter's case, irresistible. Tinged with mystery from page one, *Lost in Thought* keeps readers guessing from beginning to end, and will appeal to paranormal romance fans of all ages." – Amy Ackley, author of *Sign Language*

"Compelling and solid, this paranormal thriller has it all: love, murder, intrigue, mind games, and a bit of mystery." – *Publishers Weekly*

"X-Men meets teen romance…Fans of paranormal romance will find a lot to like in *Lost in Thought*; this vividly written tale sets the stage for an exciting series to come." – Jill Baguchinsky, author of *Spookygirl*

"…a quietly compelling supernatural romance. A promising start to a series that will find a fan base." – Danielle Serra, *School Library Journal*

"*Vampire Academy* meets *Spellbound*…Simply put, *Lost in Thought* is an absolute must. You'll fall in love with the shocking story and amazing ending." – Samantha Pomier, *Girls' Life Magazine*

"Fans of paranormal romance, as well as readers who enjoy stories that delve into 'what-if,' will certainly enjoy this first installment from Bertrand." – Beth Green, *VOYA*

"I very much enjoyed this book. I love weird goings-on at boarding schools, but this book is not as Lois Duncan as I was expecting… even though it's definitely paranormal, it feels very contemporary, too. Recommended. – *kellyvision*

"Cara Bertrand has created a world I intend to visit again…with the next book." – booksandwhatnot.com

Prologue

*M*y boyfriend is going to kill me.

It was the same thought I woke to every single morning, bolting upright in bed before reminding myself sternly that he only might kill me. The future was never definite.

I would change this.

If I could.

Chapter One

L egs a little wider, Lainey," Carter's voice sounded in my ear. "Good." He reached around me and pushed my arms up a little higher. *"Perfect."*

"I'm really getting better at this, aren't I?" Probably I shouted, but I couldn't help it.

"You're a natural," he replied. It sounded like a whisper. He caressed my arm once more. "Okay, shoot."

I sighted the target down the barrel of my Smith and Wesson and fired.

After ten rounds, I clicked the safety into position and lowered my gun, pulling off my earmuffs and safety glasses as the target came whirring up the motorized track.

"Very nice, Lainey," Jeff Revell, Carter's uncle, said from a short distance away. "All ten hits. I'm impressed."

I smiled over my shoulder at him. "Thanks! It might be my best round yet."

Carter stepped up behind me again, pulling the target out of the clip while scanning it over. "Definitely. I'm impressed too." He leaned in and kissed me lightly on the cheek, his lips lingering close to my ear, where he really did whisper this time, "And I didn't even help."

I elbowed him in the ribs. "You're right," I agreed. "You *didn't* help. Sometimes I think you *try* to mess me up." He just laughed and squeezed my arm before putting on his own ear protection and glasses and stepping up to his booth. I knew what he'd really meant though. With his Thought Mover abilities, Carter could "help" with my shooting in a way no one else could. I considered it cheating and had expressly forbidden him from doing it.

We were in the private range at the local rifle club, a place I never thought I'd visit let alone become a member. But it was a popular destination around Northbrook Academy, in the northwest corner of Massachusetts, and over the summer, it had become one of my favorites. When Carter first told me about his surprising hobby, I'd freaked out and refused to ride in his car if there was a gun in it. Of course, he'd laughed and explained he never *carried* a gun. He kept them at the range, and now I did too.

Shooting with the two of them came with definite benefits. First, they were both crack shots and excellent instructors. Second, because of Jeff's retired military status and their long-time membership, they got all sorts of privileges, including regular use of the private range. The general club range was larger, louder, and constantly bustling with distractions. I always shot better in the private room, where there were only three stalls, soundproofed walls, and never any outside observers. A private gallery kept anyone watching hidden and silent behind a dark pane of mirrored, one-way glass.

"Another round?" Carter asked, after he and Jeff looked over their nearly perfect targets. They'd stay all afternoon given the chance.

But after getting up early for a final shift at one of my summer jobs—as the counter waitress at Dad's Diner, where Carter and I had gone on our first "date"—I was exhausted. "Can't," I told him. "My arms are shaking, and I need a nap all the way until tomorrow."

"Back to reality," Carter said as he walked me to the parking lot. He grinned, but it was forced, more a sigh than a smile. Neither of us reached for our keys as we stood together. When we left, it would mean the end of our weeks of summer fun, filled with trips to the beach, trips to the shooting range, and zero hours of homework.

"Back to work," I said, leaning on my car and pulling Carter closer. "Back to studying."

"Back to you *distracting me* from studying."

He rested his hands on my hips with a *real* smile this time and kissed the end of my nose. "I am an *excellent* study partner."

"If I don't want to study." I pushed on his chest with my palm but it didn't move him. I left my hand there, where I could feel his heartbeat, and he leaned in to kiss me again.

"How about, back to friends and fires in the fireplace? It's not *all* bad."

"Back to sweaters and boots and no-more-tan," I countered. "Goodbye, beach weather."

"Hello good running weather."

"You'll miss the beach, too."

He shook his head, leaning in even further. "No, I'll miss *you* on the beach. I like fall."

"Well, I like summer, and *you,* so I'll miss the beach *and* all the extra time with you."

"Then I'll have to make the most of the time we've got."

He kissed me goodbye with an enthusiasm that made his words into a promise and I didn't want to let go. I didn't *ever* want to let go. If I could have folded myself into Carter's kisses and lived in them, I would have. Finally, I pulled back, leaning my head against his broad chest and closing my eyes.

If only I knew how much *time we had,* I thought to myself, before lightly tracing my fingers up Carter's arm. He hugged me tighter then, and I melted into his embrace, wishing it was the whole reason for my touch.

But it wasn't.

As soon as I brushed his bare skin, I opened my Grim Diviner senses—the ones that told me how people died or were *going to die*—to try again to see my future more clearly. A few months ago, when I foresaw that *I* was going to die, and that somehow Carter would be the cause, there were no details to tell me how or when.

But despite checking once, twice, twelve times a day since, there was still nothing new.

I'D MEANT WHAT I told Carter before we left the range—I couldn't wait to get back to my room and sleep all the way until the students arrived tomorrow.

When I finally walked up to Marquise House, my dorm, I discovered a pale blue chair outside the building. I stared at it, admiring how the soft fabric matched the sky. It looked comfortable, like I could curl up in it and read a book or fall asleep right there on the front porch. I contemplated doing either of those things, but I already knew exactly how comfortable the chair would be. When I'd left that morning, it had been located in my room.

I looked around and considered the possibilities. One, I'd been robbed. If that was the case, they weren't very good at it and had left behind a huge and expensive piece of evidence. Or two, Amy Moretti, my roommate and absolutely best friend in the world, had come back to campus a day early. I hurried up the stairs to find out why our furniture was leaving the building.

The second I opened the door to my room, I slammed it shut in front of me. Maybe I *had* been robbed. Either that, or I was at the wrong room—the place was a mess, furniture pushed around haphazardly and half-covered in sheets, and the wrong *color*. It used to be blue, like the chair. The walls behind this door bore a mix of soft and darker, gem-toned green.

A glance down the familiar hall confirmed I was in the right place. When I reopened the door, sure enough, there was my roommate, smiling at me from beneath a liberal spattering of green paint. She looked like she had the measles and I laughed as she engulfed me in a hug.

"Lainey!" she shrieked. "Oops! Sorry. I hope I didn't get paint on you, but where the hell have you *been?!* I've been here since, like, *sunrise!* We're almost done, and you didn't even get to help."

I pulled away, a huge smile testing the limits of my face even though my shirt looked like it had caught her illness. "I'm sorry. If I'd *known* you were coming, I would have made sure to be here…not that it looks like you needed my help. I didn't realize we were making changes." Amy and her mother, who'd waved at me from where she was hidden behind about twenty bags full of new pillows, towels, and other decorations, really must have been there all day working on redecorating.

"Well, I wanted to surprise you!" Amy tugged me further into the mess. "You're going to need a new comforter and sheets, by the way; I'll help you order them later. The old look was nice and all, but it was just so—*calm.* We're seniors now! I thought we should have something a little spicier."

Our room was definitely spicier, I'd give her that. The colors were rich, but not garish, and made me think of one of the beautiful royal bedrooms at the Palace of Versailles, a place I'd visited back when I was still a world traveler. Only Amy could have orchestrated this transformation, and only at Northbrook would it even be allowed. "I love it," I told her truthfully. "And you know I default to you on all questions of style and decorating."

She giggled and hugged me again. "Of course you love it, silly. I have excellent taste, *and* I have a surprise for you. Mr. Valser and my dad are getting ready to bring it up!"

The surprise was actually accompanied not only by Mr. Valser, the grounds manager, and Dr. Moretti, but also Caleb Sullivan, Amy's boyfriend, and *his* father too. I heard them struggling down the hall before Caleb kicked open the door with a grunt.

"Shit, Ame," he said, then swallowed and glanced apologetically at Amy's father. "I mean, *shoot,* sorry Dr. Moretti, but this thing weighs a *ton.* We barely got it up here!"

This thing was possibly the most amazing antique divan I'd ever seen. My mouth dropped open as I took in the pristine chartreuse silk, gilt woodwork, and thick rolled arms on each end. It looked like a piece that *could* have come from a palace bedroom. I didn't care how much it weighed, or how big of a pain it would be to get out of the room at the end of the year, because antique furniture was my first true love and this baby was going to live with me.

"Hello, beautiful," I breathed, trying hard not to drool. Amy glowed with self-satisfaction.

"Suck it up, Caleb," she said with a mock scowl. "You need to get back in shape for swimming anyway. You're getting paunchy." Which was hardly true. Caleb was about five feet ten inches of solid muscle. Amy poked his not-paunchy stomach before turning her beaming smile back on me. "I *knew* you'd love it! We found it over the summer and I designed the whole room around it. You'll never believe how cheap it was, either. A total steal, you'd be proud of me. Daddy even said you could keep it at the end of the year, right Daddy?" Her father was out of breath as they struggled to maneuver the couch into place but he managed to nod and smile at me.

"Well that's great news," Caleb huffed, "because that means *your* boyfriend can carry it back down the stairs."

"I'm sure that won't be a problem," I joked, forgetting momentarily that it might. That I might not be here when it was time to move out.

HOURS LATER, AFTER our room was rearranged and redecorated, our stomachs were fed, and Amy's parents were long gone, the two of us lounged in our own beds, exhausted. We left the windows open to dispel the lingering scent of paint, making the room cool and filling it with the complex symphony of the woods at night, chirps and howls and wind through leaves. I snuggled under my soon-to-be-replaced comforter. I was surprised my eyes were still open, but after nearly three months of essentially living by myself, I was excited to have my roommate back.

"Have you thought any more—" I started to say, but Amy cut me off completely.

"No, so stop asking." She fluffed her brown curls out around her, and I knew her peevishness wasn't *entirely* an act. We were both stressed about the big college decisions we were facing, sooner rather than later. "I have months to declare a major, right?"

"Sorry. I'm just curious what you're going to choose."

"Me too," she said lightly, but then frowned. "Daddy still wants me to go pre-med."

"But that's not what *you* want to do."

"Yeah. It's not. I don't want to be a surgeon, Lainey. I don't want to cut people open." She grimaced. I didn't blame her for that one. She turned onto her side and propped her head on her hand. "It must be nice to know exactly what you want to do, huh?"

I laughed. "I suppose. It must be nice to know exactly where you want to *go.*" Despite that we hadn't quite started our senior year, Amy, teen genius, had already applied and been accepted early decision to MIT. And while I knew I would go to business school, since *I'd* dreamed of running my own antiques business since I was about thirteen, which one was weighing heavily on my mind.

"You know you love Boston…" She'd been encouraging me for months to come to the city with her, even if I was at a different school.

"I do," I told her. "And it's a top contender, I promise. But…I don't want to disappoint Aunt Tessa either." My "Aunt" Tessa had actually been my mother for as long as I could remember. She wasn't technically my aunt, but really my Godmother. She also, I knew, hoped I'd choose her alma mater in Baltimore, where she'd met my parents and I'd been born.

"Lane, seriously, you could run away to join the circus and not disappoint your aunt. She'll be happy with you no matter what."

I wasn't sure that was true, but it was funny. "I'd make a great trapeze artist, don't you think? Maybe I should consider it. Where's a good circus school?"

Amy giggled too, but I could tell she was fading fast. Not before she had one more question though. "And Carter…?"

"Tiger trainer?"

"Hot! In leather pants with a whip…*that* would bring people to the circus." We laughed for real before she said, "Seriously though? What's he doing?"

Ah, the current mystery of Northbrook Academy: why Cartwright Penrose hadn't gone to college yet. Not that much of the student body minded, since it meant he still worked almost daily at the bookstore. It had a great lounge with couches, chairs, and a huge fireplace, and tall, handsome, devastatingly flirtatious Carter was a popular attraction. Lucky for me, he was *my* boyfriend.

"He's…seriously considering Boston too," I said. Technically he'd been top of his class at Northbrook when he'd graduated two years ago and a full scholarship to pretty much anywhere was virtually guaranteed. "And, well, basically any city I'm considering, or close."

"Wow. That's big, Lane. You'd actually go to college together?"

"Not the same school, but…yeah, I think he'll choose near wherever I do." Actually, I knew he would. Over the summer, he told me so, reciting his list of potential colleges arranged geographically to coincide with mine. The idea of it both thrilled and scared me. I didn't want to have a long-distance relationship, but then again, I was afraid he was following me instead of his dreams. Maybe I should have been overjoyed by that, because I *did* love Carter, totally and absolutely, but I also couldn't shake the feeling that it was too much pressure.

"Wow," Amy repeated. "I wish Caleb would be so definite about it."

She was quiet after that, and before long I could tell she'd drifted off to sleep. I clicked off the reading light next to my bed and waited to fall asleep myself. I expected it would happen instantly, but it's never that easy when you want it to be. I kept thinking about college, and Carter too.

As always, the thought lingered in my mind that maybe I wouldn't have to make any lasting decisions anyway. Carter *was* going to kill me, after all.

Maybe, I reminded myself as I finally fell asleep.

Chapter Two

I woke with a start the next morning, surprised to find I was alone. Of the two of us, I was the early riser. Amy slept as late as possible whenever possible. I'd just gotten my roommate back and already she was gone.

A hastily scribbled note on the board tacked next to our door told me she was helping Caleb with move-in over at his dorm. I smiled to myself as I slipped out of bed and over to the bathroom. Not that I ever questioned it, but this was just one more confirmation of how incredibly and crazily in love Amy was with Caleb Sullivan: she willingly got up extra early to devote her day to physical labor just to spend a little time with him. I understood though. I'd do the same just to be near Carter.

In reality, I'd do just about anything to be near Carter, not limited to running, occasionally shelving books at the store, and learning to shoot a gun. I'd risk my own *life*. If it seemed crazy that I'd be so desperate for his company despite that he was—*maybe*—going to kill me, it probably was. I knew this. It just didn't change how I felt about him.

The first things I *should* have done, after I had the vision, were 1) *tell him* about the vision and 2) Divine what other death he'd somehow caused. My mind went back and forth over which should've been one or two. But what I did was neither. Despite the certainty from the vision that he'd caused a death before, not a single part of me could believe Carter would hurt someone—hurt *me*—intentionally. And having just been through a serious trauma at the time, I couldn't handle another.

I couldn't handle being wrong.

So the longer I didn't tell him and didn't try to Divine his past, through the whole summer and into the unofficial start of autumn, the less likely it seemed I'd do either. Instead, I spent every possible moment with him *not* doing either of those things. I liked to tell myself the more time I spent with him, the more chances I'd have to catch glimpses of that frightening future and be prepared to change it.

That's what I told myself anyway.

Mostly, I was in love. Hopelessly, stupidly in love. And even though that was true, there was still one other thing we'd *not* been doing. Despite the long, romantic summer, and one almost-night, I was hesitant to take that next big step. In my mind, if I was hesitant it meant I wasn't ready. Even if I might die before I was. Even facing the distinct possibility of dying, reckless abandon just wasn't my style.

Showered and cozy in my bathrobe, I sat down for the first time on our magnificent new-old divan. And was jolted out of thoughts of my own death by the visions of not one but two others.

I leaped up from the soft silk upholstery and nearly fell backwards over the ottoman. I stared at the pretty green sofa with new eyes. No wonder Amy had gotten such a great deal on what should have been a several thousand dollar piece: it was from an insane asylum. Literally.

The visions showed me the psychiatrist's plush office in the otherwise dreary mental hospital where the divan had previously resided. As if that wasn't creepy enough, two patients had *died* on it, after going into hysterics and being forced to swallow some kind of narcotics.

Even worse, I couldn't tell if their deaths were accidental or intentional.

I shuddered. A Grim Diviner's day could be full of unwelcome surprises. I wasn't sure if I'd be able to sit on our new couch anymore, or how I'd explain my reluctance to Amy.

Perhaps the worst part, for me anyway, was that these were the first unbidden visions I'd had in weeks. Since I'd been working with my gift for nearly ten months, I'd obtained a significant amount of control over it. I thought of it like a muscle, my Diviner sense, one that the more I worked, the stronger it had become. Usually now it only did what *I* told it to do.

Classes didn't start for three more days, but that didn't mean there was nothing to do. Summer vacation was over, even if the warm weather was not. I tied my long, dark hair up in a ponytail, donned my Northbrook Academy T-shirt and workout pants, and headed across campus to help initiate the new students.

After enjoying a summer gig giving campus tours to incoming students, I'd volunteered this year to be the upper-class representative for a seventh and eighth grade dorm. Some of the student reps, including Caleb, actually lived in the bigger dorms in exchange for free room and board, much to Amy's chagrin. His was the hardest one to sneak in and out of.

Sanderson House, the dorm I was responsible for, wasn't nearly so large, but just as challenging in its own way. I didn't have to live with them, but I *did* have thirty mostly wealthy young teen girls to contend with. And, to make it even harder, most of those girls, like me, were part of a group of people who all had some form of what most of the world called extrasensory perception. Amongst each other, we simply called ourselves Sententia, and what we could do, we called that Thought. Besides helping the girls move in, I'd be the upperclassman they could approach with problems or for advice. Like getting along with roommates, or adjusting to living away from home…or how to deal with a newly developed ability to divine deaths. Just as an example.

All day I helped talkative girls and their families haul boxes up and down the stairs of Sanderson, directed the first-time students to the bookstore to pick up their start-of-year packages and supplies, and helped dry up tears. I was enormously thankful it wasn't raining or too hot. Even though it was almost a perfect late-summer day in New England, by the afternoon I was sweaty and exhausted.

When all their parents were finally gone, and all their belongings had been perfectly arranged, we gathered in Sanderson's first-floor lounge. I wanted a little time to catch my breath and try to remember all of their names before hitting the chaos dinner hours were sure to be. I decided to let the girls ask any burning questions they might have had while we were in the general quiet of our dorm. What they wanted to know surprised me, though it probably shouldn't have.

They stared at me blankly for a minute—maybe this *hadn't* been the great idea I thought it was—before a cute seventh grader was first to raise a tentative hand. I smiled and nodded.

"Is it true that Carter from the bookstore is your boyfriend?" she asked. She was a little wide-eyed but not exactly shy. Several of the other girls giggled and nodded their heads.

I laughed. "Well, I suppose this is the first lesson for the new girls: nothing is secret around here and word travels fast. Yes, it's true. Who told you about it?"

A different girl, another first-time student, chimed in. "*He* told me about it," she said. "He asked where I was living, and when I told him, he said that you were his girlfriend. He's *really* cute."

"Does he have a younger brother?" yet another girl asked, and they all laughed.

Before I could say anything, a voice from the back of the room caught me completely unprepared. It came from a new eighth grader who I'd almost immediately given the label of *future most popular girl in school.* She was slim and blond, already beautiful in a sophisticated way even at only thirteen or fourteen, and, between her parents and her luggage, struck me as possibly the wealthiest girl in Sanderson. I was pretty sure her name was Amanda, maybe Mandi for short.

"Is it true that his ex-girlfriend kissed him in front of everyone at the Winter Ball last year and then later she *died,* until you saved her anyway? Even after she kissed him?" She sounded not curious but…almost smug. The other new girls looked shocked and murmured among themselves at the scandal of it.

My mouth opened and closed once before I gathered my wits to respond. "Er. Yes, I guess all of that is true too, and I did save Jill. But I don't think Carter told you about it…"

She shook her head and smiled at me, a knowing smile that caused my stomach to twist and put me on guard, which I *should* have been on since I first met her, had I known. "No. My cousin Alexis did."

Ah ha. That explained a lot. I could see some family resemblance now despite the different last names and hair colors. I wondered if Alexis had also told her little cousin that *she'd* kissed my boyfriend on the night of the Winter Ball too, and that I'd slapped her for it. Probably not. And obviously, *I* still had the guy, despite that Alexis was the hands-down most beautiful and popular girl on campus and had been making her play for Carter for years. Now I knew I'd have to keep my eye on Amanda just as much as her cousin.

"Well, Alexis would know about those things," I said, and I applauded myself for being polite. "I'm sure she's told you all about Northbrook." Amanda just smiled sweetly and leaned over to whisper to the girl next to her. I resisted the urge to sigh. I didn't want a girl rival in my own grade, let alone her Mini-Me to contend with in my group of advisees. But I didn't have any choice about it either, so I just continued our get-to-know-each-other session with a smile of my own and an enthusiastic, "So, any more questions?"

We made it through the rest of the evening without any more awkwardness, but truth be told, I was a little distracted. Once Amanda had mentioned her, I couldn't stop thinking about Jillian Christensen. Jill.

Yes, it was true, she'd kissed Carter at the Winter Ball. She wasn't his ex-girlfriend though, actually more like his cousin. She was Daniel Astor's daughter and had been in love with Carter for years. Also, little -known fact about her: she'd tried, and nearly succeeded, to kill me. The only reason *she'd* died and I saved her was because I used my Hangman gift—the one that let me stop a person's heart with just a touch and a Thought—for the first and only time. It was that or die myself, and I really didn't want to die.

I thought about Jill a lot. That tended to happen when you killed someone. Or she tried to kill you. Despite knowing I'd do it again if I had to, I felt incredibly guilty about the whole thing. It was difficult carrying so many secrets around all the time, and this was the biggest one. My exterior bruises had healed in a few weeks, but the ones inside were the most difficult to deal with. Amanda's comment had picked the scab and made it bleed all over again.

I WAS STILL thinking about her in the morning as I made an early trip to meet with Headmaster Stewart. To get there, I followed the same route I'd once watched Jill take as she scurried away from my dorm, where she'd been spying on me. And Carter, having our first kiss. Sometimes I forgot that moment wasn't as private as it should have been.

Administration was one of my favorite buildings on campus, with its improbable lavender siding and mix of a modernly functional office with a quirky collection of antiques. It was early, so the building was as quiet as a centuries-old Victorian ever is. I climbed lightly up the stairs to the headmaster's office, where I found her in the anteroom, sipping her customary tea and waiting for me. She looked the same as always—tall, imposing, unflinchingly alert and in command.

"Good morning, Lainey. Prompt as always."

"I heard you have croissants if you get here early enough and I didn't want to miss them."

She actually smiled before gesturing to the breakfast spread laid out on her sideboard. "Help yourself." There was *always* the best food in Dr. Stewart's office, no matter the time of day.

My relationship with the headmaster was…different from other students. Not that we were friends or anything, but I liked her. I was pretty sure she liked me. We'd come to understand each other a lot better after what I called the *Jillian Incident*. Usually I wouldn't be so casual with her, but this was a casual meeting. A formality, really. Every student met privately with the headmaster at least once at the beginning of the year, for introduction or reacquaintance, but I'd seen her all the time over the summer.

Though just because it was casual didn't mean it wasn't important. After we'd settled into chairs in her office, she said, "I've reviewed your schedule, of course. It's appropriately rigorous, as I expected. How are you feeling about this year?" She watched me over the rim of her china cup.

Never lie to Headmaster Stewart is the first thing new students learn at Northbrook. If they're Sententia, they know it's because you, literally, *can't*. Her gift tells her whether she's hearing the truth, so I considered my answer carefully. "Excited, but nervous," I finally said.

She nodded. "That's understandable. Most seniors feel the same way, you know."

I did, but, "I'm not sure they're nervous about the same things. Or all the same things."

"Elaborate."

I took a bite of the famed croissants, swallowed. "Well, Jill, for one."

Dr. Stewart lowered her tea and looked at me. "Surely you know Jillian won't be returning to Northbrook."

"Oh." I didn't know. Maybe I should have suspected, or Carter should have told me, if he even knew. None of us liked to talk about the *Jillian Incident,* least of all him. I wasn't sure if it made me feel better or worse that she wouldn't return, but at least I wouldn't have to see her on campus. Now I had a feeling I'd never see her again. "But her Legacy?"

"Elaine," she said. Just the way she pronounced my name reminded me of her authority and my inexperience. Even though we got along, I was still a student, sometimes a foolish one. "Jillian is…not well. Regardless, she couldn't return to this school, where she attacked a student—*you*. No matter how few people know or who her father is."

I swallowed again. "Does Senator…is Senator Astor okay with that?"

"It was never a question."

I wouldn't have long to wait before I was finally introduced to Senator Daniel Astor in person, since, besides my aunt, he'd be the guest of honor in a few weeks at the debut of her sculpture installation. He'd been very understanding after what had happened between his daughter and me, but I still couldn't shake my dread over meeting him. If I couldn't forgive myself, how possibly could he?

And then a small voice inside me, one I tried to ignore but couldn't, kept telling me I couldn't trust him. I hated that voice, but it wouldn't go away. Sometimes when I heard it, it sounded like Jill and her crazy ramblings while she strangled me. Other times it sounded like me, asking why had everyone believed Jill and her father had no contact with each other when it wasn't true? I knew I'd caught him in a lie. I wondered if Dr. Stewart ever had.

I set down my breakfast plate, no longer hungry, and shifted in my chair. Outside, the rising sun played peek-a-boo through the trees, throwing patterns of shadow on the floor below the windows. "What's he like?" I asked.

Dr. Stewart thought for a few seconds. "He's our leader."

"I know, but—" A slight narrowing of her eyes told me she hadn't been finished. I shut up and listened.

"He's patient. A fine virtue," she reminded me with another pointed look. The headmaster tapped one finger lightly on her teacup while she chose her words, and I could see a worn spot in the glaze that told me she did it often. "I think you'll find the senator much like his nephew, minus the impetuousness that makes Cartwright so difficult sometimes."

I smiled into my own cup, swirling the remains of my coffee. She knew Carter well. Without taking too much time to think about what I was going to say, I blurted out, "Does Senator—do the two of you still talk about me?"

"Of course. You know how important you are. For a number of reasons."

"That's another thing I'm worried about."

"The Perceptum, you mean," she said and I nodded. I was glad I didn't have to explain for her to understand. I worried about the Perceptum and, specifically, its Council—the unofficial but very real and very serious governing body of all Sententia—often, almost as often as the man who headed it. For the other Sententia students, it was basically a given that they'd become members after graduation. But for me, it was different. As the last known Hangman, or *Carnifex* in the old

Latin, it was my talent they wanted most. "We don't choose our gifts, Lainey," Dr. Stewart continued. "Only how to use them."

"That's just it. What I'd have to do…" I trailed off, unsure exactly how to finish. It was a lot of things, most of which I was sure I couldn't stomach. The Perceptum Council protected the most important and pretty much only code Sententia followed: to be discreet with our abilities. Occasionally the Council determined a person, and their abilities, were too big a threat to do anything but "eliminate" them. Or in other words, *kill them*. That's where I'd come in. "Don't you think there's another way?"

Dr. Stewart shook her head. "No, I don't. Elimination is not a whim; it's a last resort, for the most egregious abusers and most dangerous. It's justice, and protection. If there's another way, we haven't found it yet."

And that was the problem.

Before I could say anything more, ask another question for which there was no good answer, Dr. Stewart moved from her chair to stand before two of her wide windows. She glanced back at me, and I joined her, surprised by the view. I could see my dorm, the ponds, most of campus. Between two of the newer buildings, I could even see the gates, and all the way across the street to Penrose Books. The sun had risen enough now to light the tops of the buildings and trees a glowing orange.

"I'd like you to do something, Elaine," Dr. Stewart said, "that I think will help you understand."

"What is it?"

"I'd like you to join the Honor Board. Ms. Kim has already nominated you. If she hadn't, I'd have submitted your name myself."

Wow. Honor Board *was* an honor, and a serious commitment. It reviewed and determined disciplinary actions for student infractions, things like cheating and other rule-breaking. It was also, now that I compared them, pretty similar to the Perceptum Council. Just without the secrecy and the killing.

"But I'm only a second year!"

Dr. Stewart shrugged, actually *shrugged*. If I hadn't been so shocked by the Honor Board nomination, I wouldn't have believed my eyes. Maybe she'd been spending too much time with me. A hint of a smile before she spoke told me she'd done it on purpose. "That's all that's required. That, and a stellar academic and participation record, and a disposition the faculty deems worthy."

"Thank you," I said. "Of course I'll do it. I promise to do my best."

"Bah." Dr. Stewart waved one of her slender hands. "It's not about 'your best.' You'll do admirably because it's what the position demands and you're suited to it. Honor Board is a challenge. You'll succeed."

I nodded, unsure what else to say. We stood there, at the windows, and I wondered if the headmaster simply enjoyed the view. A few moments later, I realized she was waiting for something, when Carter appeared, nearly sprinting down the main hill. He slammed to a stop at the gates before checking his watch and pacing back and forth to cool down.

"Is that…?" I asked, though who else would it be? Even from here, I could recognize the rise and fall of his strong shoulders, the caramel hair, lit by the pale sunshine and curling at the ends where it was damp. He looked beautiful, unreal.

"Every morning. I admire Cartwright's dedication, another trait he shares with the senator."

"You know, I wondered why you scheduled our meeting so early."

A gleam in her eye told me I amused her more than I irritated her. By way of answer, she said, "The school is blanketed in potential before it fully wakes, while one of its brightest students haunts the grounds." She was quiet for a second and I realized that she didn't hate Carter like he thought she did, not at all. She wanted more from him. Maybe everyone did. "Speaking of dedication," she added, "I think you'll find the senator is as devoted to his 'nephew' as he is to the Perceptum."

We said our goodbyes, the headmaster and I, but there was one thing I couldn't say to her, a secret she didn't share. Though I wanted to be part of the Honor Board, I was sure that all the practice with it could never erase my fear of the Perceptum. More than what they wanted me to do, the reason I hated them was this: they held Carter's life in their hands.

Only a few people—fewer than knew I was the last Marwood— knew that, like me, Carter was dual-gifted. Outwardly, he was just another Penrose, a *Lumen* with a brainiac gift, blessed with a perfectly photographic memory. Underneath, however, he was a telekinetic Thought Mover of unheard of power.

Unlike other Sententia, Carter's gift was *not* limited by proximity. He could move anything he'd seen once before, no matter where it was. And *that* kind of gift was exactly what the Perceptum would see as too powerful to be allowed to exist, regardless of how Carter used it or didn't. His family and Senator Astor's devotion to keeping his secret were all that stood between Carter and an almost certain death penalty.

So yeah, to say that I feared the Perceptum was a bit of an understatement. I loathed them, just on principal, and promised myself I would never have any connection to them.

Until I discovered I already did.

Chapter Three

This is so exciting," Amy called from where she leaned over our bathroom sink applying mascara. "Almost like getting ready for the Winter Ball, only more sophisticated."

I laughed. "I guess so." October had arrived like a blink, and with it, Aunt Tessa's art unveiling. Despite that she'd spent months planning, creating, and installing it, I still didn't know what it was. She'd forbidden me from seeing it, and though I could have peeked in the weeks since she finished her work, I knew that would disappoint her. So I kept my word and stayed out of the Auditorium and its lobby until the big day. Today.

I slipped on my sleek black heels and inspected myself in the full-length mirror on the back of our door. In the reflection, I caught Amy looking at me from the bathroom doorway, a funny smile on her face.

I smoothed my hands over my slim black satin pants. "What? Don't you like my outfit?"

Her smile widened. "No, I love your outfit. Those pants are outrageous. In a good way."

"Thanks…But so what's with the look?"

"It's just this is like the first time ever where you're the confident one, taking me to something in *your* element. An art opening seems so…exotic to me, but it's as comfortable to you as, I don't know, going out to dinner or something."

I'd not thought of it that way, but she was right. Usually things that were completely normal to everyone else were new to *me*. It was a nice change, and I was happy to finally introduce Amy to something that had been part of my life for as long as I could remember. Not that I wasn't nervous in my own way, but it wasn't about the event itself.

Amy looked fantastic. She usually did, but tonight she looked…grown up. Her skirt and jacket were a deep red, a beautiful, mature color, not garish or too sexy, and fit her to perfection. She'd smoothed her curls into a low pony-tail and dabbed a muted red lipstick on her full lips. I could have confused her for an executive—or an art dealer—if I hadn't known her so well.

But of course, Amy was still Amy. She giggled as she slipped her arm through mine and dragged me out the door. "C'mon Heartbreaker. Let's go, so you can teach me about art and we can try to sneak some champagne before everyone gets there."

WE PICKED OUR way across campus in the cool early evening. It was usually the quietest time to be found on a Friday, but tonight there was an energy hovering over the grounds, as parents and alumni arrived, and people bustled about preparing for the night's events. The air was crisp but not cold and the sky was a rainbow of sunset colors over the still green, rolling lawns of the Academy.

My early nervousness began to change into a more familiar, and enjoyable, feeling. Though I'd been to my aunt's unveilings many times before, I'd never once failed to be proud of or excited for her. As we approached the Auditorium, I let the anticipation settle in on me like an old, welcome friend.

People were already gathering outside, where there was a small group of performers from the student orchestra to entertain them and several waiters mingled amongst the crowd with cocktails and light hors d'oeuvres. The front doors were locked and darkened, adding to the atmosphere of drama and suspense. I smiled to myself as we slipped around the side of the building to the rear door. My aunt was a real pro at this kind of thing. She'd promised me a private showing before the doors opened and she became the center of attention.

"Auntie?" I called as I pushed open the back door. It creaked as it swung and opened into a dim, deserted hallway. Honestly, it would have been a little creepy if not for the five huge trays of full champagne flutes sparkling in a row against the wall. Score. I looked sideways at Amy, who winked at me, and we swiped a glass each before making our way through the stage doors at the end of the hall.

We stepped through from backstage into the auditorium itself but it, too, appeared empty, the lights glowing just enough for us to see our way down the aisles. We were headed toward the lobby proper to search for my aunt when her voice called to me from seemingly everywhere at once.

"Elaine Rachel Young! Don't go any further!" I jumped at the booming sound and spun in a circle, searching for her. "Up here, silly!" Aunt Tessa's voice echoed again, followed by a ghostly laugh. Amy laughed too and pointed up. There, at the back of the balcony, was my beautiful, bohemian aunt waving at us from behind the previously darkened windows of the lighting control room.

I warmed just at the sight of her. Tonight her small, curvy frame was showcased by the swirling print of her skirt, a simple black strapless top, and layers of entirely different but somehow perfectly coordinated necklaces that glimmered in the dim lighting. Her dark, wavy hair fell over one shoulder as she swept down the stairs to where we were standing.

"You look so beautiful!" I gushed, taking a moment to admire her before hugging her tightly. "And I can't wait to finally see what you've done for the Academy."

"Thank you, sweetie," she said before releasing me to hug my roommate too. "Good to see you Amy. Let me show you before the rest of the guests get tired of waiting." She eyed our glasses of champagne, warning, "And you finish those before the reception starts," before leading us out of the auditorium.

We followed her through the doors and into the dark hallway that led to the lobby. In fact, when the door swung shut behind us, it wasn't just dark but pitch black. I nearly stumbled over my aunt before she grabbed my hand and said, "Just walk slowly. I promise it will be worth it." Amy gripped the back of my shirt as we inched through the darkness.

When we reached what seemed like the end of the hall—even the lobby was pitch black—Aunt Tessa said, "Okay, now!" into a small walkie-talkie I hadn't even noticed she was holding. The lights blazed to life overhead.

When my eyes finally adjusted, I was no less dazzled. What had previously been a boring architectural ceiling of acoustic sound panels had been transformed into a myriad flock of hanging origami birds in an array of materials—mixed metals, plaster, wood, lacquered paper. There were at least fifty of them, all different shapes and sizes, hanging at varied lengths and in different angles of flight or rest. They weren't just the basic, familiar crane shapes either; there were swans and peacocks, swallows and herons, eagles and owls, along with a number of other birds I couldn't name on sight.

The birds would have been impressive on their own, but this was an installation, not just a sculpture exhibit. Before long, the tiny, artfully placed spotlights began to rotate and move, casting shadows across the white ceiling, and giving the entire room the impression of birds in flight. It was nothing short of magical.

I gasped in awe and gripped my aunt's hand, which I'd never relinquished, even tighter. Next to me, Amy breathed out an impressive curse.

"Oh Auntie." I pulled her into another crushing hug. "It's…amazing. I don't even know what else to say."

"It really is, Ms. Espinosa," Amy said. There was wonder in her voice, and I saw her wipe at her eyes as we continued to stare at the ever-changing ceiling.

"Thank you, girls," Aunt Tessa said. "I'm so glad you like it. I hope everyone else does too. And now, it's about time to show it to them."

THE BIG UNVEILING was even more impressive than our private showing. I wasn't sure how it would work, trying to usher everyone into a dark room to preserve the mystery, but Aunt Tessa still had more tricks in store for us. She left me with a wink and a wave to go greet the guests as they entered. Amy went out to the grounds to find her parents and Caleb while I waited patiently, in the dark, by the side wall.

I wished Carter, Melinda, and Jeff were able to be here for this part, but they wouldn't arrive until later, after they'd closed the bookstore for the night. As much as they wanted to come, the unveiling was also the beginning of Homecoming, one of the busiest weekends of the year at the store. This meant actual paying customers—alumni and families—lots of them, not just the current students they generously entertained in the lounge on a daily basis.

As I watched in fascination, people filtered slowly into the Auditorium's lobby, each carrying a faintly luminescent glow-stick, giving off just enough light to guide them but not enough to ruin the surprise. When everyone was assembled, the room appeared to be full of anxious fireflies, flitting amongst each other, their quiet, curious whispers filling the room with buzz and excitement. The door opened and closed one final time and moments later a spotlight illuminated my lovely aunt. The crowd fell completely silent.

"Good evening, and welcome," she said in her practiced, resonant voice. "I'd like to thank you all again for joining us and especially for being an important part of what has made Northbrook Academy an historic and elite institution, one I am proud that my niece attends. It is my great honor to donate this permanent installation to the Academy, and my wish that it will be enjoyed and enhanced for many years to come. Without further delay, I present you with Future Flight. Enjoy!"

Like before, the overhead lights came on in a flash, this time accompanied by a track of ambient music intermixed with subtle bird calls and songs. The crowd gave a polite and appreciative round of applause while they all admired the ceiling's flock. Just at the right moment, as voices began to grow and people started to mingle, the music swelled and the miniature spotlights went into action. The room again plunged into silence, except for a few surprised gasps and exclamations, before it erupted into a nearly thunderous ovation. Aunt Tessa was bombarded by congratulations, while Headmaster Stewart, stationed by her side, smiled broadly and genuinely.

I spotted Amy in the crowd and went to join her, swiping another glass of champagne on my way. I carried it discreetly at my side and hoped that my aunt—or the headmaster—wouldn't notice. Amy and Caleb were both grinning at me by the time I reached them.

"That was freaking *incredible,*" Caleb said. Amy nodded in agreement before grabbing my champagne and taking a big swallow. "Amy told me it would be great, but wow, yeah. I had no idea. And I wondered why the ceiling in here had been draped in black cloth since the beginning of the semester. So this is really what your aunt does all the time?"

I could feel the proud smile pushing at the limits of my cheeks before I snuck my own sip of my drink. "Isn't she amazing? It's not always the same exhibit, of course, and sometimes she just does sculptures. It's not always so exciting either. Most of the time, half the attendees have done this kind of thing a million times before too. See those two guys over there?" I pointed to the side of the room where two men stood separate from most of the crowd, chatting and gesturing. "Those are art critics from the city. I remember them from when we lived in Boston a few years ago. I think they were impressed, too, though. Usually they're just straight-faced and a little bored looking."

Caleb eyed the men with curiosity while Amy made a little pout in their direction. "I don't know how they *couldn't* be impressed," she said. "Unless they're blind or dead, and it doesn't look like they're either. Well, maybe a little dead-ish, but not *dead* dead."

I giggled. "Well, we can read what they thought in the paper tomorrow. At least one of them will write up their review tonight." The men broke from the side of the room and started toward where my aunt was standing next to a bronze plaque that had also been unveiled. "This is where she tells them all about the piece and her inspiration and all that. They could read it all on that plaque, but it's more interesting to hear my aunt tell it. She'll entertain them for a while now."

And she did. My aunt began a long dialogue with the critics, as well as a crowd of other interested listeners, and I made a loop around the room, stopping to greet Amy's parents and a few other friends, before drifting over to listen to some of her explanation. I wanted to hear it too.

"…symbolizes the diversity of the student body, but also their similarities. They're all from different places and backgrounds, cut from different cloths so to speak, and have been folded and molded in different ways by their families, their experiences, this school. They come in all shapes, sizes, and colors, but they also all have one thing in common: they're about to take flight. Their future is before them, and we can only hope we've prepared them well. I worry daily about setting my own niece free to fly,"—she gestured to where she'd noticed me lingering at the edge of the group—"but have to believe I've done my best to make sure she's ready. Sending her here, to Northbrook, is certainly one of the best assurances I could have."

She paused to smile first over at me, and then at the headmaster and other prominent Academy personalities in the group. I knew she was genuine, but after years of experience, she also knew how to spin her flattery in the perfect moments. "You'll note the many openings throughout the form where additional birds can be placed. I've already discussed a project with the Academy's art department so that student-artists can collaborate on a new bird each year to commemorate the graduating class…"

I drifted away at that point to mingle. I thought the last part my aunt mentioned was a wonderful touch, to let the students personalize the installation, and I wondered who would work on the bird for my class this year. I was speculating about that with Brooke Barros, one of my only Sententia friends, when I saw him. A small commotion at the door caught our attention, and we both turned to watch the tall, handsome man begin to make his way through the crowd.

"Oh! There's Senator Astor," Brooke said. "I'd better go find my parents—they'll insist I 'greet him properly.'"

She made little air quotes around those last words and giggled before she disappeared into the crowd. I think I nodded, or smiled, or did *something* to acknowledge I'd heard her. At least I hoped I did. I hoped I wasn't as frozen in shock and confusion on the outside as I felt on the inside. I was thankful for a passing waiter so I could deposit my mostly empty champagne glass on his tray before I dropped it.

The senator, and president of the Perceptum, progressed slowly toward the bronze plaque by which my aunt and Headmaster Stewart still stood, stopping every few steps to shake someone's hand or exchange a few words. Aunt Tessa had seen Daniel Astor, just as I had. The look of surprise on her face was probably similar to mine, though hers held only curiosity, not the fear I suspected I hadn't entirely disguised.

He was quite tall, taller than Carter, though not nearly as broad. Senator Astor was slim and elegant, in a fine gray suit that complemented his fair hair, handsome features, and blue eyes. Eyes from all over the room followed him from the moment of his entrance and he was clearly comfortable being in the spotlight. He carried himself in a way that showed his importance but also made him seem entirely approachable. I was sure he was an excellent politician.

I also didn't need Brooke, or anyone for that matter, to tell me who he was. In fact, I'd have known him anywhere, in any setting, and whether he was a senator or not.

He looked exactly like my father.

Chapter Four

For a moment, all I could think was, *this can't be happening*, followed quickly by, *how is this* possible? I stared at Daniel Astor as he worked the crowd, unsure what to do or even if I believed it. I took a step closer, thinking I was seeing things, that my eyes were playing tricks.

On closer inspection, Senator Astor looked even *more* like my father, with the same sculpted cheek bones and same friendly smile I'd seen in photographs. The only difference was his hair and eye color. No doubt the rest of their nearly identical features they both inherited from the late Jacob Astor, their father. Carter might have thought of the senator as his uncle, but in reality, he was *mine*. The identity of the older, important man Virginia Marwood had been so desperate to hide my father from was obvious now.

I was an Astor. An illegitimate Marwood-Astor and I was petrified.

I was also, as far as I could tell, the only person in the world who knew this and I intended to keep it that way.

Shaking my head, I broke from my stupefied trance and basically bolted toward my aunt. When I bumped into someone in my haste, I realized drawing attention was the absolute last thing I wanted to do.

Practice discretion, I reminded myself. The Perceptum motto came in handy more often than I cared to admit. I slowed down while I worked my face into something closer to surprise than horror.

When I finally reached my aunt, she put her arm around my waist and pulled me close to her while smiling at the small crowd still gathered. Headmaster Stewart remained nearby but was, I noted, actively tracking Daniel Astor's progress through the room. Good. I needed her distracted. Aunt Tessa lowered her voice and started to say, "Lainey, did you see—?" before I cut her off.

"I know, Auntie. I saw him. It's amazing, isn't it?" I hoped she couldn't feel my hands shaking.

She nodded and glanced back at the rapidly approaching senator. I had to get this taken care of before he reached us. "His resemblance is so...I can't even...But who is he?" she asked. "Do you know?"

I giggled softly, like this was only a strange coincidence and no big deal, and kept my voice as low as my aunt's. "Of course I know who he is. He's Senator Astor, Carter's uncle. The girl Jillian's father too, remember? He's also like the most important alum in the world right now." Here was my one chance to get her to drop it and I had to make it good. "So *please* don't say anything," I pleaded. "Please? It's just too weird. I don't want to make him feel uncomfortable and I...I don't want to talk about what happened to Mom and Dad tonight. Okay?" I threw in that last part on an inspired whim; it was actually harder for *her* to talk about them than it was for me.

She eyed me for a moment but then nodded in agreement. "Okay, I won't say anything. Yes, I promise," she added when I gave her a skeptical stare. My aunt was known for being chatty and rarely holding back what she wanted to say. "Honestly though, I'll have a hard time not staring at him."

"It's okay," I replied. "Everyone stares at him. See, even the headmaster." I gestured to Dr. Stewart, whose eyes still followed Senator Astor's every move. "I think he's probably used to it."

It was my aunt's turn to giggle, and if I hadn't been so freaked out by my own thoughts I would have realized that should have worried me. "He's certainly handsome, just like...well, you know. Yes, I'm sure he gets stares all the time."

He was also almost to us. Aunt Tess and I both put on our best smiles, hers completely natural, mine the best approximation I could come up with, just as Dr. Stewart stepped into our line of sight.

"Senator," she said smoothly and reached to shake his hand. "So good to see you, and thank you for attending. It's an honor to have you at such a unique event in the Academy's history." I wondered if I was the only one who realized the headmaster was a tiny bit in love with Senator Astor.

"Constance," he replied, grasping her hand in both of his. His voice was rich and warm, an extension of his charming smile, and as I observed them, I changed my mind. I probably wasn't the only one aware of the headmaster's feelings. "Lovely to see you, as always. And it is my honor to be here tonight. I only wish I'd been in time for the initial introduction, which I understand was extraordinary."

He turned to my aunt and me then and, if possible, turned on his considerable charm even more. I'd always thought Carter was especially charming and now I knew where he'd learned it. "Ms. Espinosa, I presume? Along with my nephew's winsome girlfriend? What a beautiful pair you make, almost as much a work of art as your magnificent installation. Pleasure to meet you. I'm Daniel Astor."

He extended his hand to my usually confident and unflappable aunt who—no joke—grasped it demurely and glanced down at her feet before meeting his undeniably appreciative gaze. Tiny warning bells sounded in my head, but they were faint and not yet enough for me to take seriously. My aunt couldn't really be *attracted* to a man who looked just like my father. Could she?

"Thank you, Senator," Aunt Tessa said. Her smile was absolutely radiant. "Just Tessa will be fine. 'Ms. Espinosa' makes me feel like my mother." She laughed lightly. "And it's certainly my pleasure to meet you and also to introduce my niece, Lainey. I understand you haven't met in person before?"

I fixed my smile in place as Daniel Astor focused his gaze on me. "No, not before now, though I've heard so many wonderful things about her, and, of course, will forever owe her a debt of gratitude. Lainey, how do you do?" He shook my hand and held it. "And let me take this opportunity to thank you again for your bravery in saving my daughter."

There wasn't much I could really say to that, especially considering the true nature of my "saving" Jill. "Thank you, Senator. I hope Jill's doing well, and it's nice to finally meet you." I did my best to sound *actually* pleased to meet him, instead of panicked. I thought I succeeded.

He held my gaze and didn't release my hand for what felt like an eternity. "You as well, Lainey. And please call me Dan. Both of you. I insist." He nodded to my aunt. "Unfortunately, my late arrival caused me to miss your introduction. Would you mind repeating the story? I'm fascinated by what you've done here…"

Aunt Tessa gladly complied and she and Senator Astor became absorbed in discussion while I lingered nearby. Headmaster Stewart also lingered in the vicinity, growing visibly more annoyed the longer the senator—Dan, I reminded myself—worked his magic on a woman other than her. I was half listening to my aunt and half trying to figure out what to do about my new knowledge, when strong arms circled my waist from behind.

I almost screamed before I heard Carter's familiar voice in my ear. "Hey gorgeous," he said, kissing me on the cheek. "I'd ask what I missed, but I can see most of it, and it's incredible." Lower, he added, "Speaking of incredible, love the pants," and my skin flushed, only partly out of surprise.

"Hi!" I squeaked. I cleared my throat and turned, unable to hide my smile as I took him in. He looked great, as he usually did, but he'd changed out of his typical daily uniform of comfortable jeans and a simple T-shirt into a blue dress shirt with a tailored jacket and slacks in a color like steel or gunmetal. The combination made his already pretty blue eyes nearly arresting and somehow enhanced the handsome angles of his features. "You surprised me," I tried again and I was relieved that I sounded more like myself this time.

He returned my smile. "I know," he said. "You looked like your body was here but your brain was in another room, or like you'd just seen a ghost. I even waved at you when I came in."

I swallowed an inappropriate laugh or, possibly, a sob. He was more right than he knew and I was suddenly glad he *hadn't* been here earlier. "Sorry. I…guess I was daydreaming. And listening to my aunt talk about the installation. I didn't hear the whole story the first time."

"It's incredible," he repeated. "I should have been here." He glanced over my shoulder and nodded in the direction of Aunt Tessa and the senator. "And it looks like your aunt and my uncle have hit it off well. Did you meet him already?"

"Yes!" I said, too quickly and far too brightly. I mentally reminded myself to relax and Act. Freaking. Natural. I would have plenty of time to worry over what to do about my newly discovered relation. For now, I *had* to pretend that everything was perfectly fine.

But Carter confused my over-eager response for something much more common. He laughed and squeezed me a little tighter. "Yeah, my uncle's been known to have that effect on women."

I blushed again, but it worked. He couldn't know how creepy the idea that I found Daniel Astor attractive actually was, so I went with it.

"No, it's not that! I mean, yeah, he's good-looking, for an old guy. He was just very nice." I lowered my voice. "You know I was…nervous to meet him."

"How many times did I tell you not to worry? And was I right?"

"You were right." I smiled and stepped closer to him. "Now kiss me hello while no one is looking."

He did, one hand running over my hair, the other slipping dangerously across the smooth black satin of my pants, before his lips pressed mine and held there longer than was probably polite. Kissing Carter was an invitation to a private world, like Oz or somewhere over Dorothy's rainbow, where time was inconsequential and my troubles melted along with my heart.

Tonight, he was exactly the distraction I needed.

THE REST OF the reception, and the dinner that followed, was actually fun, once I postponed my major freak-out and started to relax. I stuck close to Carter, letting his presence and his touch calm me while we mingled with the other students and our families. Senator Astor barely left my aunt's company after their introduction, except to spend time with Alexis and her parents. Mr. Morrow and the senator, I realized, were probably lifelong friends. Alex's cousin Mandi was with them too, and Senator Astor put his arm around her shoulders like a familiar uncle.

Alexis and I studiously ignored each other but she did manage a wave and a blinding smile for my boyfriend, not to mention some less-than-subtle glances his way throughout the private dinner for Legacy families and special guests. For my part, I barely bothered to sigh. I wasn't the only one who noticed though, and I don't mean Carter. Amy was always on top of things.

"Gawd," she said after we'd bid good night to our dates and our parents and walked up the stairs of our dorm. "Could Alexis *be* more obvious? I thought she'd have given up by now."

I was long past worrying about Alex and her designs on Carter so I actually laughed. "She *could,* you know. She has been before."

Amy snorted. "True. At least all she could do was eye him tonight. She wasn't close enough to drop her napkin and *say hello* from under the table."

I glanced back at her over my shoulder while I unlocked our door. "She wouldn't do *that,*" I said, but I wasn't sure it was really true.

"No, *you* wouldn't do that. She totally would." We both slipped off our heels and flopped onto our respective beds. She was making fun of me, but I ignored it.

"You're right. But it doesn't matter, because he wouldn't let her."

"No, he probably wouldn't."

"Probably?"

She smiled. "Never underestimate the power of a hot, willing girl, Lane. Even with Carter. He's reformed, yeah, but he'll forever and always be a guy." She talked right over me as I started to protest. "I know, I know. You're not worried. And I *don't* really think you need to be, you know that. I'm kidding around. Mostly."

It was the "mostly" that actually *did* worry me. I never questioned how much Carter loved me, and he'd been resisting Alex's advances for *years* now, but doubt still crept into my mind on occasion, quite often in the form of Alexis's voice. Or my own worked just as well. I doubted myself better than anyone though I tried constantly to stop doing it. *Tried* being the operative word. It would have been great if my Marwood genes allowed me to kill old, bad habits instead of just people.

I sighed and rolled onto my stomach. "Don't you worry about Caleb sometimes too?" I asked. I already knew the answer, but it helped to hear out loud that your usually confident roommate had her moments of doubt too.

"Alex doesn't want *Caleb*," she replied but then got serious. "Of course. Once in a while. Who doesn't worry sometimes? But then he doesn't…anyway. Yeah, sometimes I worry, but not very much." I was about to ask her what she hadn't finished saying when she got up and started to change out of her suit. I assumed she was getting ready for bed, but instead of pajamas, she pulled jeans and a sweater out of her dresser. After months last semester of spending at least one night a week in our room by myself, you'd think I'd have expected it, but somehow I never did.

"Speaking of Caleb…I guess you're not staying here?"

She winked. "Not until the sun comes up anyway." It was well known around campus how easy it was to sneak in and out of someone's room, but that you had to do it all before sunrise.

I blurted out, "But your parents are here!" and then blushed at how foolish it sounded.

Amy, as usual, laughed at my innocence. "Well, yeah, but it's not like they're sleeping in either of our rooms! I don't think they'll catch us from their hotel in Brattleboro."

The heat slowly dissipated from my face. "You're right. Well, don't wake me up when you come back."

"I never do." She hesitated then, glancing at me several times while packing a few things into her bag. I should have known what it was about, because though she loved to tell me about her sex life, she knew I *didn't* like to talk about mine, or the lack thereof. I also suddenly knew what she'd started to say earlier, something about how Caleb didn't have many reasons to be tempted by other girls. It went *without* saying that Carter did have one big reason, one he'd enthusiastically pursued before meeting me, and one that, if not Alexis, any number of girls would be glad to pursue with him again.

"Lane," she finally started but I interrupted her.

"If he's waited this long, he's not going anywhere."

She nodded emphatically. "I know that. I wasn't saying he was. But...well, I see you together and I know how in love you are—really, it's nauseating sometimes—so I just can't figure it out. What *are* you still waiting for?"

Good question. I looked at her for a long time before I finally gave the answer I'd wondered about myself.

"A year," I replied. "I'm waiting for a year."

Chapter Five

C arter was in an especially good mood throughout the weekend, between the store filled with customers and Senator
Astor's presence. He, more than anyone, looked forward to
his uncle's visits. Dan had been the one to teach Carter how
to control his Thought Mover abilities and Carter looked up to him as
almost another father-figure, different from his own father, or from
Jeff Revell. Maybe more like another Jesus, if I was honest with myself. Carter didn't just look up to him; he practically worshiped him.

Saturday night found us at a very private table in a historic, upscale
restaurant in Vermont that I didn't even know existed. Usually students weren't allowed to go so far off-campus, not without a parent or
guardian, but I *was* with Senator Astor, so my permission from Headmaster Stewart had been instantaneous. I think she wished she'd been
invited too.

"I'm sorry your aunt couldn't join us, Lainey," Dan said shortly after we'd been seated.

"Me too," I told him, though I only half meant it. I did want to
spend as much time with her as I could, but I didn't really want her in
the vicinity of the senator—my real uncle—any more than necessary

or she was bound to say something. "She wanted to come, but the critics have created such a great buzz about the installation, she felt like she had to go to the event in Boston tonight." *Future Flight* was already being hailed as creating an "undoubtedly instant trend of 'collaborative installations.'"

"It's nearly as amazing as the artist herself," he replied with a smile. Carter squeezed my hand under the table and I smiled back. Yes, this was *exactly* where he'd learned to be so charming. He was seated between me and his Uncle Dan and Melinda was on my right. We were at an intimate round table for just the five of us, but somehow it was clear that Senator Astor was at the head.

Dinner itself was delicious. I nibbled appetizers of pate and escargot, stuffed myself with roasted duck, and managed a few bites of maple crème brûlée. In fact, by the time we were done eating, I had a stomach ache. Except it had nothing to do with my meal. Though everyone was companionable, and Carter was practically exuberant, an undercurrent of tension ran throughout the evening.

Family relations between Dan, Jeff, and Melinda were…a little forced. The brothers—half-brothers, really—saw each other infrequently and spoke even less. And they were actually on pretty *good* terms right now. I was sure they'd never be a loving and laughing family. Add me, and my disastrous confrontation with the senator's daughter, into the mix and you had possibly the most awkward family gathering ever.

Dan and Carter naturally dominated the conversation, with Melinda filling in most of the rest. Jeff was as quiet as usual, and I was nearly as reserved. Unfortunately, it didn't go unnoticed.

"You've been quiet this evening," Senator Astor said casually, stirring his coffee and taking a sip.

"You have," Carter echoed. A small frown creased his brow as if he'd just realized this, which he probably had. It wasn't that he'd been ignoring me, but that he'd been happily wrapped up in talking with his Uncle Dan about the most recent events in politics, both United States and Sententia.

"I didn't mean to be," I lied. "I was enjoying listening, learning a little more about this stuff." I sipped my own coffee to try to appear relaxed. Which was pointless, because Daniel Astor was nothing if not shrewd.

"I'm glad we could teach you more about our society," he said. "I'd like to do more of it, in fact. But that's not really what's got you so quiet this evening, is it?"

Time to be honest. Or honest-ish. No chance I was telling him— anyone—*all* the concerns occupying my mind. "No, I guess it's not," I admitted.

"I suppose it's my daughter," he said gently. Everyone but Dan shifted uncomfortably in their chairs, and Carter reached over to grasp my hand. I hated thinking about what happened, so of course I thought about it all the time. I suspected that Carter and the Revells did too.

"I'm sorry," I said. What else *could* I say? I'd *killed* his daughter, however briefly. It was a difficult fact to overcome.

But the senator actually surprised me with his response. In fact, shocked might have been a better word. "Certainly not more than I, Lainey. I owe *you* an apology. It's my fault what happened." He sighed and looked around the table making eye contact with every one of us. "I am so very sorry, for what she did and especially for my dishonesty about her."

Carter and his aunt and uncle glanced at me and then at each other in confusion. "What do you mean?" Carter finally asked.

"I know she attacked Lainey, in part, because of me," Dan explained, shaking his head. As always seemed to be the case, he directed his comments mostly to Carter. "I should have kept my promise to her mother not to have any contact with Jillian, but I didn't. I'm so sorry for that, and sorry for not admitting it sooner. I should have told you."

Probably *I* should have told them too, but I'd never mentioned any of Jill's ravings, letting them believe her attack was entirely about her unrequited love for Carter. I couldn't believe Senator Astor had just admitted his deception; I'd never thought he would. In fact, the longer I spent in his company, the harder it was to maintain the fear and distaste I'd been cultivating for months. Maybe I *was* wrong about him.

Carter turned to me. I could hear the confusion, plus a little bit of anger, in his voice. "Lainey, what's he talking about?" He dropped my hand to run his hastily through his hair, his number one bad habit and clearest indicator of distress.

"I…" started to explain, but didn't have to.

"Don't blame her, Carter," Dan interjected. "She was just being discreet, I know, and I thank her for it." There was no higher praise for Sententia than being called discreet, and I'd just gotten it from our leader. He seemed genuine about it too—about *everything*. "As I said, I had, perhaps foolishly and undoubtedly selfishly, been in contact with Jillian. Phone calls and emails only, but I enjoyed them." He raised his hands as if saying, *what's a father to do?* "I wanted to know my daughter. I should have waited the few more years I promised, but that was my mistake. I made the added mistake of asking about Lainey. If I'd only been more cautious, or known my daughter better, perhaps I'd have seen what would happen…"

He trailed off before looking at me directly, the intensity in his eyes making it impossible to look away or doubt him. "I am so sorry, Lainey. Truly. The words can't convey the depth of my sorrow about what happened and my part in it. *You* have nothing to apologize for. My gratitude for saving my daughter, and for your discretion after the fact, is limitless. There's no way for me to repay you, but if there is *anything* I can do for you, ever, all you need is ask."

We sat there in stunned silence at the senator's confession, me over the fact that he'd made it, the others over what it contained. Finally, Jeff said nothing more than, *"Dan,"* but it held all the condemnation, as well as understanding, a single word could. Somehow I suspected these awkward moments would do more to repair the brothers' strained relationship than anything else. Among other things, Jeff was angry with his brother for his failures as a father; knowing that Dan had tried to correct them would earn him a lot as far as Jeff and Melinda's esteem went.

Carter said nothing, but finally regrasped my hand. He was looking between me and the senator with a number of emotions, but the dominant one was *relief.* He'd been eaten up over the belief that Jill had harmed me because of *him.* And she had, in part, but not entirely. At the time, I hadn't even questioned my choice not to tell him. Between taking that burden from him or forcing him to question his beloved uncle's integrity, I'd been certain the latter was worse. Except now *I* looked like the one keeping secrets. And I supposed I was, but not for anything but love for Carter. I didn't look forward to talking about it with him later.

"I miss her," Melinda admitted into the quiet. It was half sad, half apologetic, but all honest.

"As do I, Meri," Dan replied. I was unused to his nickname for Melinda, but no one but me seemed to find it strange.

Melinda sighed. "Sometimes I feel bad that I do—I'm sorry, Lainey—but I do."

"I'm sure Lainey doesn't fault you for it, Mel," Jeff said, and he was right. Maybe it wasn't logical, or the most typical reaction, but whenever I thought of Jill, I felt not anger but crushing sadness.

"I don't," I agreed. "Honest." Carter turned his head, but still said nothing.

I knew he *did* fault his aunt, but loved her too much to say anything. He'd found no forgiveness for Jill in the months since she left. Sometimes I thought he could still see my bruises when he looked at me, still touched me tentatively as if they were there, even though they'd long since faded. Naturally then, we did *not* talk about Jill. But I was curious.

"How…how is she?" I said to whoever might answer. "Did she go to Webber?" Webber was Northbrook's sister school, on the West Coast. After learning she wouldn't return here, I assumed that was the best place for her, where she could get the help she needed but also still be with other Sententia.

My question was met with momentarily strained silence. Dan murmured, "You don't know?" He looked at Carter with a combination of surprise and reprobation, and a look of guilt flitted across Carter's features. Perhaps I wasn't the only one keeping secrets where Jill was concerned.

I looked at Carter too. "I guess not," I said. *"Is* she okay? What don't I know?"

He ruffled his hair some more, which basically gave me my answer, before he finally said in low tones, "No, she didn't go to Webber. And…I don't think she'll ever be okay again."

"What do you mean?!" Looking around the table, I saw nothing but sad expressions and I suddenly felt like I was back a year ago, when I'd first learned about Sententia and my strange gift. Here I was again, on the outside of knowledge, surrounded by the pitying insiders. My temper started to rise. *"Carter?"*

But it was Dan, again, who responded. "It seems I have much intervention to do this evening," he said, and I almost thought he sounded amused, which seemed a strange reaction to me. The sad look in his eyes and his tired voice had me dismissing the thought. "Don't be angry with him. My nephew, too, is nothing if not discreet, and I'm certain he didn't want to upset you. But no, she won't be going to Webber, or any of our schools."

"Is she…being punished?" I asked tentatively. In truth, she probably should have gone to jail, or the juvenile equivalent, if not a mental hospital, but that wasn't something local authorities knew. The Perceptum did, of course. I assumed they handled the situation, arranging things as best for her as possible. But you know what they say about assuming, and I was about to prove it true.

Dan shook his head and I swore Melinda's eyes started to tear up. "That turned out not to be necessary, Lainey," Jeff said.

"Oh my God, she's dead, isn't she!" I blurted out. Despite that our table was quite private, I still saw one or two heads turn in our direction. Had Dr. Stewart been hinting at that and I just couldn't understand? I just couldn't think of what else they meant except that she'd killed herself. After all that happened, I couldn't believe she'd died anyway.

But she didn't, not exactly.

Everyone gave some sort of denial before Dan said, "No, no. Jillian is…physically fine. But you see, Lainey, her gift, it's…"

"What?" I pleaded. "What about her gift?"

"It's gone."

Chapter Six

"Gone?" I echoed. "That's…" impossible, I started to say, but I knew better by now. "Crazy," I finally decided on, then cringed. I knew better than to use that word so wantonly too. Jill had taught me that. "Does that always happen?"

Carter shook his head. "To our knowledge, it's *never* happened before."

"But then, what *did* happen?" I said. "Jill can't be the only Sententia ever resuscitated."

With a sad chuckle, Carter said, *"You* happened, Lainey."

I didn't have time for more than my eyes to go wide and my mouth to drop open before Dan interjected. "What he means is though, yes, other Sententia have been resuscitated, it's never been after an encounter with a Hangman."

I shuddered. God, I hated that term. "But…I thought my ability stops a person's heart."

"It does," Melinda said.

"But perhaps that's not all it does," Dan finished for her.

"The truth is, Lainey, none of us knows exactly what your gift can or cannot do," Jeff said.

My brain went numb at this news—I swore every time I started to feel comfortable, a new surprise was thrown at me—so all I thought to say was, "Poor Jill." If she hated me before, and she surely had, then she must *really* hate me now. I sipped my coffee, which was cold and bitter, kind of how my heart felt at the moment. My cup clattered on the saucer and sounded very loud to my ears. "Sorry," I said, though I wasn't sure just what I was apologizing for.

Dan folded his napkin neatly on the table and gave a gentle smile to all of us. "I suppose we've lingered here long enough," he said, effectively ending our dinner—and the conversation—much to my relief.

AFTER ABOUT FIVE minutes of silence in the car, Carter and I said at almost exactly the same time, "Why didn't you tell me…" though we were split on what we wanted to know.

"About Jill?!"

"About my uncle?!"

"You answer first," I said.

He glanced at me from the driver's seat. "Whatever happened to 'ladies first'?" he joked, and if he weren't driving, I'd have smacked him. I considered it anyway. Leave it to Carter always to make light of a serious situation. It was probably one of his better traits, actually, if it didn't irritate me so much.

"Shut up and answer."

"I can't really do both…"

"Argh! Carter, seriously. Please." *Before I throttle you.*

The headlights swept over the dark curves of the road, illuminating the trees on both sides. It was "quaint" up in our little intersection of three states, meaning pretty much the middle of nowhere, with miles and miles of nothing and no one around. I waited impatiently for my boyfriend's response.

Finally, in soft, more serious tones, he said, "It should be obvious why I didn't tell you. It upset you. I didn't want to."

"Ditto," I said.

"I *hate* upsetting you."

"Same." Then I sighed. "But…maybe we need to share the things that'll upset us before the not sharing them *really* pisses us off."

"Agreed," he said, and reached over to hold my hand. "I'm sorry," he added.

"Me too," I murmured. I closed my eyes and powered up my Diviner senses for a quick check of our future—still nothing new—and then, despite that we'd just agreed to be honest with each other, still didn't tell him. If only I would learn to listen to myself. Sometimes the hardest advice in the world to take is your own.

When the new silence in the car felt comfortable, not tense, I said, "There's another thing I'm curious about." Carter's thumb traced slowly, back and forth, across my hand. I wondered if he was even aware he was doing it, or of the way it gave me little shivers, both inside and out.

"What's that?" He gave my hand a squeeze before letting go to downshift.

"Why does Dan call your aunt *Meri?*"

"Well, it is her name." And it was. Her full Penrose name was Meriwether Avalinda.

"Yeah, but no one else calls her that."

"He does." Carter glanced at me and looked back out the windshield. "My father did."

"Oh." I stared out the windshield too, thinking about that.

"It's a brotherly thing. She pretends to hate it." He paused. "Uncle Jeff *does* hate it."

"Interesting." And it was. I was going to say *then why does he do it?* but I suspected that *was* why. I'd never had siblings, so it was hard to really know what it was like. Aunt Tessa and her brother, my Uncle Tommy, loved and annoyed each other with equal passion, though. Maybe it was as simple as that.

The comforting weight of Carter's hand returned to mine, his thumb finding the same path as before. It was odd how such a light touch, a whisper of a touch, really, could have such an effect. I shivered again.

"Cold?" he asked.

"No."

His grin lit up the car.

It wasn't long before we pulled into the parking area behind the bookstore. It was late, and dark, but clear—a perfect early autumn night. Almost exactly a year since I first arrived at Northbrook. It was crisp out, too, and an extra-chilly gust blew into the car as we came to a stop.

"Hey—it's cold! Why are you rolling down—?" I asked, but too late. Carter had already started our little game, where he would race to open my door for me before I did it myself. He'd employed all sorts of techniques to beat me, including liberal use of Thought and, once, duct tape, but I was almost always out of the car by the time he got there.

As soon as the ignition was off, he Thought down my door lock, a typical diversion, and then—*hoisted himself out his open window!* Wearing dress pants and shoes no less! Like a gymnast, his strong arms pulled his torso up in one quick, fluid motion. And just like that, he was gone, planting his foot on the door rim to propel him smoothly across the roof of the car, all while I watched like an idiot. I was still disentangling myself from my seatbelt when he thumped down outside my door and opened it with a flourish.

"My lady."

"Wow. Congratulations, Dukes of Hazzard," I said, stepping out of the car and into the blinding glare of Carter's grin. He Thought the door closed behind me. "Have you been practicing that?"

"Maybe." The grin never wavered as he moved forward, putting one arm on each side to trap me against the car. It *was* cool out, but it didn't feel that way when he was so close to me. When he kissed me, it got even warmer. Blazing. After a few moments, he paused just long enough to repeat softly, "I'm sorry."

"Me too," I breathed, though at that moment, as his lips traveled down my neck, I was honestly having trouble remembering what we were apologizing for. Above me, in the slice of sky between the trees and the towering bookstore, I counted a thousand glittering stars. Wisps of smoke drifted high overhead, the smell of wood fire mingling with the constant scent of pine trees. Against the car, my back felt icy compared to the heat of Carter's body pressed to mine.

"You want to come up?" he said, voice low and rough in my ear.

"What?" His fingers found skin under the hem of my shirt and I gasped.

"You're already cleared for curfew. You could come up. It would be just us."

It would, I realized. Jeff and Melinda had gone with Dan for a drink at his hotel after dinner. They wouldn't be home for a while.

It would be just us. Just us. My heart took off at a sprint and my fingers felt too hot, then too cold, with my manic pulse. Not for the first time I wondered what was wrong with me. How could I want something so much but be so afraid to take it? Part of me screamed *Just do it already!* But that was a reason to jump into the cold ocean, not *this*.

I wanted, but I wasn't ready to have. I wasn't sure what I was afraid of, but I wasn't ready, not tonight.

I exhaled. "Um. I told Amy I'd meet her at the bonfire."

Carter nodded, his hair tickling the crook of my neck. "Okay." He pulled back so I could see his smile. "Long shot, I know. I had to try."

"Are you mad?" He didn't *look* mad, but still.

"Only because you just asked that."

"Do you want to come with me?"

He shook his head. "I have to open."

"I should go then, I guess." I hugged him, laying my head on his shoulder, and he ran a hand down my hair.

"I love you," he said, almost loudly, as if he was sharing his feelings with the entire night. And then softly, just for me, "And whenever *you're* ready, I'll still be here."

THAT NIGHT I spent many sleepless hours listening to my roommate's soft, even breathing while I tried to tame the tornado of thoughts in my head. Carter, of course, whirled near the top. As soon as I left him, I regretted not staying, but I was still too afraid to turn around. I wondered if my subconscious was to blame, that underneath I feared if I deviated from my plan, everything would fall apart. The plan felt safe, somehow. Nothing bad could happen if I stuck to the plan.

Later, I thought about Jill. It dawned on me for the first time that she was my cousin and that I had probably, quite literally, ruined her life. Yes, she'd tried to take mine completely, but that was beside the point. I wasn't sure what it was about me that couldn't hate her—it was probably a *good* thing about me—but hell if I wouldn't take even a healthy dose of apathy where she was concerned. Instead, I lay in bed feeling guilty.

Her Sententia ability was gone. *Gone.* Part of me wanted to believe she was lying about it, but I knew she never would, not about something so very important to her. Being Sententia was as critical a part of her world as it was Carter's. Even I knew that much. And I had taken it from her. One more thing to add to her list.

I wished I could give it *back,* but I didn't think that was in my apparently expanding arsenal of tricks. Frankly, I'd have given her *my* gifts, either or both of them, I didn't care, if I could have. But I knew I could never escape my Marwood gift, so instead I moved on from Jill to wondering about it.

Was there more to it than I, or anyone, had thought? I knew it stopped hearts, but was that all it stopped? Maybe Jill was a fluke, but I'd pretty much stopped believing in flukes or coincidences over the past year. *Something* in my touch had negated whatever inside her made her Sententia. I mentally flexed my Sententia muscles, but I didn't feel anything inside that would answer this question. I could command my Diviner ability pretty well, but that didn't help me here. The Hangman in me wasn't exactly something I could practice.

Naturally, my thoughts drifted next to Daniel Astor. Uncle Dan. Lately it seemed like eventually *all* my thoughts drifted to him. In fact, my obsessive fear of him or, more specifically, being related to him, had given me a bit of reprieve from dwelling on my impending death and Carter's roll in it. I wasn't sure if I should be grateful to him. And, in fact, what I was starting to fear most was that I'd misjudged him.

I couldn't detect anything but sincerity in everything Dan had said at dinner, not in his pained confession or his offer to help me any way he could. He was either the real deal or one hell of an actor. I wondered if it wasn't time to give him more of a chance. He was my uncle, after all.

Maybe someday I could even tell him that.

IT WAS ALMOST as if he'd known I was thinking about him. When I arrived at the dining hall the next morning, I could tell something was going on. There was a buzz throughout the room, something more than all the parents in town making it extra crowded.

After only a few steps, I figured it out. It wasn't too hard. Daniel Astor stood from the table where he'd been sitting with Alexis, Mandi, and their family just as Amy rushed up to me. The most amazing thing about this was actually that Amy had beaten me to breakfast.

"Lane, oh my gosh," she gushed. "The senator has been waiting for you!"

All I got out was, "Um," before she continued.

"My dad just about *died* when he stopped by our table and remembered his name,"—apparently politicians were Dr. Moretti's version of celebrities—"and he did talk to us for a while, but he was really looking for *you*. You're so late!"

I looked at my watch and laughed, mostly because she was right. It was almost ten o'clock, which by most students' standards was *early* on the weekends, but usually I'd have been and gone by then. "I took the rare opportunity to hog the bathroom myself," I told her, smiling, and she stuck her tongue out at me.

"Whatever. I *don't* hog the bathroom." She really did. "But seriously, you shouldn't have kept the senator waiting!"

"I didn't mean to! I had no idea he was going to be here. And stop saying 'the senator'."

She mock-glared at me. "Bitch. Anyway, *the senator* seemed to think you did. But it all just adds to your mystique around here! Of *course* the Chairman of the Board and United States Senator is waiting for *you*. As if the seventh and eighth graders needed another reason to follow you around."

Over her shoulder, I could see Dan shaking hands with Mr. Morrow and Alexis glaring at me. Unlike Amy, she meant it. Mandi noticed my presence moments later and followed suit. Not *all* the underclassmen were following me around.

Senator Astor looked handsome and relaxed this morning, casual and approachable in a button-down shirt and jeans. Eyes from all over the dining hall followed him as he made his way toward *me*. I felt worried, and maybe cautiously excited too. I didn't understand why he thought I'd expect him, but I was still flattered.

"Ah, here she is, Miss Moretti, before ten, just as you promised," he said. Amy beamed next to me. "Good morning, Lainey."

"Good morning, Senator, I mean, Dan," I amended at the jokingly disappointed look he gave me. "I'm sorry if you've been waiting for me?" In my nervousness, I caught myself making my statement into a question, a bad habit I usually reserved for Headmaster Stewart.

"Nothing to be sorry for. I enjoyed the chance to spend some extra time with a few old friends and new." He turned toward Amy, and we both knew it was a dismissal, but at least it was a good one. "Miss Moretti, it was a delight to see you again. Please tell your father I'll have someone contact him about that grant opportunity for the hospital."

"Of course, Senator, I'll tell him! Thank you again," she said and backed away still smiling.

We watched her go. "A lovely young woman, your roommate," Dan said to me and I nodded in agreement. "Quite brilliant, in fact. A shame she's not one of us." Though the dining hall was crowded, no one was close enough to hear us over all the noise.

I nodded again. "I wish she were too."

"Nothing we can do to change that, I'm afraid," he said. "But there *is* something we can change this morning…"

"What is it?" The seriousness in his voice had my nerves jangling.

After a beat, he laughed, and what I could only describe as a mischievous smile spread over his face. "Well, I know I'm famished, and since you're here, I'm guessing you're hungry too. Let's fix that. Join me for breakfast?

OBVIOUSLY I COULDN'T decline his request, but I was surprised when instead of moving farther into the dining hall, Dan led me outside to a waiting town car. I was even more surprised when we pulled up outside Dad's Diner. I hadn't been in weeks, not since my last shift the day Amy had moved back in. Despite my nervousness about being with the senator, which our pleasant small talk in the car did nothing to cure, I was excited to be back at Dad's.

After all my hours there over the summer, walking through the doors felt a little like coming home. I basked in the warmth of the tin walls, the scent of eggs and potatoes on the griddle, and the mismatched collection of dingy booths and tables. Also, the happy greeting from Mercy Jenkins, the head waitress.

She bustled over, deftly managing both coffee pots in one hand, and grabbed my hand for an affectionate squeeze. "Lainey! What a nice surprise! And you've brought the *senator!* What a happy Sunday!"

Dan laughed. "It's been too long, Mercy." He even leaned in and hugged her. "The table in the corner, if you don't mind."

She frowned. "Well, sure I don't, but where's that nephew of yours? Y'all won't fit in the corner."

"Just the two of us today, actually," Dan replied. "I wanted the chance to get to know the newest member of my family a little more myself."

He had no idea just how right he was about that. I managed to smile, and Mercy had no trouble being delighted by his smooth charm. Plus, I thought she considered me part of the diner's extended family too. "You'll love her as much as we all do," she promised. "Lainey's a hard worker, especially for a city girl," she added with a wink, as she led us to the most private table in the far corner of the small space.

Orders placed and coffees in hand, I started to relax and Dan started his interview. After a while of telling him stories about my aunt and our life on the road, and his telling me what it was like to be a senator,

I really believed he just wanted us to get to know each other. As I was taking the last bites of my eggs and toast, I felt so relaxed—an effect he must have had on most people, if he wanted to—I forgot completely I was supposed to be afraid of him. In fact, I was so relaxed, I asked the question I'd been harboring since I learned about his Sententia gift so many months ago.

"What's it like to be a Thought Mover?" I blurted. Immediately, I sipped my coffee to hide the damnable blush creeping over my cheeks, but I didn't take it back. I really wanted to know.

He didn't respond for a moment, but studied me instead. It should have made me feel nervous, but it didn't. He seemed to regard me with a mixture of pride and intrigue, as if this was what he'd *really* wanted to talk about and been hoping I'd ask all along. But his answer was not what I expected.

With a smile, he finally said, "You tell me."

I coughed around the coffee I'd just choked on. "I'm sorry?" He laughed lightly, but I knew he was serious.

"You're as much of a Thought Mover as any of us, though perhaps you don't realize it."

"Carter said the same thing once," I told him. "I thought he was just making a comparison."

He shook his head and said, "A *distinction*. It's a rare gift to be a Thought Mover. Carter should know. And you, Elaine, are probably the rarest of all. Undoubtedly," he amended. "It's remarkable that the two most powerful Thought Movers of their generation, of the entire *Sententia,* would meet so young and fall in love, purely by chance."

Actually, I found it a little scary, but I supposed remarkable was another way to look at it. "Dr. Stewart once told me she doesn't believe in fate, but sometimes I wonder," I said.

Dan smiled fondly so I knew he wasn't being cruel. "Constance doesn't like to believe in anything she can't control," he said. "But that's one of the reasons she's such an excellent headmaster. As much as possible *is* in the control of her very capable hands."

"Carter said something like that before too… But I think you like Dr. Stewart a lot more than he does," I added.

If anything, his fond smile grew wider, though I wasn't sure if it was for the headmaster or his headstrong nephew. "Were Constance here, she could tell you that is an undeniable truth."

I dropped my eyes and said softly, "I wish I could trade my gift for hers." And I meant it.

The fleeting touch of Dan's fingertips to the back of my hand jolted my eyes up to meet his. With utter seriousness, he said, "No, you don't."

"But…why? Knowing the truth is so powerful."

"It is," he agreed. "When it's a truth you want to know. You're young, but someday you'll understand that lies are often told out of compassion and being able to believe them is a gift in itself. Constance never experiences that. It's one of the things that has made her so…hard. No, Lainey, *your* gift is powerful."

"I'm afraid of it," I admitted.

He nodded, as if there was no other answer I could give. Maybe there wasn't. "As well you should be. If you weren't, I'd be concerned. But you've already proven you can carry the weight of your gift without falling to the temptations of it. You should be proud of yourself, Elaine."

I looked at him for a while, weighing my emotions, wondering if this was how Carter felt around him. He'd called me Elaine again, not in anger or reproof, but out of…affection, I guessed. Like my aunt did sometimes, and Mercy too. I found myself proud to have made him proud. Somewhere in the course of a day, I'd gone from fearing him to being curious about him to being eager for his praise.

"Your abilities are powerful too, Carter tells me. Will you…move my thoughts? Show me?" I asked.

"I can't," he said, and for the briefest second he seemed vexed by this.

"Huh?" I was so distracted by what I thought I'd just seen in his expression, and by anticipating what it would be like to have my mind, literally, changed that I barely understood what he'd said.

But I forgot whatever I thought I'd seen when, with deep sadness, he said, "What I mean is, I won't. I'm not strong enough, Lainey. Not like you. I never use my gift, not anymore. Not even to demonstrate for you, I'm sorry."

In all that he'd told me about the senator, this was not something Carter had mentioned, even hinted at. "But…why?"

"You don't know what happened to my father, do you?"

I shook my head. I didn't really know anything about the elder Senator Astor, save that he'd died not long after his son had joined him in the Senate. And that he was my grandfather, something I was sure the man sitting across from me, turning a cold mug of coffee round in his hands, didn't know.

"My nephew tries to spare you, perhaps too much," he mused, and then he told me the story, sparing nothing. "My father was the last, as well as the first and only, Perceptum President to be executed."

Chapter Seven

I forgot how to speak. I think I even forgot how to blink. When he'd told it all, I stared at Dan dumbly for what seemed like minutes. I'd always assumed the late Jacob Astor had died of natural causes, because I had no reason to think otherwise. But no, it was much sadder than that. It was ego and greed that ultimately killed him.

Finally, I said, "I just don't understand. It seems so…so pointless." Mr. Astor had been a Diviner with a gift for seeing outcomes—exactly as I'd assumed about my own father, and what had translated into my ability to determine a person's *final* outcome, so to speak. From everything Dan told me, it sounded like his father abused his gift, and his positions in both the Perceptum and the Senate, to further nothing but his own bank account and sense of superiority. "He basically stole *from* the Perceptum, like it was a game. But what did he have to gain that he didn't already have?" Money and esteem had already been his in abundance.

Dan met my eyes with something like respect. "You *are* perceptive. Carter told me that. And the terrible answer is: I don't know. If there were other motives, better ones, he never shared them with me."

Eventually, maybe inevitably, his manipulations grew so extensive they caught up to him. And it was Constance Stewart who did the catching.

"Really?" I asked stupidly. Shock, like alcohol, disconnected my mouth from my brain.

"It was a sorely misplaced lie," Dan said. "When you've told so many of them, you sometimes forget who *not* to lie to."

I nodded, sagely, I thought. Like of course I knew this already. And in a way, I did. Lying, blatant or by omission, had begun to feel like a job I didn't want but couldn't afford to quit. I wondered if that's what Mr. Astor had felt like, before it was too late. But *I* was only trying to protect people, I reasoned.

I looked down at the table, toying with my teaspoon. "Couldn't he predict what was going to happen? In the end, I mean." If only I'd known my paternal grandfather, I might have told him exactly where all his efforts would lead.

"Probably, if he'd tried." Dan lifted his coffee, as if he'd take a sip, but set it back down without drinking any. "We can't use our gifts directly on ourselves, but...well, I'd say it should have been obvious, but I was as blind to what he was doing as anyone."

"I'm sorry. This must be hard for you to talk about."

Dan met my eyes. "I've made peace with it. I've *learned* from it."

"What do you mean?" It seemed like maybe the saddest thing he'd set yet, which made no sense.

"I mean that my father's fate could easily have been my own." I gasped, and Dan smiled sadly. "That shouldn't be surprising. There's a reason I don't use my gift anymore. I *know* I'm not strong enough to resist the temptation of abusing it because I did. My father's disgrace was what finally made me admit it. I haven't used it since the day he died."

The most powerful drug in the world, I thought to myself. Moving thoughts had to be difficult to resist and infinitely harder to quit. Despite what he'd said, it was clear it pained Dan to talk about what happened, just as it pained me to learn my grandfather had actually been a pretty terrible man. I had a million more questions I decided to keep to myself, but I couldn't resist asking one more thing I'd wondered about. "Is that why you and Jill's mother never married?"

"Yes," he said. "I won't deny it. I should have learned my lesson when it cost me my daughter. I loved Angela, but it's Jillian I truly lost. Nearly twice, if not for you."

So we'd come full circle, back to me and my gift. "Why don't you hate me?" Another question I'd been dying to have answered but never thought I'd ask.

He said nothing for a few long moments, regarding me not with hostility but a fatherly sort of warmth. "Carter also once told me you don't see yourself as others do. He was certainly right. Your humility is perhaps an even rarer gift than your heritage," he mused. "What I hate are the actions you were forced to take, along with my part in them, but I can't imagine anyone else who'd have followed them with such compassion. If not for you, I wouldn't have admitted the additional mistakes I was making, and never would have gotten my daughter the help she needs. No, I *needed* you, Lainey, and I'm not alone. *We* need you too."

Here it was, the moment I'd been dreading, all the more since my suspicion of Daniel Astor had begun to change into something else. I knew who he meant—*We* was all of us, the Sententia, and the Perceptum Council specifically. They wanted me to do my family's job, and I was sure I couldn't.

Instead of answering, I studied the chip on the edge of my empty mug. As I stared at it, I realized it was strange that my mug *was* empty, since Mercy was usually so prompt about filling them. I glanced over my shoulder and was shocked to see the restaurant was nearly empty. It was almost closing time, and time for us to go. Mercy was sitting at the counter, enjoying her own cup of coffee. A lifetime of waitressing must have told her our conversation hadn't really been one to interrupt.

The senator's smooth voice broke into my jumbled thoughts. When I looked at him again, he was smiling. "I'd have been surprised if that compassion didn't make you hesitate," he said, and stood, pulling his wallet from a back pocket and depositing at least twice as much as our breakfast cost on the table. "You have plenty of time to think about it, don't worry. You are exactly who we've needed for probably a very long time. We'll wait until you're ready."

If it hadn't been such a serious topic, the possibility of my joining the Perceptum as assassin-in-residence, I'd have laughed at the similarity between the senator's words and Carter's. He was talking about something entirely different, of course, but once done, I couldn't go back from that either. I'd given myself a year until I was ready to take that big step in our relationship. Somehow I knew that was about how long I had until the Perceptum would expect a definitive answer.

A WEEK LATER, I was no closer to an answer, but Amy had other concerns.

"Isn't that Maddi Worthington one of your campers?" That's what she'd taken to calling my dorm girls. The one in question had just come into the bookstore lounge where we were seated on our favorite couch by the fireplace, working on homework.

"*Mandi* Worthington, and yes. Why?"

"Mandi. Whatever," Amy said. "I saw her talking to Caleb at the reception and another time or two since then. I can't figure out why. Isn't she a seventh grader? And Alexbitch's cousin, right?" That's what she'd taken to calling Alexis.

"Eighth actually, and yes again, Alexis's cousin. I don't know why she was talking to Caleb though, and come to think of it, I don't know why she didn't come here last year either."

Amy watched Mandi's progress toward some of her friends in the sitting area. "Well, she's not a Legacy. I put together mailings for all of them—you—the other day." Amy's work hours were spent at the Admissions office, which also coordinated fund-raising for the Academy. Considering the size of the Academy's endowment, she must have mailed a *lot* of things. "She's not on the swim team, is she?" she pressed.

I glanced at my roommate over my economics book. She was back to rapidly scribbling numbers on her paper, but she was wearing an uncharacteristic frown while doing it. When it came to math, usually that was *my* expression. "You know she's not on the swim team; you come to our meets."

The frown deepened and the scribbling slowed but didn't stop. "Oh, right. Sorry."

I put my hand on her notebook. "What's going on here?" I asked. She seemed…suspicious. That was also not like her.

"I just can't figure out why Caleb would be talking to an eighth grade girl, is all."

I sighed. "Did you *ask* him why he was talking to her?"

"Talking to who?" Carter said as he wandered into the lounge, a few pieces of wood under one arm, a book under the other. He settled the logs in the fireplace and himself onto the couch next to me, throwing his now empty arm around my shoulders. I loved break time.

"Mandi Worthington," Amy said, voice tinged with distaste. "She was talking to Caleb."

Carter glanced in Mandi's direction and frowned, his eyebrows drawing together in a look of obvious concern. I barely had time to think *Oh, no,* before Amy pounced on it. *"What do you know?"* she hissed.

"What? Nothing!" Carter replied. "It's just that she's right over there…" Which was a bullshit line, but Amy seemed to accept it. I made a mental note to get the real scoop on young Mandi as soon as I could.

"Sorry," Amy whispered. "But…anyway. I don't like it." She frowned some more and I laughed at her.

"No, really?" I mocked. "Why are you so bothered by this anyway?" I was trying to get her to relax, but in the back of my mind, Carter's reaction kind of had me wondering if she *should* be worried.

"Bothered by what?" Caleb himself asked as he squeezed onto the end of the couch next to Amy. "What's the matter, babe?"

We both squealed in surprise and Caleb grinned. Carter looked amused, like he'd known he was here. Instead of answering, Amy asked, "Where the hell did you come from?!"

Caleb grinned a little wider, just like Carter often did. They were definitely spending too much time together. "Upstairs. Picking up a book for Bio extra credit."

The second floor housed, in addition to my favorite section of the store—First Editions—all the health-related books. Amy might have been unsure about her future career, but her boyfriend was decidedly on his way to becoming Caleb Sullivan, MD. It was also impossible to see the staircase from our seat by the fire, which explained how he snuck up on us.

"N…nothing, really," Amy finally stammered. "Just having trouble with this problem set." She hastily scrawled a few more numbers on her paper in pretend confusion.

It was Caleb's turn to frown, and I couldn't blame him. *"You're* having trouble with math?" he asked, as he glanced over at her now-messy notebook.

"*That's* why it's so bothersome," she replied. It might have been a poor excuse to start with, but she sold it well. "I just need quiet to concentrate. Come with me?" she said to Caleb, who nodded but was obviously perplexed. Amy gathered up her books to head back to campus, Caleb trailing after her, and I looked at Carter expectantly.

"What?"

I rolled my eyes. He never was very good at feigning ignorance. "You know what."

He sighed, and then ran his fingers through his hair, instantly confirming my suspicions. "She's a Siren," he said in a low voice.

"Like a warning or, uh, like Odysseus…?"

"The latter. Sirens are…hard to resist. She's a kind of Herald, like Alex. Except worse."

"That's a tall order," I said drily. In the Sententia hierarchy, Heralds were one step below Thought Movers. Their gifts projected onto others, though they had no impetus. They influenced—sometimes strongly—but couldn't compel. Alexis was *persuasive;* whatever she said, people were likely to believe.

"Honestly, Lane, from what I've heard of her, Mandi makes her cousin look like a saint. Alexis does things for a reason, even if it's a selfish one. Mandi…she just seems to do shit for fun," he said, and *that* made me nervous. If I remembered correctly, Odysseus had to be shackled to a mast in order to resist the feminine allures of the sirens.

"So then I should be worried about a Siren, even an eighth-grade one, talking to Amy's boyfriend, right?"

He gave a small nod. "Probably. She's fourteen," he reminded me. Carter hadn't been a saint at fourteen. Neither had Amy, for that matter.

"Great," I said. Now I'd need to investigate just why she was talking to Caleb. "Should I be worried about her talking to *you?*"

One of the sexy smiles I lived for spread over his face and he leaned in close, his lips practically touching mine as he said, "Even a Siren can't make me think of anyone but you." He kissed me after that, and I forgot completely that we were in the middle of the crowded bookstore.

Kisses like that made me forget a lot of things, including that he was destined to kill me.

FINDING MYSELF ALONE in the lounge, with Amy gone and Carter back to work, I decided to go hang out with Melinda. It was late Sunday afternoon, so I knew she'd be upstairs making dinner. I'd dined with them almost every Sunday night for the last year, but over the summer, I'd started helping her. Slowly, but surely, under Melinda's patient tutelage, I was becoming a halfway decent cook.

When I got up to the apartment, I was greeted by the delicious aroma of oregano and comfort. A lasagna was already bubbling in the oven.

"Jeff?" Melinda called from the living room.

"No, it's me."

"Lainey!" She popped into the kitchen and dropped her latest Sudoku book on the table. "It's not closing time already, is it?"

"No, not yet, but I guess I'm too late to help with dinner."

She glanced at the clock over the sink and then at a bowl of apples on the counter and said, "But it's never too late for dessert, right? Let's make a crisp. The boys will appreciate it."

So we did, Melinda chopping apples while I measured and mixed. It was comfortable and familiar. We worked well together, and I'd missed my cooking lessons since school restarted. I tried not to think about the homework I *should* be doing.

I tried, too, not to think about the things Dan had revealed to me, but it was hard not to. Initially, I'd intended to confront Carter about his conspicuous omissions right away. I couldn't believe how in all our time together he'd never told me about Mr. Astor, or about Dan vowing not to use his gift. But eventually I realized that wasn't true—I could believe it. I could even give several reasons why he'd done it. I just wasn't happy about it. I was also, I reminded myself, still omitting some big things of my own.

As I stirred my flour and sugar and chatted about this and that with Melinda, I realized Carter wasn't the only one I could talk to. "Mel?" I started.

She looked up from the apples and smiled. "Are you ready for these?"

"Um, sure," I said, handing over the baking dish. "But that's not what I wanted to ask you."

There must have been something in my tone that tipped her off, because she stopped scooping apples and frowned. "What's he done now?"

I almost laughed. "It's more about what he hasn't done. Why didn't anyone tell me about Mr. Astor?"

She shook her head, caramel curls bouncing lightly, and her frown deepened. "I knew this would happen," she muttered and then sighed. "I'm sorry, Lainey. I…well, there's no good excuse. We should have. I suppose Dan did though?" She said it like a question, but it really wasn't. She couldn't hide the traces of anger in her voice either.

"He did. It was…pretty shocking." Obviously. I had a gift for understatement.

Melinda brushed a hand across her forehead, a motion reminiscent of her nephew's nervous tic. "I suppose that's one of the reasons we never told you. It's not something any of us likes to think about. In fact, it's probably the worst moment in our history." By "our," I knew she meant Sententia.

"Was Mr. Astor really that terrible?"

She thought about it. Something in my expression must have told her I hoped the answer was no. "I…didn't know him, not really. Evelyn"—Dan and Jeff's mother—"would probably tell you he was *worse*. The Council believed he was."

"But elimination?" *That* was what I really wondered about. It seemed extreme, for an already extreme measure. I hadn't wanted to ask Dan about it.

Melinda leaned on the counter. She said, "It shouldn't have come to that," the words thoughtful and measured. "I—I'm sure Dan explained what he was up to. He manipulated everyone, including other Sentenia, other *Council* members, *his* people. The people he was meant to *lead*. He took our gifts and used them against us. I think, in some members' eyes, that was a worse offense than indiscretion."

I nodded, pushing the baking dish in a slow circle in front of me. "So it was a little bit revenge."

"No." She gazed at me with her pretty pool blue eyes, so much like Carter's. "He threatened to expose us. That's what did it. His ego. But…like I said. It shouldn't have come to that. It didn't have to." She cleared her throat. "It *did* change his son, though. Even tragedies can have silver linings, I suppose." She reached over her hand to pat mine, still covered in apple and sugar. We both gave a little laugh when we realized, breaking the tension of the story. "Have a cup of tea with me? We can talk about it more while we wait for Carter and Jeff."

As I set the table in the dining room, Melinda made tea. She brought in mugs for each of us before returning to the kitchen to check on dinner. I'd never seen the mug she gave me, an old one with a fading picture of a bear, clearly well-loved and probably from the back of the cabinet. It was the perfect vessel for something hot and soothing, which seemed perfect right about then. With no thought for the steam clearly rising from it, I took an eager sip.

And unceremoniously spit it all over the table in front of me. Simultaneously, I dropped the mug, which hit the edge and split in two, spilling hot tea all down my front. I yelped, and Melinda came rushing back into the room just as I jumped up from my chair and tried to mop up the damage with my tiny napkin. "S...sorry!" I stammered. "It was hot, and I burned myself, and then I dropped my cup which just made it worse..."

"Oh, you poor thing!" She grabbed another napkin to help, but since most of the tea had been absorbed by my shirt, she told me, "You go clean up. I'll bring you something to put on and then we'll take care of this."

I made it to the bathroom before I started to hyperventilate, but just barely. I sat down hard on the toilet lid and put my head in my hands, willing myself to take deep breaths. The tea had been hot, true, but that wasn't what caused me to spit it out and drop my cup. No, it was the vision of another cup of tea that had been served in that mug.

The one that killed Mark Penrose.

It lasted only a second, the vision, but long enough that I saw Carter's father sipping from that same mug while reading a newspaper. I knew instantly that there was poison in the tea and that Mark Penrose would not live out the day. But that was all I saw before I dropped it.

I didn't know how the poison had gotten there or by whose hand. It could have been Mark's own, for all I could be sure. Carter had said he died of a broken heart. Maybe he decided he couldn't live with it anymore. Maybe it was a terrible accident at the tea manufacturer. I wanted to believe that one, but I knew that wanting to believe something and it being true were two very different things.

I also knew that maybe neither of those scenarios was true. Maybe the poison had been added by someone else, even someone who lived here still. I didn't want to believe *that* but I knew better than to rule it out. I couldn't rule *anything* out until I got my hands back on that mug.

A soft knock on the door jolted me out of my thoughts.

"Lainey? You okay, honey? Do you need to go over to the infirmary? I brought you a shirt to change into," Melinda's slightly muffled voice said warmly. I roused myself and opened the door a crack.

"Thanks." I reached out to take the shirt from her. "Most of the damage was to my T-shirt, but I…I think I burned my stomach. Let me help you clean up, and then yeah, maybe I should go over to the infirmary to have them check it." In actuality, I was fine—the damage was entirely within my mind—but I *really* needed to get out of there for a while.

"Oh, don't worry about cleaning up," she said. "It's already done. You just go ahead back to campus. I'll tell Carter what happened."

"Thanks," I repeated. *Shit!* I said in my head. I changed as quickly as possible and raced back to the dining room, but I was too late. Melinda had indeed finished wiping up my mess and the broken mug was already gone, along with my chance to read more from it. Melinda was in the kitchen, so it wasn't like I could pick through the trash on my way out. Unable to do anything else, I apologized and thanked her again before escaping downstairs and across the street to my room.

Later I called Carter to give excuses for not coming back for dinner, half of which were true, because I did have a lot of homework and I *wasn't* hungry. As much as I wanted to see him, to take comfort in him, I just couldn't, not tonight. And not about this.

I couldn't sleep either. After tossing and turning for too long, I quietly slipped out of our room and down to the porch. Technically, I was breaking curfew, but I needed the fresh air. I settled into one of the pair of antique reed-back rockers and pushed the checkers around the board that rested on the low table between them.

I sat there for I didn't know how long, listening to a chorus of owls charm the night around me. Owls were supposed to be wise birds, and I hoped maybe I could learn from their refrain. In a matter of days, my head had become crowded with things I'd rather not know and their burden was heavy. Sharing them would lighten their load, and Carter and I had even promised each other that we would, but when I thought about telling him, my stomach formed a cold, tight ball.

If my fleeting vision last spring had been correct, I only had a limited amount of time left before he killed me, and I *still* hadn't been able to see why. Could this be it? How *did* one tell the boy she loved— loved so madly that she risked her death daily to be near him—things like his father didn't die of natural causes and his uncle, whom he idolized, was really *her* flesh and blood? For all I knew, I'd just discovered the keys to my own demise.

What I needed was more information. To find it, tomorrow I'd visit a place I hadn't been since I'd killed a girl there.

Chapter Eight

hat are you doing here?!" Amy and I said at almost the same time. It was Monday afternoon, right after classes ended, and I'd just opened the door to our room to find my roommate frantically rummaging through a dresser drawer. Usually she was at her work hours during this time. We were both surprised, and not entirely pleased, it seemed, to see each other. I decided to answer first.

"My study group got changed to later tonight." I didn't mention that *I'd* asked to change it. "What are you looking for? And why aren't you at work?"

"I, uh, spilled something on my pants," she said sheepishly, "but I can't find the ones I wanted to change into." And it was true, I suddenly realized, that she was not wearing pants. Thankfully, her long sweater covered everything I didn't want to see, but the problem was, she was searching through her underwear drawer. And, on further inspection, it wasn't *her* sweater she was wearing. I eyed her messy hair and slightly flushed cheeks.

"Is he in the bathroom?" I asked. For possibly the first time ever, Amy blushed as deeply as I usually did, which answered my question for me. I didn't even wait for a response. "Caleb," I called, "if you're not wearing pants either, please stay where you are." I heard him chuckle from the other side of the bathroom door.

"Sorry," Amy said, pulling out her underthings and holding them behind her back. She eagerly shared all of the details with me after the fact, but apparently being almost-caught in the act wasn't as fun.

I looked at the clock and did some mental math. Classes had ended not even ten minutes ago. "Did you guys skip final hour?" I asked, even more surprised about that than finding the two of them in our room. Amy was on her way to being Valedictorian. It wasn't at all like her to skip classes, not because she was totally against the idea once in a while, but because she actually enjoyed going to them.

"It was just test review," she muttered.

I finally let out the laugh I'd been holding in and turned around so she could get dressed. "Right. Now could you please put some pants on? And we seriously need to get a ribbon-on-the-door system or something, so this doesn't happen again."

"If you'd gone to your study group like you're supposed to, we wouldn't need a ribbon!" Caleb shouted from the bathroom and Amy giggled. "And Lane, are you staying? 'Cause I really need to get out of here…"

I laughed again. "Only long enough to change my shoes. Keep your pants on…"—I spied his jeans half-hidden under Amy's bed—"or not for a minute."

"Where are you going?" a now fully clothed Amy asked as I sat on my desk chair to put on my sneakers.

Shit. I had no excuse, because I hadn't thought I'd need one. "A walk," I finally said. It was the truth and, also, the only thing I could come up with.

She eyed me speculatively, but all she said was, "Okay, then. And I am sorry, Lainey." For some reason, she was more embarrassed about this than she should have been. I'd ponder that later.

"It's okay," I assured her. I grabbed my keys, phone, and earphones. "See you at dinner. You too, Caleb."

"Bye," I heard her say, with a muffled, "Later!" coming from the boy hiding in the bathroom, as the door closed behind me.

SINCE IT WAS the middle of the afternoon on a regular school day, I had to be extra careful sneaking off campus. I'd already been wearing leggings and an Academy sweatshirt—not my best fashion day—so I took off at a light jog, as if I were just going for a run. Being on the track team in the spring, and dating Carter, it was something I did with enough regularity that it wouldn't seem strange to see me trotting past the ponds and through the gates.

I turned left on Main Street and continued running past the bookstore on the other side of the street, hoping no one would notice me. "No one" mostly meaning my boyfriend. The bookstore was usually empty this time of day, and it would be just my luck that he'd look out the front windows as I ran past. When I reached a particular spot in the trees that lined the street, I stopped as if to stretch but really just to make sure I was alone. Seeing no one, I darted into the woods.

On a day I didn't care to remember for other reasons, Carter had shown me this shortcut into the seemingly endless trails that zig-zagged through the vast forest bordering campus. Carter knew them all like the back of his hand, but even after my summer of exploring them, I could still get lost. I did, however, easily know my way to the trail that led even farther off campus, into the cemetery where Carter's parents were buried. Where Jill had tried to kill me, but I'd killed her instead.

It was a good mile and a half from where I'd entered the woods to the Penroses' grave, but I didn't mind the walk. And I did walk, dropping the facade of my jog as soon as I was hidden in the trees. The fresh air and moving slow were good for me, helping me clear my head for what I planned to do next. Instead of dwell on Mark Penrose's death while I walked, I thought about my roommate.

I was confused about what was up with her. Amy was always so happy and solid, much like Carter. The two of them really had a shocking number of things in common; it was no wonder they made such good friends. But her behavior today—her embarrassment and skipping class, not to mention her suspicious inquisition the other day—was so out of character, I couldn't help but be concerned.

It definitely had something to do with Caleb, but as far as I could tell, he seemed perfectly normal. Something was going on, possibly only in Amy's mind, and I determined I'd get to the bottom of it. Right after I figured out who killed my boyfriend's father.

I paused where the trail opened into the large St. Cecilia's cemetery, with its acres of neat graves amidst manicured, park-like grounds. It was undeniably beautiful, in a melancholy way, and I was surprised how reluctant I was to enter. There was nothing sinister about the place, except for my memories. I fought the urge to turn and run, instead taking a deep breath and stepping out of the forest.

It was sunny out and the grounds were lovely in the fall. I suddenly wished I'd brought flowers, but all I had were my own regrets. They would have to do. I picked my way over to the Penroses' grave slowly. I'd only been once, but it wasn't hard to find. I imagined I could find it blindfolded, it was so indelibly etched in my mind. Sometimes I swore I could still feel where it dug into my back as Jill had kicked me again and again.

Their headstone was a smooth, pearlescent gray marble, simple and elegant. PENROSE was carved in the center, with BELOVED WIFE and

BELOVED HUSBAND the only other inscriptions below their names and the dates of their too-short lives. Geneviève Marie Gosselin was buried on the left. Markham Loughran on the right. I made a silent apology and sank to the ground on his side of the grave.

I had no idea what to do, or even if this had a remote chance of working, but I had to try. I had no other plan. Without asking, I didn't know of anything else in Carter's apartment that would have a connection to his father's death. So, I closed my eyes, put my hands to the ground, and opened my mind, praying my Diviner sense could reach the thread of Mark's past.

Nothing happened. Not even a tingle or a hint of dizziness. I moved my hands and tried again. I touched the headstone. I even laid down on the cool grass over the length of the grave. Nothing. Clearly, I was not close enough to Mark Penrose, and I certainly couldn't get closer.

With a resigned sigh, I got up. I touched the headstone again in a brief goodbye and started back to campus.

ABOUT HALFWAY BACK to school, without warning, someone grabbed me around my waist. I was so surprised, I didn't even scream.

Finally—*finally!*—my instincts kicked in and my years of martial arts classes paid off. I used my elbow and foot simultaneously, to break the hold, sending us off balance. But I was rusty, and the arms around my waist only loosened as we fell toward the ground.

We hit with a thud and I tried to roll away. During the fall, the headphones pulled from my ears, and I thought I heard a familiar voice, cursing roundly. I landed on top of my attacker and hands grabbed my wrists from behind. I kicked out with my foot once, twice more, connecting solidly with a knee.

The person groaned again, before a definitely familiar voice, in a mix of pain and exasperation, shouted, "Fuck, Lainey! It's *me*. Stop kicking me!"

I whipped my head around. Sure enough, it was Carter beneath me, still holding my wrists and pulling me tight against him. I struggled once more, just out of instinct, as I waited for my heart to slow and my brain to recognize that I wasn't really in danger.

And just like that, it did. All of a sudden, fighting didn't feel so much like fighting anymore. If anything, my breathing quickened. Carter's did too. I felt it, puffing faster across my bare neck, along with the increasing beat of his pulse and the heat of his long, solid body.

In seconds, and without my even realizing how it happened, I was facing the other way. Carter grasped my wrists again and pulled me toward him, kissing me deeply, almost desperately. Like he might never get another chance. Before long my wrists were freed, letting my arms twine around his neck and his hands slide down my back to grip my hips.

For a minute or two, kissing Carter there, in the forest and with the sense of danger still sparking in my veins, felt like the sexiest moments we'd ever had. But then reality seeped in along with the cold, damp dirt at my knees. I broke away, reluctantly, and sat up to catch my breath. After a moment, Carter followed suit, pulling me up to stand.

Once we were upright, I shoved him, demanding, "What the hell were you doing?!"

With a sly, sexy grin, he tugged me close and said, "I was kissing you." Then he did it again.

I refused to be distracted. Much. Finally, I pushed him away again, though not as roughly this time. "I understand that part," I said. "I was *talking* about your grabbing me in the first place. What are you even doing out here?"

His good humor left abruptly and he raked his fingers through his hair. "Waiting for you," he said. "And I could have been *anyone,* including someone who actually wanted to hurt you."

"Well, but you weren't." I grabbed his hand and started walking back toward campus. He came along willingly, but I still felt tension radiating from him. "You were you and there's no one else around. But...how did you even end up out here?"

"Last time you disappeared and I couldn't reach you, this is where you were. And your roommate told me you'd 'gone for a walk.'" Damn it. I hated doing it, but I probably should have lied to Amy outright. Then she couldn't have informed on me. Through my irritation, I realized Carter was still talking. "...*trying* to scare the shit out of me? Why would you even come out here, in the middle of the afternoon no less, after what happened last time?"

It was a valid question, one I *couldn't* answer truthfully. I hadn't planned on answering it at all. Thankfully, a plausible lie presented itself. I ducked my eyes and lowered my voice. This lie worked because it was partially true.

"I think about 'what happened last time' all the time," I whispered. "And with meeting your uncle...that made it worse. Probably it wasn't healthy to go there; I don't know. But it did make me feel better to walk away and know we're both still alive."

Carter was silent for a long minute before he came to an abrupt halt and pulled me into a bruising hug. "I'm sorry," he breathed. "I'm so sorry."

I am too, I thought. I felt like shit for lying to him.

We were nearly to campus when Carter finally got around to the questions I'd been waiting for. The slight change of pressure in his grip on my hand warned me it was coming. "You didn't really burn your stomach with that tea, did you?" he asked. I shook my head. There was no point in denying it. "So is this all about my uncle?"

"Yes," I said. Mostly.

"He really liked you."

That really wasn't the problem. "I know he did. And I…liked him too," I said, and I was pretty sure it was true.

"But?" Carter asked, even though I knew he didn't have to. He just wanted me to say it.

"He tried to recruit me, Carter."

He nodded. "I know. He didn't tell me what you said, though I suppose I can guess it."

"I didn't say anything."

That brought him to a standstill. We were about twenty steps from the edge of the tree line; I could see campus, and freedom from this discussion, just paces away. Carter stood in front of me, a wary hopefulness in his voice that pained me. "You're considering it?"

I wasn't. Was I? I *thought* I hated the Perceptum. But maybe it wasn't that I didn't want to work with them at *all*; I just didn't want to do…what they wanted me to do. I didn't even like to think it was necessary. But most of all, I didn't want anything to hurt Carter, including me.

"I don't want to disappoint you," I told him and he hugged me again.

"I love you," he said into my ear, kissing just below where he'd spoken to punctuate it. "There's no way you could."

I very much doubted that was true.

Chapter Nine

Thank *God for coffee,* I thought as I waited in line with my class-mates in front of a folding table manned by one of the lower grade teachers. She was not a Sententia, I noted, but she did look bored and tired, much like the rest of us. Amy shifted restlessly in front of me. I sipped from my travel cup and pictured the thousands of other kids standing in similar lines in similar hallways across the country. This forced waiting was as much a rite of passage as taking the SATs, the reason why I was there. The reason for my already-accepted-at-freaking-MIT roommate's presence was another matter.

"You're here again, why?" I asked her, though I knew the answer. I just liked to goad her.

She made an exasperated noise and tapped her pencil on her calculator. She had to be the only person in line eager for the test to start, not just to be over with. "I *told* you; I have to try." By which, she meant she had to try for a perfect score. To avenge the whole one question she got wrong the first time. "I swear I just filled in the wrong bubble," she muttered and I laughed.

"You probably should have had Penrose tutor you first. *He* got them all right," Caleb said from behind her, giving her hip a playful squeeze. Amy shoved him without even turning around and I laughed even harder. The one wrong answer was made even sorer for Amy by her unofficial rivalry with Carter. His score was perfect the first time.

Speaking of rivals, my official one was laughing a few places back from us. There was no reason for her to be so loud, or sound so smug, for that matter, so I knew it was on purpose. Sometimes I forgot that Alexis and Amy had a little rivalry of their own. "…just here for the hell of it," she said. "Georgetown's already waiting for me. I'm so *relaxed* this time, I'm going to *ace* this."

Amy's face was murderous, and I could tell it was taking all her control not to turn around and glare at Alex, or worse. It might have been okay for Caleb and me to make fun of her little neuroses, but *not* Alexis. I imagined myself saying something like, *Ace* this, *bitch,* and slapping her again, but all Amy ever needed was words.

"The only test she's ever aced was the quiz in Cosmo last month on the A to Z of blow jobs," she said, in the same smug, too-loud voice Alex used. She started to tick them off on her fingers. "In an Airplane, on a Boat, *behind the Chapel,*" she added with a little extra emphasis.

Alexis's laughing immediately cut off, and I dared a glance over my shoulder. Her face looked as murderous as Amy's had a few moments ago and I wondered what I was missing. I only had time to catch Amy's smirk before the teacher up front called us to attention. It was time for the tests. She made me leave my coffee at the door.

Several hours and one fried brain later, I joined the line to hand in my test booklet. I flexed my aching fingers as I inched closer to freedom, watching my classmates leave one by one before me. We'd been sorted alphabetically, so I got the lucky last chair in the last testing room. Caleb grinned at me and said, "Later, Lane," over his shoulder as he left.

I knew I hadn't really needed to be here either. My first scores from the spring had been pretty decent, and might be moot in a matter of days or weeks anyway, but I still wanted to have as normal a senior year as I possibly could, however much of it I managed to get. So, I'd dutifully taken the test again along with everyone else, and I really did hope my scores improved. I'd never come close to perfect like my roommate, but grades still mattered to me too.

"Thank you," I told the proctor as I handed over my materials and practically bolted for the door.

"Oh, wait!" she said to my back, halting my escape. I spun around to see her frowning at my booklet. "You're Elaine Young."

"Um, yes? Is something wrong with my test?"

She shook her head. I thought she looked sheepish, for some reason I couldn't imagine. "No, it's fine. I'm sorry. I was supposed to give you this before," she said and held out an envelope with my name on it.

"Thanks," I told her again and finally made it out of the room, opening the envelope as I went. Of course, I stopped in my tracks as soon as I pulled out the note.

It was from Daniel Astor.

Lainey, he wrote,

My wishes for good luck today, though I understand you don't need it. I have on good authority that a certain university in Baltimore is expecting your application with approved stamp in hand. In fact, I've taken the liberty of setting up dinner for us and your aunt with the university president next week during your visit. I so look forward to seeing you then.

Yours, D.A.

Whoa. I didn't know how to take this. Was I flattered? Bothered? I was standing in the middle of the hall, staring at his words, when I thought I heard my name.

"Lainey? You okay?" Brooke Barros was right in front of me, waving a hand in front of my face. Her arms were full of testing materials. I shook my head, but said, "Yeah, sorry. Hey, Brooke. You at work hours?"

"Yeah. Mr. Wislowski sent me to help the test proctors," she confirmed. "Though seriously, I almost took the test myself just to get out of this. So. Boring. Anyway, what's got you all statue in the hallway? You're the last one in the building, you know."

"It's a note from Senator Astor," I told her. I couldn't see any reason to lie.

"Wow, you really are a rock star! Personal notes from the senator." She studied me for a beat, her eyes flashing a tell-tale amber. "And you want him to like you." It wasn't a question, not from Brooke, a Sensor with a handy gift for reading what people wanted. I guess it answered how I felt about the note.

"I suppose I do," I admitted and I blushed.

"Don't we all, yeah? Nothing to be embarrassed about. Sorry," she added. "I couldn't resist." She looked as if she wanted to say something else after that but hesitated for some reason. It made me wary.

"What?"

Brooke bit her lip and sighed. "Lane, listen. I've been trying to figure out how to tell you this, or if I should even mention it but someone…someone *wants* something to do with you. And I don't mean all the boys who've got the hots for you. Some of the girls too. I mean something…not good."

I'd almost have laughed if she didn't sound so ominous. Instead, I said, "Alexis wants my boyfriend. That's nothing new. In fact, she probably wants me to disappear or maybe explode in a cloud of dust."

Brooke shook her head. "No, that's not it. Well, it *is* true. Still. But that's not what I mean this time. I felt it first, I don't know, a few weeks ago? Just by accident. Maybe it was at the unveiling? I keep checking, and every once in a while, I feel something again, but I can't quite figure it out. I probably shouldn't have said anything, but it doesn't feel right, Lane. Lex is harmless. This…isn't."

I frowned, and before I could stop it, my mouth said, "Is it Carter?"

But Brooke didn't understand. And really, who'd have thought I wanted to know if Carter was going to harm, possibly kill me? "I don't think so, no. Alexis is the only one who thinks she still has a shot at him. I'm sorry. I'll keep trying to find whoever, whatever it is. Shit, I've probably freaked you out now. It's probably nothing, but…just in case. I just couldn't keep it to myself."

I leaned over and hugged her and her test books, putting on my brave face for reassurance. "Thanks, Brooke. But I'm sure it's nothing. Don't worry."

In reality, I was sure it was something. I just wondered where it would rank on my ever-growing list of things to worry about.

I'D BARELY MADE it out of the building when I heard my name again.

"Young!" someone called. It was Derek Wei, a sophomore on the swim team. He'd been headed around the side of the building, walking quickly toward the auditorium. "Sullivan's girlfriend is about to get into it with that hot eighth grader. You probably want to see this."

I almost couldn't understand what he meant. "Amy?" I asked, but who else could he be talking about? Caleb was the only Sullivan at school. I nearly stumbled down the steps as I hurried to follow him.

Sure enough, by the side of the auditorium, in the middle of an excited group of students, were Amy and Mandi Worthington. Mandi had her back against the wall and was smirking in that irritating way only bitchy pretty girls can. My roommate looked ready to slap the smirk right off of her.

"Hey!" I shouted. The crowd easily parted for me, most probably hoping I'd get into the fray. "What the hell's going on?" I inserted myself between them.

Mandi paused in her smirking long enough to tell me, "Your crazy roommate was just threatening me to keep away from her boyfriend. I told her I can't, since he *volunteered* to be my algebra tutor."

"The hell he did!" Amy shouted, and when Mandi laughed, I actually had to put my hand on Amy's shoulder to keep her away from my charge.

I was in a very awkward position, literally, what with trying to restrain Amy, and also because she was my best friend while Mandi was one of my students from Sanderson. And I was on the Honor Board, which would be tasked with disciplining either or both of them, if necessary. I couldn't win here, so I had to get them separated, and fast.

"Mandi, go wherever you were going," I told her. "Amy's sorry."

"The hell I—" Amy started to say, but I squeezed her shoulder. Hard. She turned her angry glare on me, but thankfully she did shut up.

"Amy's sorry," I repeated. "Now go ahead." I smiled at Mandi and nodded toward anywhere that wasn't right here.

"Thanks, Lainey," she replied, her words dripping with faux-sincerity, before she slipped past me to leave. But not before she gave Amy one more sly grin and added, "Caleb is probably wondering why I'm late for our study date."

That answered one question, at least. *I'd* wondered where the boy in question was during this altercation, since we'd just been in the same testing group a few minutes prior. I threw my arm around Amy's shoulder and headed us in the opposite direction of Mandi, toward the athletic fields and the other side of campus from our dorm. I could practically feel the disappointment wafting off the gathered students. Too bad.

After a few steps, Amy shoved me away. "Thanks, Laincy," she said in a mocking imitation of Mandi. Her voice was colder than I'd ever heard it directed at me. I didn't like it, but I was angry too.

"I'm sorry, Ame, but what'd you want me to do? And actually, what were *you* doing? I swear you were going to hit her. In front of that whole group!"

"I don't know!" she shouted back and then she started to cry. I stopped, stunned, and put my arm back around her. Amy was fiery and dramatic on a regular basis, but this was something different. This was almost hysterical. "I don't know," she repeated on a sniffle. "Something about that girl just makes me crazy. And she won't leave Caleb alone! He even talks about her. 'Did you know Mandi blah blah blah?' Like I care what Mandi Worthing-twit did or said. I swear, he spends more time with her than with me lately."

I sighed, and for approximately the millionth time, wished I could tell Amy about the Sententia. Hell, I wished I could tell Caleb too. It would make all our lives so much easier. But I couldn't, not without facing the inevitable wrath of Headmaster Stewart, and I really didn't want to risk that. On top of that, I didn't know what game Mandi was playing or how much of this problem was in Amy's head. I didn't trust Mandi as far as I could toss her tiny butt, but I also spent plenty of time around Caleb and couldn't remember him mentioning her even once.

Whatever was really going on, what I needed to do right then was calm my roommate down. "That's not true," I said gently. "He's just her tutor; it's his job, Ame, four hours a week, just like the rest of us."

"Six," she reminded me, and she was right. Caleb did extra work hours along with his dorm duties as part of his free room and board. Still, he didn't spend all six hours with one student and I said so.

Amy sniffled again and, in the most un-Amy move ever, wiped her nose on the sleeve of her wool sweater. "You're right," she said. "I don't know what's wrong with me. But I do hate that girl. I know that much."

I gave her shoulders another squeeze and turned us around, heading back toward Marquise House and the rest of civilization. It was windy and cold out on the soccer fields. "That's fine," I told her. "You don't have to like her; you just can't go around threatening her. You're not losing Valedictorian over Mandi Worthington. Even if MIT wouldn't care. *You* would, and I would too. And so would Caleb."

Her eyes started to water again, and she swiped at them angrily. Not knowing what else to do—I'd never seen my roommate so off balance—I grabbed her hand for comfort. "Ugh, Caleb," she said. "I'm sure he's hearing all about this right now."

"Probably," I agreed. "But he loves you, crazy and all. You'll apologize and then you'll make up. It's what you guys do." I squeezed her hand again and changed the subject. "So anyway, what's the story about Alexis behind the Chapel?"

LATER THAT NIGHT, I asked Carter, "Have you ever visited the Cove?" and it caused exactly the reaction I hoped it would. He stopped and stared at me, hand hanging in the air where it had pushed open the door to his room. Hopefully he forgot how he'd just caught me poking through his nightstand.

"The Cove?" he said, a slightly strangled quality to his voice. I was standing now, hiding the drawer I'd just hastily closed. I smiled, put a hand on my hip and licked my lips. His eyes flicked between the movements as growing interest lit his features.

"Yeah. Amy told me about it this afternoon." *Kneeler's Cove* was apparently a little, well, alcove in the outer walls of the Chapel where kids went to fool around. Carter stepped farther into the room, his bright blue eyes flashing dark as he Thought the door behind him all the way closed. The little click of the latch felt very loud.

"Is this an invitation?" He took another step toward me, and another.

"Have you ever gone before?" I countered. Right in front of me now, Carter leaned in closer, *closer,* until I fell back on the bed and he trapped me there.

"No."

"Why not?"

He was propped on his forearms, leaning over me, just barely touching the length of my body with his. Our lips were close enough to kiss if either of us bridged the last little distance.

"Because it's a place you only go with Academy girls. So. Are you inviting me, my Academy girl?"

I licked my lips again. "Maybe."

And then the distance was gone and he was kissing me. *Serious* kissing, the kind that means business. The kind that leads to other things. Like T-shirts landing on the floor and hands and lips on skin.

"Lainey?"

"Yeah?" He kissed my shoulder, the hollow of my throat. Every nerve in my body wished he wasn't talking.

"Rain check on the Cove tonight."

I ran my fingers down his back. Lower, dipping below his waistband. He inhaled one quick breath, like a gasp. "This is more comfortable anyway."

Comfortable, and *dangerous.* With every kiss and touch, I was losing clothes and restraint. I hadn't wanted to visit the Cove anyway. Privacy seemed so much sexier to me than cold stone walls and the chance of getting caught. I didn't want to be caught. I wanted *Carter.* Here, in his room, just the two of us, I had nothing *but* Carter. I could have all of him.

Maybe I would.

"Lainey?" he said again, lips brushing my ear and down my neck. I wished they would keep going.

"Yeah?" My voice was nothing but eager breath. It sounded…hopeful to me. Like tonight, I wanted him to ask. If he asked, I thought I wouldn't say no.

"What were you looking for in my drawer?"

SHIT. I'd been ignoring how I'd *already* been caught tonight. I tensed, which meant he tensed too, the muscles in his back bunching beneath my fingers. Carter was nothing if not expert at reading my signals. Even when I wasn't sure I meant them.

"Nothing." The word burned like ice, numbing my lips, while a deeper chill spread across my overheated skin. Why was reality always so cold?

"Nothing?" he said, still tense, waiting for me to relax. To say stop, or go. I knew what he thought—hoped—I was looking for and had found. I *should* have just said, *"These,"* and pulled out the package of condoms I'd known were there anyway, just in case or for whenever I was ready.

But I wasn't ready, not anymore. I'd said a year, and this wasn't my plan. Most of my body was screaming *to HELL with your stupid plan!* and if Carter hadn't just asked that question—the wrong question—I might have listened.

"Nothing. I'm s-sorry," I breathed. The plan was safe.

Carter rolled off me, his weight gone like it hadn't even been there. I shivered. Next to me on the bed, he stared at the back of his eyelids while doing what I suspected was the same yoga breathing he always made fun of me for. I'd really been looking for something—*anything*—connected to his father's death, because in weeks of trying I hadn't found a single damn thing in the rest of the house.

"I'm sorry," I repeated. I went about retrieving and righting clothes before trying to sit back down as if I were no heavier than a feather. But the bed tilted under me and, worse, squeaked, practically announcing my return with a bullhorn. Carter still hadn't moved.

After another few deep breaths, he said, "Have you lost something? What are you looking for?" His eyes were still closed.

"I…" I faltered. What could I say? *No, you've lost something, your father, and I'm trying to figure out what happened.* I couldn't say that. Or *No, I haven't lost something—my virginity. It's right here, and I'm afraid to let it go.* Carter knew that. Boy, did he know that. I wanted to cry, or crawl into a cave and hide.

"Because the other day it seemed like you were randomly searching the kitchen, and then today—" He paused for another deep breath. "So I think you must have lost something, but why won't you just tell me what it is?"

"I'm sorry."

"*Fuck.*" He sat up, fast, running his fingers through his hair and across his face. "Stop apologizing."

"I—" was going to do it again. Instead, I swallowed, while my brain shouted at me, *Lie, Lainey, lie! Come up with* something *for God's sake!* "I was looking for antiques." Ah, my old fallback. "Or things original to the apartment. I was…curious."

Carter looked at me, hard. His arms rested on his raised knees, hands clasped between them. "You were looking for antiques. In my nightstand."

I cleared my throat and toyed with a piece of my messy hair. "Not exactly. It's all related though. I was trying to find ideas…for Christmas presents. You know?"

The hard look didn't change and I didn't blame him. Lying was not my strongest skill, not on the spot. "Did you find any? Ideas?"

"Not really. Except for the dining room set, and the sink, everything seems contemporary here." Finally, a truth!

He stood, searching for his shirt as an excuse to pace. He might have been captivating when he smiled, but more than I cared to admit, I thought Carter was sexiest when he was angry. Tonight was no exception. He moved like an athlete, graceful and powerful, as he stalked across the room, eyes glinting and one hand scrubbing through his hair again. When he dipped to grab his T-shirt, I held my breath, watching with a painfully thumping heart as all the muscles in his broad shoulders down to his perfect stomach tensed and shifted in concert.

As he slipped it over his head, he said, "Aunt Mel remodeled when they moved back in." After his father died. This explained why I'd touched basically *everything* in their apartment, but so far found nothing connected to the day of Mark Penrose's death. When he'd crossed the room several times, Carter paused and said, "I'm not coming next weekend."

"What?!" I dropped the piece of my hair. We were supposed to be going to Baltimore and D.C. together to visit schools. And my aunt and Uncle Dan. We had that special dinner Dan had set up, and it would be Carter's first time on an airplane, and now I'd ruined it.

"I can't."

"Carter, I'm *sorry*—"

"No. It's not—*fuck!*" He quit pacing and returned to the bed, punching down the pillow as he sat. "It's not that. Not you. Well, not really. I don't understand what's going on with you. But Uncle Jeff has to make a trip and I can't leave Aunt Mel alone with the store. I was going to tell you tonight."

"Oh." If I weren't feeling so miserable at the moment, I'd have been disappointed. Mostly I felt guilty. For everything.

"I'm sorry."

I put my hand on his leg, just lightly. "It's okay." He didn't move but to nod.

"Maybe it is," he agreed. "Maybe it's good. You can figure out if you're going to tell me whatever you're not telling me."

Chapter Ten

Lainey!" Aunt Tessa was waving and practically running through the baggage claim area.

"Whoa, Auntie. Tone it down," I said as I hugged her. Really though, I was excited to see her too. I told her I'd take a taxi from the airport but she insisted on picking me up herself.

She released me to arm's length and appraised me. "You look tired, sweetheart."

I nodded. I was sure I did. The weight of so many secrets was keeping me awake at night. "School is so stressful this year," is what I told her.

"Well, let's go get dinner and see if we can't help you relax."

She took me to her favorite neighborhood place, a little Italian restaurant with paper tablecloths and the most amazing manicotti. Watching her during dinner, it was obvious she was happy, comfortable, and…home. She was back in Baltimore for the second time in as many years, though not in the same apartment as before my "migraines" took me to Northbrook and changed my whole world. The major difference between the two places was that this one felt as close to permanent as I thought her life could get.

I was unsurprised when about halfway through dinner she finally told me she'd accepted a full-time position at the University for the next fall semester. In other words, the same time I'd be starting, if this is where I chose to go.

"I know I don't have to tell you this," she said, "but I'd love nothing more than if you were here with me."

Yes, I'd certainly known that without her telling me, but I appreciated hearing it all the same. I reached across the tablecloth and squeezed her hand. "That would scare a lot of kids *away* from a school, Auntie," I said, and before her threat of a frown became real, I added, "but not me."

She beamed. "It was quite nice of Dan to set up our dinner tomorrow night. I'm looking forward to it."

The light in her eyes made it clear she was *more* than looking forward to dinner with Senator Astor. In the weeks since her visit to the Academy, she'd repeatedly mentioned her disappointment over seeing him only once. I hadn't had the heart to tell her she sounded like a school girl with a crush, since it was so rare she got excited about anything other than me or art, let alone a man, but mostly because I couldn't figure out how to feel about it.

"Me too."

After a pause for a thoughtful bite of dinner, Aunt Tessa tilted her head and asked, "And how is Carter, honey? By which I mean, how are the two of you?"

Crap. How were we? Strained. But I hadn't mentioned that to my aunt. "What do you mean?"

"I *mean,* are you okay?" When she pushed her hair over her shoulder, a pile of bracelets jangled on her wrist. "He was supposed to come, and, well, I thought maybe the store was an excuse. You haven't seemed yourself since I saw you last, and… Frankly, I wondered if you weren't getting ready to break that boy's heart."

I started at her words, nearly jumping out of my seat and spilling my cappuccino across the table. "What?! No!" I said. "I can't even believe you'd think that!" But there it was again. An echo in my head reverberated with, *She'll break your heart, Carter.* And this time it was my *aunt.* When Alexis had said it last year, I knew she had a vested interest in it coming true. My aunt, on the other hand, loved my being with Carter possibly as much as I did.

"I'm sorry, sweetie. I just wondered, that's all. You've seemed…" She frowned and flipped one hand over and back. "And you're my daughter in your heart, if not your blood. I know a little about fearing comfort more than change. For you, change *is* comfort. It's almost a year you've been with him…"

Before I'd known what being comfortable in one place really meant, I'd have agreed with her. But it turned out, maybe since I'd already had so much change in my seventeen years, I *liked* permanence. My psychologists had been right about that anyway. Or so I'd thought, until my aunt had just given new life to an old seed of doubt.

"I know," I said. "And I'm not planning to—*never.* I *love* Carter. He just couldn't make it. The store *wasn't* an excuse. They've got one new employee since, well, you know. Jill couldn't come back this year. But the new woman is off this week. And school is stressful for me…"

I realized I *sounded* like I was making excuses, and maybe I was. There was so much distance between us the last week, and Carter was right—so much I wasn't telling him. I just wasn't sure I was ready yet, for *so* many things.

Aunt Tessa cocked her head at me again, in the other direction this time. From somewhere she'd produced a pencil and had been idly sketching on the tablecloth. Me, I realized. I recognized my long hair and the contours of my face. "So," she said, "you haven't had sex with him yet, have you?"

Flames leapt instantly to my face, especially because I'd just been thinking about it. "Auntie! Jesus!" My aunt was liberal enough when it came to sex, and had never been afraid to talk to me about it. She and Amy had that in common.

"You haven't. I can tell. I'm surprised, honestly. Aren't you ready?"

"Auntie!!" I repeated. If you could pass out from blushing too hard, I was about to do it. I eyed her wine glass, but it was still half full. No, this was just my aunt being herself.

She laughed at me. "It's okay, Lainey. I just thought…" She shrugged. "Anyway, there's no prize for hurrying the first time, so don't. Just don't forget to be careful when you finally do."

My mortification complete, I nodded. "You've reminded me enough times since I was ten. I've learned that lesson well, I promise." But inside, I laughed a little. The first part of her totally non-traditional sex talk was proof Aunt Tessa didn't know about Sententia, since having sex could jumpstart, or spark, a developing ability, like it had for Carter. Sometimes there *was* a prize.

WE SPENT THE next day like a normal mother and daughter, going on the campus tours, eating at the student union, and meeting other prospective students and their families. My aunt pretended she wasn't an alumna with her sculptures featured in the school museum, and I pretended I wasn't maybe going to die before I had the chance to become an alumna myself. It was actually a fun day.

Dinner that evening was possibly more fun, despite Carter's absence. The university president was friendly, down to earth, and seemed genuinely interested in me, even if it was only because of my aunt and Senator Astor, but I didn't think so. I got the impression he cared about and would have been the same with any of the over seven thousand students.

We, naturally, talked about art, politics, and the business school, none of which was boring, and we laughed often and genuinely. My aunt flirted almost shamelessly with Dan, who seemed equally interested in charming her. I felt worried about that but entirely unsure how to stop it. Otherwise, it was a great evening, and the best part of the whole thing was the absolutely zero mention of Sententia. Up until the very end.

"Have you given any more thought to my offer?" Dan asked, almost casually, while my aunt had gone to the ladies' room and the president had taken his leave.

Of course I had. I thought about it pretty much all the time I wasn't contemplating my own impending death. Unable to tell him that, I decided to be straightforward with him.

"I don't honestly think I have it in me."

He nodded, as if he'd expected my answer. "I understand," he said firmly. "It's a hard thing to have to do. Tell me this—do you not believe in our mission?"

"No, it's not that. I do, sort of." And I did. The Perceptum did a lot of good. "But…just the part that really bothers me would be my part."

"Of course. You've heard the stories though; you know the caliber of person who receives such a vote, and the rarity."

I sighed, wishing my aunt would just hurry up and free me from having to talk about this. My stomach churned, in part because he was right. I nodded. "Of course. Dr. Stewart said almost the same thing, but…it's not just that. It's, well honestly, it's Carter. I know what would happen to him, just because of what he *can* do, not because of what he *does* or who he *is.*"

Dan's eyes lit on me like I'd made some connection without knowing it. "Objectivity is the greatest challenge, is it not? And doing things you don't necessarily want to do for the good of others. Don't you see the most important advantage to working *with* the Council, Lainey? Why do you think I've become its leader? *That* is where you have the most power to *protect* Carter."

I inhaled so sharply the breath stabbed my throat. It had never occurred to me Dan didn't *want* to be leader of the Perceptum. It had never occurred to me there'd be any advantage to being a part of it. But there *was*. I'd been too caught up in my own fears to see it. Now, I was more confused than ever.

I opened my mouth to say…something, *anything*, when Dan patted me on the shoulder and smiled at my aunt coming up behind us.

"Tess, Lainey and I were just talking about the future, and I think she's got some important things to think about. Shall we go for a nightcap?"

ALL THE FLIGHT home, I replayed the conversation in my head. Was it that simple? Well, it wasn't *simple*, but…it was a good question. What *would* I do to protect Carter? I liked to say *anything*, but I'd never thought anything would include killing people, even the kind of people I'd be asked to eliminate. And I always thought my morals would stand up and say *never!* But never was a tricky word when you loved someone and that someone was in danger.

It was with these thoughts that I stepped outside the terminal, on hold with the dispatcher for the car service as they tried to locate my strangely missing reservation, when I saw Carter. He was standing next to his car and holding a sign with my name on it, just like the driver should have been. I hung up the phone and threw myself at him. He caught me and held tight. Kisses became our mutual apology.

Until another driver honked his horn, I forgot where we were. Which was at the airport, in *public,* in a taxi zone where we shouldn't be stopped. Sheepishly, I broke away and, in what had become a habit of mine just about every time I touched him, gave a quick check with my Diviner sense to see if my death had become any clearer.

At the same time I was saying, "What are you—" Carter practically leaped backwards.

"What the hell, Lainey?!"

"—doing here?" I finished. He was running his fingers through his hair and staring at me from his new distance. "What?"

"Are you trying to kill me or figure out when I'm going to die?" His low voice was harsh, angry.

Shit. He must have seen my eyes flash. Caught up in the moment, I'd been careless. And now, I was stuck. It took me so long to reply, Carter cleared his throat. He fidgeted, shuffling his feet like he wanted, and *not* wanted, to move closer.

"Wow. *Are* you trying to kill me or *am* I going to die? Is that what you didn't want to tell me?"

I shook my head and stepped toward him, lowering my voice to match his. "Neither." And then, without any further thought or gentleness, I plowed straight into a confession. *"I'm* going to die—and you're going to kill me. At least, that's what I saw a couple months ago."

"What?!" He actually tried to back up further, bumping into the car and nearly slipping off the edge of the sidewalk. The impatient taxi driver behind us honked again. Carter looked at him, looked back at me, and opened the passenger door. "Get in. Apparently we need to talk, and we can't do it here."

WE WERE HALFWAY out of the airport when I started to talk but Carter cut me off completely.

"We are *not* having this conversation while I'm driving." He wouldn't look at me, his eyes strictly focused on the road while his white knuckled fingers gripped the steering wheel at ten and two. Minutes, then miles, ticked by in silence. Slowly.

I was beginning to wonder if he planned to drive us all the way home first. In the right lane. Going five miles below the speed limit. "It's not tonight, so you don't have to drive like my nanny," I joked.

He glanced in my direction but didn't smile or otherwise relax his stiff posture. "You may be wrong. Right now, I'm trying to keep myself from killing you just for not telling me, so don't push it," he said. Sometimes I forgot how passionate Carter could get when he was angry, but this was something more, something he so rarely showed I didn't recognize it at first: fear.

I reached out to touch him but thought better of it and dropped my hand back into my lap, where I recommenced wringing it with my other one. For the first time ever, I didn't think my touch would be a comfort. Instead, I apologized with all the sincerity I could infuse into two insufficient words.

"I'm sorry."

Carter said nothing but he glanced at me again. His wet eyes shimmered in the dark. After we were about halfway home, he rather abruptly pulled off the highway into the kind of rest area with picnic tables and no bathrooms, where truckers stopped to sleep, not the bright, busy kind with gas stations. The kind where, over the summer, we'd had our almost-night. It was cold out, so he left the car running. I listened to the hum of the engine and blow of the heaters, a familiar sound not unlike the ocean, and thought how *this* night couldn't feel further from that other one.

Next to me, emotions warred on Carter's face in the glow from the dashboard, processing the thought of my death and his possible role in it. I'd had so long to accept it, I'd practically forgotten how freaked out

I used to be. Seeing Carter fight through denial, anguish, anger—all the things I felt at first—was heartbreaking. Maybe my aunt had been right.

Finally, he turned to me. "It must be an accident."

"I don't honestly know. But the vision was real. Just…brief."

"Tell me everything. Please. We've done it before—We'll figure out how to change this." Desperation had crept into his voice, giving it a rough quality I'd never heard in it before. He sounded like an adult, a man, rather than a teenager. I reminded myself that he'd be twenty in only weeks.

"That's what I'm trying to do!" All of my pent-up frustration rushed out with my words. "I've been trying since that day, but I can't see any more. I can't see *anything!* I saw my face, and, the way I *know* things, I knew you were responsible, but that's it. I've seen flashes of it since, just the same little glimpse, but I can't get any closer to what happens! And—" I broke off.

Carter ducked down to look into my face and leaned toward me from his seat. "'And?' How could there possibly be something worse you don't want to say?"

"It won't be the first time," I whispered. "For you. I won't be the first." It was stupid, I *knew* it was stupid, but I'd still been unable to make myself read Carter for that detail. Whatever happened before had never forced itself on me like some visions did. I'd gotten good enough with my Diviner sense that I could concentrate only on the future or the past, and this was a past I just didn't want to know. I *should have,* I knew that too, but I couldn't bring myself to find out.

He slumped back into his seat and, if anything, seemed *relieved,* which made no sense to me. "Well, that's no secret."

"Wh…what do you mean?"

"I've been a murderer since the day I was born, Lainey. You know that, and besides, even if it wasn't common knowledge, how could *you* of all people not know? I mean, didn't you try to *see* it?" He was shaking his head and grimacing in the way that was almost a smile, like if this were any other topic, it would have been amusing.

I dropped my head into my hands, feeling like a fool. In my quest for bliss-in-ignorance, I'd overlooked the obvious. "Your mother," I murmured. "Of course." She'd died in childbirth.

He tipped my chin up with gentle fingers and, for the first time since we got in the car, gave me a very small smile. "Did you really not check?" Heat crept up my neck and flushed my cheeks as I shook my head. Carter leaned over again, practically scooping me up in his arms. "God, I love you," he said into my ear.

With a little maneuvering, I repositioned myself onto his lap, my back to his door and my long legs extending all the way into the passenger seat. It wasn't exactly comfortable, but it was comforting to be close to him. I rested my head on his shoulder while he ran his fingers through my hair. I always loved it when he did that, which was often, but tonight it felt especially good. Like home.

Eventually he asked the question I'd been waiting for. "Why didn't you tell me?"

"Because saying it out loud to you makes it real."

He kissed my cheek. "That's illogical."

"I know."

"I *knew* something's been wrong," he said. "You've seemed so lost in your own head lately, and took that trip to the cemetery…That wasn't really about Jill, was it?"

"No," I admitted, though I still didn't tell him what it was *really* about. "I'm sorry."

We were quiet again for a while, the sounds of our breathing mingling with the hum of the heaters. It was already late, and only getting later every minute we sat there, but I knew Carter wasn't ready so I didn't push to leave. He needed time to come to terms with the future, but more than that, he needed to formulate a plan. Carter was incomplete without some kind of action he could take. "It has to be an accident," he repeated.

"Most likely." Before he could get angry, I added, "but it's more like it...wasn't definite. Like God or whoever hasn't figured out the details yet. I've never had a vision so vague before."

He thought for a moment. "Are you sure it wasn't just a...a possibility, something that might happen?"

Sometimes I liked to let myself believe that same thing, but, "It felt pretty certain."

"Then it must be an accident. I'd *never* hurt you intentionally."

"I know." I wondered if this would still be true if he knew all of the other things I'd been keeping from him lately, but I couldn't dwell on that. One problem at a time. I kissed his neck and hugged him a little tighter. "It's late, Carter."

"I don't know what to do yet," he replied. "How do I fight a future you can't even see?"

This time I kissed his lips before pushing myself over to my own seat. "You don't," I told him. "You let me do it."

"You're telling me *everything*, right? And you'll tell me if anything changes?"

It was strangely easy to say "I promise," knowing the promise was already broken. To *myself*, I promised no more lies—if I managed to live through this one.

Chapter Eleven

The next note arrived the following week while I was at my library hours. Wednesday nights were busy times—Northbrook had a world-class library and the students were expected to use it. Last year, I had to dodge my classmates while I snuck up to the Special Collections floor for Sententia practice with Carter. This year, I had to dodge my classmates to get anything done. I spent most of my two hours with my head down and earbuds on to keep myself from being distracted.

I'd just pushed my empty cart into the elevator and was about to push the top floor button when small, slender fingers did it for me. I snapped my head up to see Mandi Worthington smirking at me. I hadn't even realized she'd followed me in. The doors shooshed behind her and we started up.

"Hey, Mandi," I said, turning off my music and giving her a smile. "You here studying?"

"Mrs. Hastings wanted me to give this to you," was her answer. She held up a familiar cream envelope with my name in the center. I easily recognized the strong script as Daniel Astor's.

"Uh, thanks." I reached across my stacks of books but Mandi made no motion to hand over my note. "Mandi?"

Anger turned down the corners of her smirk. "I know who it's from," she said, still holding it just far enough that I'd have to lean over to snatch it from her. Not that I'd do that. If I'd learned anything in the last year, it was to be patient long enough to figure out what game girls like Mandi were playing.

I tried very hard not to sigh before I said, "And?"

Mandi leaned toward me, putting all her considerable bitchiness into her next question. "And why is he sending *you* notes too, like he is to Alexis?"

"I don't know," I blurted out, because I was too surprised to stop my mouth from saying it. I reminded myself that I should never play poker before I added, "Why don't you ask Alexis?"

Frost formed on her words as she replied, "I will," finally handing over the note. "She's going to help him become President, you know. Don't get in the way."

As if she'd timed it, the elevator dinged and the door opened behind her. She disappeared between the stacks on the fourth floor before I even had the chance to close my mouth that had dropped open in surprise. The door slid shut before I remembered to get out.

I read the note as I rode down and back up again.

Dear Lainey,

As always, I delighted in your company, and that of your aunt's, this past weekend. I urge you to join us here next year, as your acceptance is guaranteed, so that we may make dinners together a regular occurrence. However, so you can make the most informed choice, I've also arranged dinners for you and my nephew in Boston with several prominent alumni of both your prospective schools.

I understand the difficulty of your decision, Lainey, but feel certain after our last meeting that you now understand all the possible advantages. I know you'll make the right choice. Let's talk again soon.

Yours, D.A.

It was strange how the note could make my stomach flutter with excitement and apprehension, but then, much in my life was strange. Though I knew the difficult decision he wanted to talk about had nothing to do with colleges, I looked forward to the dinners he'd arranged—it made me feel a bit like a celebrity, in the best possible way. I wondered if this is how people close to the senator always felt.

My biggest concern in all this was actually Mandi. Not her revelation, but her threat. What was she up to, and why? I'd heard the rumors about Senator Astor becoming the next President—we'd even talked about them over dinner last weekend—but I'd gotten the impression he wasn't as decided on running as everyone else was. He already had one presidency to deal with, and I couldn't imagine it would be easy to hide his connection to the Perceptum as President of the United States. Though, for all I knew, it might help him *get* the job, not disqualify him from it.

Maybe it was an odd notion that Dan would approach a high school girl to help his potential presidential campaign, but it made perfect sense to me. Not only was she a close family friend, I counted many ways Alexis could be an asset. She was going to Georgetown, too, so she'd be right there in D.C.

But she wasn't there yet and something was up. Except for Honor Board, we generally ignored each other this year, almost as if by unspoken agreement. But then here was Mandi, complicating everything. I wondered if *she* was doing Alex's dirty work, between her flirtation with Caleb and her new threats. This, at least, was a problem I could handle directly.

I'D NEVER ACTIVELY sought out Alexis before—usually it was the other way around—but it wasn't like she was hard to find. For one, we had two classes together, and otherwise, she was a campus star. If I didn't know where she was, all I had to do was ask anyone. Tonight, all I had to do was guess.

After I left the library, I headed across the street, grabbing a to-go cup from the coffee shop right before it closed and then over to the bookstore. Since I usually *wasn't* there, and Carter was, I figured that was Alexis's most likely location. And I was right, because that's where I found her, sitting on the couch where I usually did. Next to the guy I usually sat next to.

Carter stood up when he saw me, leaving Alexis alone on the couch and glaring at me from behind his back. He didn't look guilty, not exactly. More like apologetic. Like he hoped I wouldn't be mad.

"Well this is a nice surprise," he said as he met me at the edge of the lounge, plucking the coffee out of my hand and sweeping me into a tight hug. That was one thing about Carter; he was never afraid to be affectionate, even in the middle of the crowded bookstore, even though it always made me blush. "What's up, gorgeous?"

I planted a quick kiss on his cheek before I squirmed out of his arms and reclaimed my coffee. "Maybe I should ask you that," I said. It was not entirely sarcastic.

In return, I got his measured look, the one that meant he was deciding whether to say something. "Sorry. She needed help with physics and I couldn't resist." After a pause, he leaned down, a sexy smile spreading from his lips to his eyes, and added, "But I kind of like it when you're jealous."

Ignoring my usual reserve, I stepped even closer and ran my hand down his stomach. I was rewarded with an intake of breath and an eager look in his eyes. In my most seductive voice, I said, "Well, I actually came here to see *her,* not you, so maybe you're the one who should be jealous."

Carter's eager look morphed into confusion and then curiosity, before he laughed and grabbed my hand. He kissed it lightly and took a step out of the lounge. "I *am* jealous. And I'm also done here tonight. Come upstairs after"—he glanced over his shoulder at Alexis— "whatever you're doing with her?"

I shouldn't have, but I agreed, and then watched Carter stride off to the staircase behind the counter that led up to their apartment. I waved at Melinda where she sat behind the register. Alexis was still glaring at me when I returned my attention to the lounge. It was clear she'd been watching our entire exchange. Interestingly enough, none of her friends had claimed the rest of the open couch. I wondered just how often she sat here alone on Wednesday nights and needed help with her physics.

Without invitation, I sat next to her, taking a sip from my coffee and watching the fire while I decided what to say. Alexis looked as effortlessly beautiful as ever tonight. Her dark hair, so similar in color to mine, fell perfectly over her shoulder to catch the flickering light from the fireplace.

"Lainey." She said my name like it tasted bitter. "This *isn't* a nice surprise, by the way."

Her attitude loosened my tongue and excused my manners. "I just want you to call off your little dog."

She glanced at me. "I wish I knew what you were talking about, but I don't."

"Right." I felt her shrug next to me. When I finally turned to face her, she was watching the fire, just like I'd been. I truly sensed no dishonesty from her. In fact, if asked, I'd have said she was trying to hide her curiosity behind indifference. "I mean Mandi," I clarified. "You know, your cousin."

"I know who she is, Young. What about her?"

I was starting to feel kind of stupid and the answer tumbled out of me awkwardly. "She…threatened me at work hours today. And she's up to something. With Caleb."

Alexis actually frowned before the annoyed mask slipped back into place and she began examining her pristine fingernails for chips. "I haven't the slightest idea why she's interested in Sullivan. Though maybe I should be telling you to keep your *roommate* in line. She started the threatening, as I understand it." Alexis put on her best sneer. "Mandi's probably just trying to keep your crazy away from me. She's protective of her family that way."

Touché. After taking a sip of my coffee and counting to five, I did the hard thing. "You know what? I'm sorry, Alex. I assumed you were involved and I was wrong." She looked at me with open confusion as I gathered my bag and stood. "And that problem set from physics was hard, so I'm going to go get some help of my own. Bye." I was just stepping away when she called to me softly.

"Lainey? I don't know what she's up to. Honest."

I nodded. "I believe you." And I did. Mandi might have been her cousin, but apparently she wasn't her puppet. I hoped she wouldn't turn out to be something worse.

WHAT SHE TURNED out to be was a pest. Like a mosquito, buzzing close to my ear but never in reach. I barely *saw* Mandi in the following weeks, but she seemed to be in everything. This is what I was thinking while I sat on that same bookstore couch and listened to—another— argument between my roommate and her boyfriend.

"Seriously, Caleb? You're *already* leaving?"

"You knew I couldn't stay!"

"But you've only been here, like, *five minutes.*"

He'd really been there closer to an hour. Long enough for them to have spent possibly more than five minutes making out while I tried to ignore that, too. I carefully shifted my foot out from underneath me on the couch, before it fell asleep or my pants got too wrinkled, while trying not to draw attention to my continued presence.

Caleb dropped his head back and rubbed his eyes. "I told you already: I. Have. To. Work." Which meant tutoring. Which meant Mandi.

"You *always* have to work." Amy flopped her legs off his lap with a huge sigh.

"That whole scholarship thing, you know? It's kind of important." Caleb shoved his books in his bag with great determination. From across the room, Carter caught my eye, frowning in our direction. If he could hear them, *everyone* could.

I was about to say something when I heard a gentle throat clearing next to me. I startled and turned to find one of my Sanderson girls, Mandi's roommate, standing at my elbow and looking entirely uncomfortable.

"Hi," she said.

"Um, hey Chels." I glanced over my shoulder at my bickering friends. "Have you been standing there long?"

She shook her head, though obviously she had. "I was hoping I could talk to you."

"Sure." To Amy, I called, "I'll be back," but she wasn't really listening.

"I'm *sorry* my dad's not a *surgeon,*" I heard Caleb saying as I mercifully followed Chelsea to one of the small tables by the windows.

"Sorry about that," I said to her, even though it wasn't *my* fight, but she nodded like she understood. Which maybe she did.

"Are they fighting about Mandi?"

"Um." I, along with everyone else in the room, watched Caleb stomp out the door and close it too hard, making the little bell ring like it was caught in a storm.

Chelsea traced lines on the table with her finger. "I hear her talking to him sometimes," she said, voice low. "She likes to say *tutor* like it means *boyfriend*. But then she sneaks to the Cove with Patch Jacobsen, you know? And I think his roommate too. Geoff?"

"Is that what you wanted to talk to me about?" *I* didn't really want to talk about the Cove with a seventh grader, or about Mandi's romantic endeavors. But it was my job to be here for the girls, so I tried not to look like I'd almost rather be back listening to my roommate fight.

"Not really," Chelsea said. "I just…I was wondering if you thought it would be possible to change rooms? Maybe after Winter break? Or Thanksgiving?"

Oh. "Are you uncomfortable with your current situation?" That was what I'd been coached to ask.

"No!" she said, too quickly. "No, I just, I'm really good friends with Sejal Daga, you know? And we're both in seventh, and we hoped we could switch to room together."

"Have you talked to your dorm attendant?"

She shook her head. "I thought I'd ask you first. I didn't want Mrs. Devlin to think…I just wondered if it was possible?"

Truth was, I didn't know. "Part of the boarding school experience is learning to resolve differences." Another thing I was coached to say. "But if you're uncomfortable…"

Chelsea looked down again. "Mandi and I just have really different interests." She looked back up at me. "It's not that she's…she's just hard to be around. I feel like it's all boys *all* the time, and I…I'm not even sure…"

Oh. "That's a lot to be dealing with." She nodded and drew in a breath like it was the fullest one she'd had in a while.

"It's even worse, with my—you know."

I nodded. It was hard enough to be thirteen, but even harder as a Sententia—that's when our gifts typically started to manifest. That's also why Northbrook eventually added the lower grades. "How's that going?"

"It's mostly easy, so far. It started last year, so it's not, like, new, but…" She looked around, checking if anyone might overhear. "Well, I sense love."

"A Cupid!" That's what Carter had once called love detectors. I thought that would be a delightful gift, despite the name. Like my inverse.

"Yeah."

"That's great!"

Except Chelsea didn't look like it was great. "Yeah, I guess. My mom already wants me to become a marriage counselor and join her practice." She sighed. "But it's not *always* love, the nice kind I mean, like you and Carter have." Her eyes flicked to Carter, who was momentarily sitting on the couch with Amy. When he glanced our way and saw us looking, he smiled. Chelsea smiled back and quickly ducked her eyes, but I caught their telltale flash as she powered up her gift.

"See?" she said, voice low as it all poured out of her. "Well, you can't, I guess. But I can. He's so sweet, and he, I mean, he *loves* you. Totally. I see it like shades of colors, I guess, and yours—yours is real love and it's like nuclear bright. That's the best, and it's *so* uncommon. My mom tells me to look for those. Mr. and Mrs. Revell are like that too. You guys are really lucky."

"Thank you," I said, which seemed a better response than *I know*. "But it's not always what you see, huh?"

She shook her head, and I didn't miss how her eyes darted to Amy and back. "Sometimes…sometimes it changes. What used to be red is turning purple, fracturing. And then, well, around Mandi there's always so much *yellow.*"

I could guess what yellow was. "And that's more like…"

She nodded. "Lust, I guess. It's not *real* love, though people don't always know the difference. Sometimes she means to bring it out and other times not. And I mean, there's tons of yellow all over school. You should *see* how much yellow is in the dining hall when you or Alexis walk around, or even in here"—she gestured just with her fingertips toward the rest of the lounge—"but it's different with Mandi, because of what she is. That's not…well, she doesn't do it on purpose *all* the time. It's hard for her. I get that. But it's hard for me, too. It's just so *bright.* I don't *try* to see it, but I can't help it. It's exhausting." She dropped her voice to near whisper. "Especially when I don't even *like* boys."

I thought Chelsea was being very mature about this and I told her so. I don't know why I was forever thinking that other gifts were better, or easier, than mine. They all came with challenges.

"Thanks, I guess." She smiled shyly, but seemed pleased. I remembered how she was the one to tell everyone about me and Carter on our first day at Sanderson.

"I don't know about changing rooms, but I think your reasoning is fair. If you want me to go with you to talk to Mrs. Devlin, I will. And I'm glad you felt you could talk to me. About everything."

Chelsea gave a great shrug of her small shoulders, though she was still smiling. "I mean, I'm supposed to talk to you, right? And…I thought you wouldn't tell anyone. You're not like that."

She was right. *So* many secrets were safe with me.

Amy was glaring at her homework, and the rest of the world, when I sat back down with her. "What was that about?"

"She just needed to talk for a while. She wants to change rooms."

"Isn't that Worthing-twit's roommate?"

"Yes," I sighed. I shouldn't even have told her that much. Though she would just have assumed the problem anyway.

"See, she's a menace." Amy closed her notebook with a thwack.

She kind of was, it was true. Two Honor Board meetings had mentioned her on the periphery, though she wasn't in any real trouble. But she *wasn't* a menace to the extent my roommate believed. She'd blame Mandi for it raining today, if she could. In fact, Mandi was under Amy's skin so deep I wasn't sure how to dig her out.

"She's done nothing wrong to Chelsea, as far as I know. Things are sometimes more complex than you think."

"*As far as you know,* she's flirting with my boyfriend over algebra and earth science *right now*. Did you know he's tutoring her in science too?"

"Ame." I grabbed her hand and she bit her lip. Sometimes my fiery friend didn't realize she'd gone overboard until someone pulled her out of the water. "Yeah, I know. But it's what he's supposed to do, and he's *good* at it. I think you need to give Caleb a little break. *He* hasn't done anything wrong."

She looked down. "So everything is *my* fault?"

I squeezed her hand again and resisted the urge to sigh. "Ame, no. Listen, let's go get a coffee? And *talk.*"

"Don't you have to leave?"

That's right; I did. And I could see Carter striding out from behind the counter, hair newly combed and car keys in hand, for our final trip to the city. I'd practically forgotten. With everything else going on, college seemed impossibly far away, a figment of my imagination. But it wasn't, if I made it that far. The last of the college dinners Dan had arranged was tonight.

I gave Amy a swift hug before I stood up and slipped on my coat. "You're right. I'm sorry. We'll talk later, okay?"

"Sure," she said, like she was saying *whatever*. "Have fun."

"Ready?" Carter said to me, as he took first my bag and then my hand.

"Yeah. Bye, Ame."

"Bye," Carter echoed. She waved at us, but it was more like a dismissal than goodbye.

On our way out of the store, I leaned in and asked Carter, "So what'd you say to her? When I was talking to Chelsea." He looked awesome tonight, having changed into the stylish jeans I called his "fancy pants" and a button down that made his blue eyes *bluer*. I wished we had special dinners all the time.

He shook his head. "Nothing, really. She apologized and said she 'didn't want to talk about it.' Which is fine, because I don't really think I'm the guy she needs to talk to about the scene they were making." I sighed and he squeezed my hand. We both said bye to Melinda as we passed behind the counter and into the back room. "What were *you* talking about, with Chelsea Agro?"

"Switching rooms and…other stuff."

"Stuff about her roommate?" When I shrugged, he chuckled. "Seems like Mandi Worthington is part of every conversation we have lately."

"So let's not talk about her the rest of tonight then. Did you know Chelsea is a Cupid?"

"No, but it would have been my guess."

I glanced over at his pretty profile, lit only by the service lights in the back of the store. "She said you *loooove* me."

His eyes met mine and he smiled. "Well, if a Cupid said it, it must be true." Without warning, he swept me into a tight hug and dipped me backwards. I squealed and clutched at him until I got my balance but he just laughed. And then he kissed me, a soft press of his mouth to mine that was better assurance than any Sententia gift that he, in fact, loved me.

"I'm wrinkling your shirt," I said against his lips. Up close like this, his eyelashes looked miles long.

"Like I care," he replied, but he righted us before long. Just before releasing me, he held his hand against mine for a second and whispered, "Anything?" So playful a moment ago, his eyes were serious now, searching mine for some kind of answer.

After a quick burst of my Diviner sense, I shook my head. Suddenly, it felt like it could have been *any* day since I told him about the vision, when *Anything?* had replaced *Hello* in Carter's vocabulary. Every single time we saw each other he asked and so far, my answer had been the same. I checked the vision again and again but still nothing new. He frowned as he opened the back door and we hurried to the car through the rain.

Carter closed the door behind me a little harder than he needed to, but I knew he was just frustrated by the lack of clarity. *I'd* have been frustrated by it too, if I allowed myself any time for frustration. During the few weeks since my trip to Baltimore *school* had become my primary focus. I had a million problems to address—the vision, Mark Penrose, Mandi Worthington, and on and on—but no time for ones that didn't start with *home* and end in *work*.

On the weekends, if there wasn't swimming, there was this: Carter and me in the car together. The long drive to Boston and back had started to feel not quite so long and I liked that. Because the more times I visited, the more I was reminded just how much I *loved* the city. My aunt was in Maryland, but I thought my heart was here. If I stayed, Amy would be right across the river, a T ride away. And, probably, Carter too. He wouldn't say, but I was pretty sure Harvard was his favorite. Something about the prestige and the historic feeling of it.

Carter backed out of his parking spot fast, pressing too hard on the brakes and throwing me against the seatbelt. "This is driving me crazy."

I rubbed my shoulder. "I can tell."

"Sorry." He accelerated at a more appropriate pace and pointed us toward the city.

"It's okay."

"*Nothing* about this is okay." In between shifting gears, he plucked my hand off my leg and trapped it with his.

Northbrook breezed by outside my window and I marveled at how the grounds could look so beautiful still, even on the verge of winter, even with a few hundred kids tromping all over them every day. I loved the Academy. I *hated* talking about the vision. I wanted back the playful Carter I'd had so briefly in the store room.

"I just don't understand," Carter continued. Sometimes my silence only encouraged him to ruminate. "How are you not seeing more?"

I lifted our linked hands and dropped them, a driving version of a shrug. "If I could explain it, I would. If I could see more, I *would.*"

"I mean, is it actually gone? Are you not seeing anything?"

I wished. "No. Well, sort of, but it's…weird. Sometimes I don't see anything, but I still, I *feel* it. It's like an echo. Lately it's like the echo's getting further away." And I didn't know whether or not to feel good about that.

"That's good. I think." His fingers twitched and I had to hold his hand tighter to keep him from messing up his hair before we made it to the city. "Like that *future's* getting further away. Becoming less likely. That's good," he repeated, convincing himself.

I couldn't be sure enough to agree, so I just kissed his hand and left it at that. In truth, the uncertainty made me *more* nervous, and I tried not to think about it. I preferred to distract myself with something else. Before he could talk any more about the future I couldn't fully see, I asked a very important question.

"What do you want for your birthday?"

I was hoping he'd say me.

No such luck. The grim face he made was answer enough. "To change your vision," he said. He kept his eyes fully on the road.

I sighed. "Besides that."

Finally, he glanced over at me, and a tiny, sexy grin appeared on his handsome face. "How about some time alone with you *not* in the car?"

Now *that's* what I was hoping to hear. I thought about it more and more, since the disastrous night a few weeks ago when we'd been so close, to every single day when he asked about the vision and I felt like time was running out.

Our year anniversary was right around the corner and I was ready now.

Chapter Twelve

ou'll be there on Tuesday, right?" Amy asked for at least the tenth time on the Friday afternoon before her mother arrived to pick her up for our week of Thanksgiving break.

I was lying on my bed, reading one of her magazines. I flipped down the glossy pages to look at her. "Yes. For the thousandth time."

"Sorry," she muttered. She zipped and unzipped her weekend bag over and over again without taking out or putting anything in. On Tuesday, my aunt and I were driving out to spend the day with Amy and have dinner with the Morettis and the Sullivans.

I was beginning not to recognize my roommate. Bubbly and carefree had always been the words I used to describe her, but more and more she'd become irritable and distracted. I was worried about her. Her pants were looser, but she wasn't dieting. Just not eating. Her side of the room was more cluttered than usual, and it seemed like she was up later with her homework or sneaking back from Caleb's a little later each night.

Not for the first time, I wanted to talk with her, *really* talk with her about what was going on, but we never seemed to get the chance. Either I was too busy or Amy joked it off. I felt horrible that she wouldn't open up to me and even more horrible that I'd basically ignored my roommate's problems for weeks because I was caught up in my own. Looming death or not, I hadn't been a very good friend lately.

It wasn't how I wanted to go into my afterlife, as a crappy friend. Amy seemed to be getting into desperate territory and I didn't understand why and especially didn't know what to do. I was hoping our first real school break would help, putting our problems—and Mandi Worthington—miles away for a while. I remembered wishing about a year ago that my life could just be simple for a while and now I double wished it.

So tonight, I was letting it all go.

Before I had the chance to say anything at all, Amy, as always, beat me to the punch. Even if I hadn't been paying attention, she had. She didn't stop playing with the zipper on her bag, but sly eyes peeked over at me. "So are you going to show me what you got to wear tonight now or after?"

I dropped the magazine again. "What do you mean?"

She abandoned the bag and came over to my bed, nudging herself next to me after pulling open my nightstand drawer and taking out the contraband candles I'd been hiding and the package of condoms she'd gift-wrapped for my last birthday. She arrayed the candles in front of us and left the condoms next to the bed.

"Lane, please. You think I don't know what you're planning tonight or that you kind of can't wait for me to leave so you can get ready? No matter how nonchalant you're pretending to be, I know you've been 'reading' the same article in my magazine for the last hour, and I pick up our mail, so I've seen the packages from that expensive lingerie place I know you don't usually shop at. Also, you put away the pictures of your family so they won't 'see' anything and there's that sexy-as-hell new dress hanging in your closet. It's a year. Tonight, it's a year, and you're going to do it. *Finally*. So, can you just show me now, please please?"

Busted. She threw her arm around my shoulders and batted her eyelashes in my face until I relented.

When I got up to get out my special lingerie set, she shouted, "Yay!" And when I showed it to her, even *her* eyes got wide. "Daaamn. Oh, Heartbreaker, I hope that get-up doesn't kill him before you even get the deed done. Also, does it come in my size?"

I blushed my best blush and stuffed the set back into my drawer. Pretending I wasn't nervous wasn't working and Amy wasn't helping.

Yes, I had planned this. A few almost-nights didn't change the fact that I'd imagined this one for months. I'd spent weeks perfecting the minor details, from my dress to my underwear, to testing where I'd put the candles.

As soon as Amy left, *finally,* I went into hyper mode, picking up the room, smoothing my sheets, putting out the candles where I'd planned them. I spent a long time straightening my hair until it was like glass, and making sure my dress fit just so. Maybe it was all silly, and not very spontaneous, but I'd waited long enough for this. I wanted it to be perfect.

OUR ANNIVERSARY DINNER was amazing—romantic, relaxed, everything I hoped it would be—and totally worth "sneaking out" for. I hadn't asked permission to go off campus, but on the first night of break, pretty much no one was around to care. We were on our way back in time for curfew though, just in case. Not that I wasn't planning on breaking a few more rules.

Carter held my hand, as usual, and gave it a brief squeeze as he made the turn onto Main Street. He'd worn a suit tonight that might have been new and unexpectedly even a tie. I really wished we had more opportunity for fancy dinners. I knew my dress was a hit too, from the impressed look on his face when I'd finally slipped off my long coat at the restaurant. I felt sexy, the way he looked at me, and desired in exactly the way I wanted to be.

"Didn't you have a good time?" he asked, swinging my hand up to his lips for a quick kiss.

"What? I had a *great* time. The best. Didn't you?"

He kissed my hand again. "Of course. You're just quiet. You seem a little tense."

Okay, I was both of those things. I just didn't think it was that obvious. "No!" I said, a little too tensely, and cleared my throat. "It's just…almost curfew."

"Well, we're home now, with minutes to spare." He turned down the narrow road that led behind the bookstore and pulled into his spot. Tonight I actually waited for him to come open my door. When I stepped out, he added, "We even have time to walk the long way back."

Exactly like we had a year ago.

We took the same route, with the same quiet around us, and the same entwined fingers. Unlike a year ago, they were comfortable that way, natural. My fingers didn't tingle anymore when he held them; they just felt *right*.

When the curfew bell started to ring, we stopped under the oak tree, *our* oak tree, for a kiss. *That* still made me tingle, in all the right ways. When I pulled away, to lead us to my door, Carter hugged me even more tightly, whispering in my ear, "Not yet." He kissed me one more time before taking something from his coat pocket and holding it out. Whoa. I'd thought the fancy dinner date and sneaking out were his gift to me. I expected this less than the tie.

It was a small box in an unmistakable shade of blue and tied with a white ribbon. I sucked in a breath and couldn't seem to make my hand close around it. If not for Carter's help, I'd have dropped it.

"I love you, Lainey," he said. "I have since the first time you kissed me right here, and even before. Happy year." When my fingers shook as I tried to untie the bow, he laughed. "It's safe. I promise." He pulled the ribbon himself and eased off the cover.

Inside *was* a diamond, but not the kind I was way—*way*—too young for. Nestled in the white interior was a single bezel-set diamond solitaire on a slender platinum chain. It was too much, but I loved it anyway. In fact, I thought I might cry.

In the bright moonlight, it threw sparkles across my fingers and glittered like the frost that covered the ground. It also matched perfectly the ring I always wore on my right hand, the one my aunt had made for me from my mom's engagement ring for my thirteenth birthday.

"I love it," I told Carter as he clasped it around my neck. "I love *you*. And I have a present for you, too," I told him, and started toward my dorm building.

I kissed Carter on the porch steps, like we always did when he dropped me off, but this time it wasn't the kind of kiss that said good bye. I stepped backwards, pulling him with me, shushing anything he might say with another kiss. Quietly, I opened the door behind us and, for the first time ever, tugged him inside. His eyes were a little wide, but knowing, and he followed me up the stairs without a word or a sound.

Once we were in my dorm room, I locked the door behind us and let the moonlight guide me to the candles arranged on our wide windowsill. The green walls looked romantic and warm in the soft light, like my roommate had chosen the colors just for this. Maybe she had.

Carter waited patiently just inside the door. He hadn't moved except to take his coat off and fold it next to my dresser. Much like the night a year ago when I'd first kissed him—really kissed him—when we'd first started dating, I knew Carter was entirely aware of what was about to happen, but he didn't rush anything, didn't make any moves at all until I was ready.

His gaze took in my room in the flickering candlelight, and I knew they saw the package of condoms still on my nightstand, before returning to linger on me. That look, full of equal parts love and desire, was all I needed to solidify my decision. I was nervous but excited and, for all my planning, not entirely sure what I meant to do next.

Carter made it easy for me. He smiled and cleared his throat before saying, "No more waiting?" They were the first words we'd spoken since we'd entered my dorm, and the last we'd say for what I'd remember was a very long time. He never took his eyes from mine and I smiled back, shaking my head. No more waiting.

To punctuate my answer, I unzipped my dress, letting it fall to the floor at my feet, and waited for *him*. After an intake of breath, he crossed the room and stood before me. His hands traced down my arms, so lightly and slowly it made me shiver, and he kissed me once before scooping me up and placing me gently on my bed.

It took him almost no time at all to take off his suit, shoes, and watch, the last thing he'd do quickly for the rest of the night. He stood before me, achingly beautiful in only a pair of boxer briefs that left nothing to the imagination, and I was nervous again. And excited and curious and a million different emotions that made my heart beat rapidly in my chest. I'd made the decision but now I needed him to make a move.

Like most times though, he understood this instinctively, without any prompting on my part. Carter joined me on the bed, where he proceeded to ease my nerves and make my pulse race in a different, much more pleasant way.

LATER, I RESTED my head on his bare chest, luxuriating in the sensation of his fingers running through my hair and the pleasant warmth of his body next to mine. I let my fingers play with the necklace he'd given me, the cool of the metal a contrast to the heat in my skin and my memories.

When I thought back on this night, our first night, I'd always remember how Carter had been patient, gentle, and tender. Pretty much everything I wanted for my first time. After all my talking and thinking and hearing about sex, I was prepared for every possibility—pleasure, pain, something in between—but it was a little bit of each of them. All the talking and thinking in the world couldn't compare to experiencing it. Sex was something new, and foreign, and full of possibilities. I wanted to do it again.

As the candles burned out, one by one, Carter said, "I love you, Lainey," into the growing darkness. It was a simple sentence, one I'd heard many times before, but this time it settled over me with gravity, like a soft, heavy blanket. I'd never felt so safe or loved or *right.*

"I love you too," I told him, before I fell asleep for the first time in the warmth and comfort of his arms.

CARTER KNEW THE unspoken Northbrook rules as well as anyone, so it was shortly before dawn that he slipped out of bed, kissing me in my half-sleep before he quietly closed my door and left for home. My bed felt cold and empty in a way I'd never thought it was before, but I drifted back to sleep before long.

My phone woke me. I grappled for it with an odd feeling of déjà vu, wondering what time it was and if it was my aunt, or Carter, calling like a year ago. But it was neither. It was Amy.

"So?" Her voice was excited, and far more awake than it usually was at whatever time of morning it had to be. It sounded like she was bouncing on her bed.

"So I was asleep?" I said vaguely. I rubbed my eyes and looked at the clock. God, it was earlier than she usually got up but it wasn't *that* early. Not for me.

She giggled. "It must have been a *really* late night then. So, spill. How was it? No, scratch that, I can guess how it was. How many *times?*"

"Amy! Jesus!" The heat from my face could probably melt the phone.

"So at least twice then, huh?"

"AMY!" I rubbed my eyes again and sat up, slipping on my robe to go sit on the horrid divan. I couldn't have any of this conversation laying in the same bed she wanted to hear details about.

She laughed again but her next words were all genuine concern. "Seriously though, Lane. Did you do it? How are you?"

God, I thought again. *She's* worried *about me.* Before coming to Northbrook, I'd thought I was going crazy. It had turned out I wasn't, not in the way I thought, but I realized that didn't mean I *wasn't* crazy. But I loved Amy for her concern, and she wouldn't have been Amy without her curiosity. So I owed her some answers, if only I knew what they were.

How was I? I stretched, took a mental tabulation of my body, my brain. Blushed again as I remembered every moment of Carter slipping off the last of his clothes, and everything after that…

A *thump, thump, thump* sound interrupted my mental replay, like Amy had knocked the phone on her bed. For a moment, I'd actually forgotten I was talking to her.

"Lane, hello? Now you're worrying me."

"Sorry! I was…remembering."

"Now that's what I'm talking about! So remember *out loud.*"

I couldn't do that. I'd never, and she knew it, but I did answer her question. "I feel…different."

"Like a woman now?" she tittered.

"Shut up."

"Really though, I know what you mean."

I wasn't sure that was true. Something was different that I couldn't put my finger on.

Amy's voice interrupted my thoughts again. "Okay, Lane, I get it. You're still in ooh-la-la land, not really on the phone with me right now."

It was only half right, but I couldn't help but laugh. "I'm sorry."

"Just tell me this—did you like it, or at least not, you know, hate it? You're kind of a freak about things you've never done before, so I figure you're a little extra freaked about this one."

After a brief hesitation, during which I really thought about the answer and also told myself to just *relax already,* I decided to tell her the truth. I cleared my throat. "Well, it wasn't magic and rainbows," I said, as she'd once joked, "but…I wish he was here right now, so yeah. I liked it."

"That's my girl! So, how many in—?"

"AMY!"

After we hung up, I went back to thinking. Really, what I liked most about it was that I was doing it with *Carter.* And it was true I wished he was with me right now, but really more for comfort than for sex. I was fidgeting. I couldn't figure myself out. Yes, my body felt different in a not entirely unpleasant way, like when you exercise muscles you haven't used in a long time. Or ever, as the case was. But that wasn't what was bothering me. I liked that feeling. No, something was wrong.

I shook my head to try to clear it. My aunt's flight would be landing soon and she'd be here before I knew it. I had to get myself together before then. What was it? Why did I feel so…off?

Maybe the problem *was* simply that I wanted to see Carter. I was feeling strange and lonely and I needed to kiss him. To see the delighted expression he never hid whenever I walked into the bookstore, and remind myself that everything was fine. Better than fine. He wasn't just my boyfriend anymore. Now, he was my…lover. I'd never imagined using that word in relation to *myself*, but that's what he was. He'd make me feel better.

I decided to send him a message, or call, just to hear his voice. By this time, he'd already have run and showered and be downstairs in the bookstore, reading a newspaper or four. I reached for where I'd tossed my phone onto the divan next to me, sliding my fingers across the beautiful—creepy—silk when I stopped. That was it. I couldn't feel the couch. Not the silk, that was still there, but its history.

I couldn't feel the couch's *imprint,* the tiny bit of nausea it never failed to cause me, as its memories tried to force their way into my brain.

The whole reason I'd sat on it was to help wake me up while I tried to talk coherently to Amy. But it hadn't worked. I ran my fingers across it faster, but nothing came. Nothing but a tiny tingling, a spark of not warning but intuition, telling me there was something to know about this couch.

A spark.

I closed my eyes and opened my mind, letting loose the Diviner sense I usually kept tightly controlled. The vision that played out was clearer, and more precise, and more informative than any I'd ever had. I opened my eyes not a moment later and understood.

My Sententia gift had been sparked.

Chapter Thirteen

I laughed. It wasn't exactly funny, but the longer I spent in the Sententia world, the more morbid my sense of humor became. Sparked! Me! Carter had told me about it, the way sex could fast-forward the development of Sententia gifts, but it wasn't a possibility I'd entertained a single thought of. I'd been far busier thinking about *other* things, or not *thinking* at all.

But now! If I hadn't been laughing, I probably would have screamed. All the migraines, and all that time I'd spent working and fretting and passing out, trying to develop control over my Grim senses. And all that time I'd spent worrying and fretting and waiting to have sex too—what a waste! If I'd just gone ahead and done it months ago, I'd have solved all my problems and had a whole summer of lots of easy private time with Carter.

What. An. Idiot.

I mean, how often did that happen? Once every *never?* I was the girl who actually *waits* to have sex and it turns out to be the *wrong* choice. Just my luck. I wished I could call Amy and tell her *this. She'd* understand and laugh along with me.

But I couldn't, so I decided I would call Carter, like I'd originally planned.

"HEY YOU," CARTER said, sounding so sweet and serious and happy that I called, all at the same time, that I temporarily lost the ability to respond. My mouth opened, but no words came out, like the right thing to say got lost and was trying to fight its way past my vocal cords.

All I managed to produce was a breathy, "Uh."

"What's wrong?" Just like that, the delight of a few seconds ago was gone.

"Nothing!" I lied. "I just…miss you. My aunt will be here soon, and I have to get ready. But I, uh, really want to see you."

He exhaled. "Okay, well, maybe I can help with the first problem. Your timing is perfect. Come downstairs."

I guessed that meant he was on my porch. Just like last year. "Um, can you give me a few? I'm not dressed." And not sure how to tell him what I needed to tell him, but sure I didn't want it to happen on the porch.

"I don't care. Seriously. Just go downstairs and you'll understand why." I sensed he was smiling on the other end of the line. I hated disappointing him.

"Okay, I'm going." I tied my robe tightly and tramped down to the front door.

Behind it was not Carter but a woman I didn't recognize, her back turned to the door. When I opened it, she turned around and smiled. "Oh, there you are. Lainey Young?" she asked. When I nodded, she handed me the exquisite bouquet of roses she was holding.

They were lush and full, a perfect mix of red, fuchsia, and deep orange blooms, and smelled like love and happiness. They also must have cost a fortune in November and probably came all the way from Vermont.

"They're beautiful," I told Carter, after I thanked the florist and closed the door.

"So are you," he said. Dropping his voice, he added, "So beautiful, it hurt me to leave you this morning."

At that I sighed, and almost thought I might cry. No matter what happened, I wondered sometimes how I got so lucky to have someone love me so much. As I stepped back into my room, and before I could think any more about it, I said, "Carter, I have something to tell you."

If he was concerned earlier, he was absolutely frantic now. "What? Are you okay? Did I...? Is it, it's not the vision, is it?"

"No! I'm okay, I guess. It's just, I...*think I was sparked.*" The last words came out all in a rush. I wasn't sure why it seemed such an embarrassing thing to say.

Silence. "Carter? Did you hear me?" I slumped back down on the divan. Now that I felt more in control of my connection to it, it no longer bothered me as much.

He finally said, "Which, uh, gift?"

Now that was an interesting question. I hadn't even thought how the *other* gift, the one I didn't like to think about, could have been sparked too, or what that might mean. I wondered, though. "Are they really even separate?"

"I don't know."

I looked at the roses, in all their blooming loveliness, where I'd placed them on my dresser. And decided to kill one.

The petals were like satin memories between my fingers, and I hated to do this to them, but I couldn't think of another way to test my theory. I was ready to Think the flower to its possible demise but decided the stem would be a better place to touch. Careful to avoid the thorns, I pulled one from the vase, closed my eyes, and Thought.

Nothing happened. The rose was still as beautiful as when I first touched it. I'd felt none of the electricity of Thought in my blood either.

"Lane?" I heard Carter say.

"Sorry, I was…testing something. I don't know about the other one, but Divining, yeah. Definitely."

"Shit," he muttered. "I can't leave. You'll have to come here."

"What?"

"I'm the only one at the store. I can't leave. I need you to come here. I'm sorry."

"Why? You mean now?"

"As soon as you can anyway."

"But my aunt—"

I could almost hear his fingers running through his hair. "The *vision*, Lainey. Maybe you can *see* more now. God, why do I feel like *I'm* more concerned about this than you are?"

"I…" honestly hadn't thought about the vision, not yet today. Usually it was my first thought every morning, but Amy had woken me up and then I'd been thinking about Carter for *entirely* different reasons. I felt a little foolish. "You're *not*, I swear." But then again… "But, well, nothing can happen right *now*, can it? I'm here and you're there."

"Shit," he repeated. Then, muffled, like the phone was in his lap, "No, no, I'm sorry. You'll need to go upstairs. I'll be right there…Lainey?"

"Customer?"

He sighed. "Yeah. I'm sorry. I'm…just get here when you can, okay? As soon as you can."

"Soon," I promised. Because now that he'd brought up the obvious, I couldn't get there soon enough.

THE SECOND I ducked under the century-and-a-half-old counter of Penrose Books, Carter grabbed my hand and tugged me through the door behind the register. "C'mon."

"But, the customers—"

Once out of view in the service area, he turned around and pulled me into a crushing hug. "I don't care if they steal the whole fucking *store* right now. You're okay, right? I…the spark, I know it's disorienting, and everything el—"

"I'm great," I told him. Truth. "About everything."

"Okay." He nodded his head—I could feel it, against my shoulder—and absently patted my back with his hand. He was *nervous,* I realized.

"Carter." I pulled back to look at him. "Everything's okay. Seriously."

He held my eyes and nodded again. "Okay," he repeated. "Let's do this." He led me to the dated floral couch that rested against the wall between the store and the stairwell. I'd always wondered why it was there, since no one ever used it, but it made itself useful this morning.

We sat down together, tiny puffs of dust floating up around us. It was dim in the small space and quiet. I reached for his hands and held them. Before I closed my eyes, I told him, "Don't be scared."

He nodded his head once but that was it. He *was* scared, and how could I blame him? We were talking about my life and his part in taking it.

I didn't *need* to close my eyes, but it helped me concentrate. It also meant that, whatever I saw, Carter wouldn't be able to gauge my reaction until I was ready. I took a deep breath and opened my Diviner senses. What I saw surprised even me. I thought I'd been ready for anything, any possibility, even the worst—that it *wasn't* an accident.

But it wasn't that. It was *nothing.*

There was nothing. No vision, no details, no nothing. No image of my face and the certainty that Carter would kill me. My future demise was a great, blank emptiness.

I couldn't believe it, so I kept trying. I'd been seeing it or feeling the echoes for *months,* and now *nothing.* It was gone. Carter held still, but the longer we sat, the more I could tell his nervousness grew. I held on for a long time. His hands were warm, even a little damp, but he felt solid and whole and strong, just the way I always thought of him.

But also, *alive.* When divining produced nothing, I tried everything, including my *other* gift. Not *using* it, but sort of *seeking.* It was strange at first. I wasn't sure anything would happen, but the longer we sat there the more clearly I felt it. Life. All the life I hadn't felt with the rose, here it was. Carter thrummed with *life.*

I wondered if anyone had ever done this before, felt the life resonating within another person. If any of my ancestors had felt it within their victims. I hadn't with Jill, but I hadn't tried. I hadn't been sparked then either, so maybe I couldn't.

Or maybe it was something about *me.* Maybe my Diviner gift had influenced my Hangman gift in the way I'd become only a *Grim* Diviner. Maybe it was just chance, by a miraculous accident of genes and the way they combined, I could *divine* life, the paths and beats of it, before I took it. I wondered if it went any deeper than that. Was it only hearts I could stop? What if that was only one path, the simplest?

When I opened my eyes, Carter was staring at me, pleading for whatever would be the least terrible answer. I gave him what was probably the best: "I see nothing."

He didn't say anything for what stretched into an uncomfortably long time, watching me with his measured look combined with an expression that was parts incredulity and relief. "Nothing," he repeated.

I shook my head and he ran *both* hands through his too-long hair. He was past-due for a cut. I kept trying to get him to go shorter, shorter than his usual and much shorter than it was now. Not that he'd admit it, but I think he felt like if it was too short, he couldn't tug on it. It was a sort of stress relief for him.

"Try again," he said next.

"I don't have to."

"Please. Just humor me."

So I did. I closed my eyes once more, squeezed his fingers, and tried again. Still there was nothing.

I shook my head again. "No vision."

"Nothing *at all.*"

"No."

He dropped my hands and it was as if all the tension that ever existed in the world rushed out of him. Before I knew it, he'd grabbed me into a deep hug, pulling me up off the couch and swinging me around.

"We *did it,*" he said. "We did it again! I can't...I...*thank you.*" He was practically laughing. Once he came to a standstill, he kissed me, recklessly, the kind of kiss that threatened to burn a hole in the very thin wall behind us, setting fire to the store and everyone in it. The kind of kiss that made me forget my name, the date, and even where we were.

For a long time, there was nothing in the world but Carter's lips moving on mine and a joy so deep it almost scared me. Finally I was able to say, "We really didn't *do* anything."

It was hard not to be caught up in Carter's elation, but I couldn't completely unravel the knot of dread that had been living in my stomach for so many months. That was me, Lainey Young, the consummate buzz-kill.

"Maybe we did," Carter countered. "Maybe it doesn't have to be as active as when we saved David this summer. Maybe it was our choices, or just by sticking together. Maybe…are you sure it was a real vision?"

"Yes." I was sure. I knew what I saw. What I felt and what I *knew*.

"The future is never def—"

"Definite, I know." One of the first things he'd taught me about being Sententia. "I can't explain why I can't see anything now, but it was as real a vision as any I've ever had."

Carter sank onto the couch, seemingly exhausted—in the best possible way—by his relief. He leaned his head back and closed his eyes. "It doesn't *matter* why you can't see it anymore. Maybe it was a real vision…at that *moment*. *Something* made that our most probable future. But the future *isn't* fixed. There's constant flux. Maybe that's why you had only hints of it since then, and now, none at all. It's changed. It's *over.*"

My response was interrupted by the ring of the bell on the counter out in the store. "Customer, shit." Kissing me quickly once more as he stood, Carter murmured, "Here's to the future. *I love you.*"

I didn't follow him immediately but stayed on the couch for a minute longer, trying to come to terms with the prospect of a wide-open future, of the sudden weightlessness without the vision hanging over me. I wanted to wrap myself in Carter's optimism, to feel as free and confident as he did. Instead I felt strangely…let down.

That was it? The months of stress of keeping the secret, telling the secret, wondering and worrying about how I was going to die and why I couldn't predict it better? It all amounted to *nothing?!* For the second time in the day, I wanted to laugh and cry. I couldn't believe it was that simple. The vision *had* been real. I had no doubts about that. But I trusted that it was gone now, too. I had no reason not to.

So far, my gift had never been wrong.

THE NEXT WEEK did wonders for convincing me everything really would be fine. For all I knew, it would, and Thanksgiving break was an entire week of forgetting my problems and living my life. With my aunt visiting, I got to pretend the Sententia didn't exist and let myself forget that I was one of them. The year before, I'd been worried about being able to keep my new secret from Aunt Tessa, and I'd spent half the time intentionally hunting for objects that would give me visions.

This year, I relished the chance to let it all go. We visited the city, spent time with Carter and the Revells, humored Dr. Stewart, and acted like girlfriends who hadn't seen each other in months. At the movies on the day after Thanksgiving, we ate every last bite of popcorn, and when it was over, I told my aunt I was no longer a virgin.

What actually happened was she guessed it without my telling her, which is why I told her at all. I should have known it would be obvious to her, and I should also have known what she'd do next: insist I get a prescription for birth control first thing Monday morning.

"That's for *you*, remember, not for him," she insisted. "And a little bit for me. I love you more than anything, but I was too young to be a mother when I got you and I'm way too young to be a grandmother yet."

In all the times she'd brought it up since I was eleven or twelve years old, I hadn't believed anything could be more embarrassing than talking about sex in theory with my parent—until theory became practice and that parent was explaining how contraception worked and making sure I used it properly. I *shouldn't* have been embarrassed, but privacy was in my nature despite Aunt Tessa's years of trying to get me to loosen up. Sometimes I thought my roommate was the daughter she never had. If Amy had been there, they'd probably have high-fived.

When my aunt left at the end of the week, I didn't even have time to miss her. Seniors at Northbrook called the weeks between Thanksgiving and the end of December the Winter Push, or just Push. It seemed like *everything* was due in that little stretch of time. Mid-term and semester assignments, schedules, and for us, college applications. It was the most intense academic period I'd ever had, with multiple all-nighters and one group project catastrophe. I was exhausted, but with Christmas only two days away, I was packed and headed to the airport for my customary weeks in Mexico. After Push, I'd never needed them, or deserved them, so much.

Carter volunteered to chauffeur me one more time to the airport, an offer I wouldn't refuse. I didn't mind taking the airport shuttle services, but I didn't really want any of those drivers to hold my hand or kiss me goodbye for the holidays. We took my car, but I was so tired from Push I let Carter drive. I loved my little red coupe, but I didn't stress out about letting someone else behind the wheel. In truth, I liked it when Carter drove.

My flight left in the evening, so it was dark by the time we were halfway to Logan. Traffic was light in our direction at that time of day. As the sun set somewhere behind us and the evening gloom began its quiet rush past the windows, I decided to ask a question I'd had for the longest time. I'd been thinking about it, off and on, since meeting Dan Astor.

"How does it work, Carter? Thought Moving."

He tapped his fingers on the wheel. "What kind?" If he was surprised by the question, he didn't show it. If anything, he was intrigued. He loved talking Sententia.

"Not yours. Your uncle's."

"He knows better than I do."

"I know, but just give me the basics." I could tell he was working up some of his standard disclaimer, something about *we don't know, exactly,* so I clarified. "Mostly I mean making people forget. Last year, your Uncle Jeff told that story about the man…the rapist, and how he made the women forget. How could he do that?"

"It's not complex, but not easy either. You have to do it in advance. Once a memory's there, it's there. You can't move it away…can't kill it once it's taken root. You can move thoughts around it, when you're in the person's presence, but as soon as the influence is gone, the person goes back to themselves. But before a memory, it's a different game. What you can do in advance is plant *suggestions*. Strong Thought Movers can plant a seed of forgetting, basically, just before something happens and carry it through to the end."

Carter reached over and deliberately covered one of my hands with his. He continued, "And it has to be the right Thought, specific enough to what's going to happen. 'Forget everything' apparently doesn't work very well, but something like 'Don't remember *this*'"—he pinched my hand and I yelped—"or '*This* didn't happen'"—he picked my hand up and kissed it—"can work well for strong influencers. The best could make you remember the pinch *was* a kiss, instead of just forgetting altogether."

Outside, the twilight deepened, made darker by a moving cloud cover that had threatened all day. I thought I understood. "What about…like a trigger? Could someone move a thought to do something, or even forget something, in the future?"

"Nope." He squeezed my fingers before returning his hand to the wheel. "Our gifts work with immediacy, now or never. You have to be there for the whole thing. Some of us can predict the future, but no one can project into it. You couldn't touch someone today and have them die tomorrow."

And thank God for that. We were quiet for a while as I thought about Thought Moving, and what I'd just learned about it. At least Sententia had to be present to do their dirty work, unless, I supposed, that Sententia was Carter. He didn't have to be nearby, but his power wasn't limitless. He was still bound by immediacy, by time.

Something else he'd said kept rattling around in my head, about memories. Memories were thoughts. Thought Movers moved thoughts. *I* was a brand of Thought Mover, or so Dan and Carter had both said to me. Pieces of things I'd learned about my abilities in the last year and the last few weeks began to come together. I stared out the windshield as a theory tried to coalesce, watching the few red tail-lights that dotted the darkness ahead of us on the highway.

Watching them swerve and brighten. Watching a pair of white lights coming toward us, but that had to be wrong. They shouldn't have been white.

But they were.

Headlights, traveling the wrong way on the highway.

And then they were right in front of us.

This is it, I thought. *It really was an accident and there was nothing I could do.* I hadn't bothered to check our future today, and now it was about to end.

In my last moments, I heard Carter swearing, along with tires screeching, metal crunching, and glass breaking. I thought I might have heard a scream too, and that it might have come from me.

And then I heard nothing at all.

Chapter Fourteen

Opening my eyes was an enormous, wonderful surprise. Especially since I hadn't expected to open them ever again. Dying, or sincerely believing I was dying, was nothing like people claim. It was just like blacking out, and after years of doing that while my Sententia gift was developing, I was practically a pro at being unconscious.

There'd been no life flashing before my eyes, and the only bright lights I saw were the ones shining down on me when I came to. There was never any concept of the lost time either. You're aware and then you're not and then you're aware again. I had no idea how long I'd been out, whether it was seconds or hours or days.

But no matter how long it had been, when I opened my eyes, I saw Carter, and he was beautiful. It was hardly the first time I'd been unconscious and woken up to his face, but since my whole being had been convinced I'd never see it again, this was definitely the best time ever. His lips formed a little grin as he noticed my open eyes, and I finally realized that he actually *wasn't* that beautiful.

In fact, he looked awful. There were red marks across his forehead, nose, and cheeks, like severe windburn or a rash, his bottom lip was split, and dark circles filled the hollows beneath his eyes. He also looked absolutely disheveled and exhausted.

And relieved.

"Hey beautiful," he croaked and then cleared his throat. "It's good to see those pretty hazel eyes. I've missed them."

I tried a smile but my face felt tight and wind burned, much like Carter's looked. When I reached my hand up to touch the marks on his face, I found my arm was much heavier than I remembered. I looked down to see it was encased in a thick cast that covered most of my hand to halfway up my forearm. And it was *purple*. Frowning hurt as much as smiling.

My head felt foggy and too heavy to lift, so I looked back up at Carter and said, "What happened to your face?" My voice sounded scratchy and out of practice.

He reached forward and brushed my hair back before tentatively surrounding my fingers where they protruded from the cast with his own. My other hand sported an IV. "The same thing that happened to yours," he replied. "It's from the airbags. No one ever mentions how much they *hurt.*" I must have grimaced because he laughed and gave my finger ends a gentle squeeze. "You don't look quite so bad, don't worry. No split lip or black eyes, but a pretty good rash."

I didn't remember airbags. I didn't remember much of anything but an overwhelming sense that I should be dead. Except I wasn't. I *loved* not being dead. Even with whatever was wrong with my arm and my head. Even with whatever my face looked like. Though, honestly, I hoped it wasn't too terrible.

Carter pushed the call button to let them know I was awake and nurses and doctors came and went. They told me my wrist should— not *would*—be fine, after weeks in the cast and more weeks of therapy. If I weren't so thrilled about the being alive part, I'd have cried. So much for volleyball season. It had only just started, and now I'd miss the whole thing. Brooke would be pissed, especially since we were supposed to be co-captains.

When the medical action was finally over and it was time for me to rest, I said to Carter, "Tell me?" and closed my eyes to listen. Keeping them open was a challenge, and the lights seemed so, so bright.

He spoke softly, like a lullaby. "What do you remember?" he asked and my answer was a tiny shake of my head.

"There was a car, going the wrong way. The driver, she's old. I guess she was confused. I think she's here now, too." He took a breath and let it out. "I almost missed it, babe. It was so close, and I'm sorry. I…just…I wasn't fast enough. She clipped our rear bumper and that was it. We spun. Into another car and then the guardrail." *Just like my parents,* I thought but didn't say. "They're okay, though, the other people. The driver helped me try to get you out."

He paused then, and I wasn't sure how much time passed. Through our connected fingers, I felt him shift, and I imagined him running his other hand through his hair until it went in all directions.

"I thought…" His voice broke and he took another breath, then another. "I thought I'd killed you, Lainey. Just like the vision. You were slumped and broken, and…God, I thought I'd lost you. I *could* have lost you, *again,* and it was all my fault. If I'd been paying more attention, or reacted faster. I let my guard down, and I'm sorry. I'm so sorry. I don't know what I'd do, if you…if you hadn't been okay. I'm *sorry.* I love you." I'm not sure if I squeezed his fingers then, or he squeezed mine, but his voice was stronger as he told the rest.

"Your car—it's totaled. I'm sorry. Most all the damage was to your side, and it was just worse because you were wedged against the guardrail. They had to cut you out, Lane. We tried, the other driver and I, but—we didn't know if we'd hurt you more, or if…so we had to wait. God, it was like forever, before the ambulances and fire trucks got there. Watching you barely breathing and not knowing how to help.

And then they *were* there and they were swarming and I *couldn't* see you and that was worse. Hearing the screech from the tools and the police trying to ask what happened. What the hell did it *matter?* They were *cutting you out of the car.* But that was it, and then you were here and your *wrist.* God. And I had to call Tessa. I don't know if they're even supposed to let me in here, but I think they realized I just wouldn't leave. Your aunt is in *Mexico,* and it's almost *Christmas,* so they let me stay. I'm *sorry,* babe. I—"

I drifted off to sleep then, and would never know what he said next. I'd only ever remember the accident as Carter's voice and a dream.

"WHAT ON EARTH is *that?"* I set my phone down on the rolling tray that was never far from reach and watched Carter unpack a surprising number of bags and boxes in my hospital room. I'd been forced to stay for a few days, to monitor my concussion and the pain in my wrist.

"Merry Christmas!" He threw a devastating grin over his shoulder as he pulled a truly ugly two-foot-tall tree out of a box.

"Happy birthday!" I countered and his smile flattened out. Carter was twenty today.

He plugged in the tree, which lit up like Las Vegas, and pushed a button on the star. A tinny rendition of "Have Yourself a Merry Little Christmas" blared out of a speaker hidden somewhere in the gaudy branches.

I laughed. "How can something so small be so *loud?"*

"And terrible," he added. "Isn't it great?!"

"Tell me you didn't spend money on that."

The Vegas Tree transitioned into "Let it Snow," which, actually, it *was,* both outside and in. Snowflake garland and icicle lights appeared around the room in a flurry, as Carter emptied the bags and turned my bland little hospital room into a Christmas Extravaganza. When a multitude of presents appeared around the tree, I started to feel like a jerk. We were forced to spend Christmas/his birthday in the hospital, and I didn't even have anything to give him.

"Hey! Now what's *that?* I hope those are only decorations." Carter's sly grin told me they weren't. "But I already gave you all your gifts!"

He sat next to me and reached for my hand. My good hand. I gave it over and he pressed it to his cheek. *"You* are the only gift I care about this year."

That's about when I melted. Then he unpacked a beach-ready snowman, wearing sunglasses and swim trunks, that sang "Feliz Navidad" when you touched one of his buttons and I almost died again. Of laughter.

"Seriously, where did you *get* this stuff?"

"It's amazing the quality holiday decorations you can still find on Christmas Eve at the drug store." He pushed the snowman again, and the sounds of the Christmas-I-was-missing filled the room.

I'd just hung up the phone with Aunt Tessa and the rest of the family in Mexico when Carter returned. Aunt Tessa would have been here, had, in fact, been ready to fly back last minute at exorbitant cost and with about seven layovers to come get me, if I hadn't convinced her that was ridiculous. I wasn't dying, I had Carter with me, and I'd be *fine.* And, also, would be delivered to her by private jet when I was released the next day, compliments of a very lavish and unexpected gift arranged by Daniel Astor.

Except for the broken wrist and wrecked car, this holiday was turning out rather better than I expected.

It improved even more when Carter unpacked dinner, a home-cooked feast compliments of Melinda. "Did she make all this *yesterday?"*

"And this morning, so it would be ready before I left to come here. And Grandma gave us a whole pie."

"Pecan?"

"Of course."

Evelyn Revell's pies were legendary. After more than a day of hospital food, I was ready to eat the entire thing myself. And also, maybe ready to cry. I blamed the industrial-strength pain killers I'd been downing at regular intervals as my eyes filled with moisture. "Carter, this…this is too much."

"Hey." He left off unwrapping our silverware—plastic, scavenged from the tiny cafeteria when he'd reheated our plates—and sat on the edge of my bed. "It's not anything," he said. "We love you. *I* love you. It could be better circumstances, but there's nowhere I'd rather be." He rested his forehead against mine while I took deep yoga breaths, fighting the urge to cry. His skin was warm, but the fresh, wintery scent of the cold still lingered around him from his trips back and forth to the parking lot. After a moment, he kissed me. "It *is* a Merry Christmas."

"I can think of a few places *I'd* rather be, but yeah, I guess it is. And a happy birthday," I added. When all he did was frown, I said, "Why do you do that?"

"What?"

"Every time I try to wish you a happy birthday, you make this face." He almost smiled at my imitation.

Running his fingers through his hair, he said, "We just don't really celebrate it. Christmas is enough for one day."

In a way, I got it. His birthday was also the twenty-year anniversary of his mother's death. But at the same time, "Carter, you don't have to apologize for being alive."

"I don't have to celebrate either."

"Well, *I* do. Let me be happy to have you."

The frown he'd been sporting morphed into a sly smile that I knew meant trouble. The good kind. "You were happy to have me—"

"OH look. Presents!" I pushed my hair forward to cover the pink in my cheeks, though really I don't know why I bothered. It was just the two of us. And possibly any number of nurses and doctors at any second.

Carter laughed, dropping a kiss on my nose before retrieving the presents and resting the boxes on my lap. "Biggest to smallest," he advised, so I started with the heaviest one. Books. A bunch of them, including an early edition E. M. Forster that Melinda had probably been saving for my birthday.

"Is it cheating to shop at your own place of business?"

"*Someone* has to buy the books. Plus I get a sweet employee discount. Besides, I thought you could use them, since this"—he tapped on my cast—"probably won't be compatible with the ocean."

Crap. I hadn't even thought of that. I hadn't thought of a *lot* of things beyond that I couldn't wait to get the heavy purple thing *off* of me. The second box was filled with sunscreen. "I'm sensing a theme here," I told him, "but I can't figure out what this one could be." The third box was tiny, tied with a misshapen bow that clearly indicated fastidious Carter had *not* wrapped it himself. "Did you go all the way to the *mall?*" He shrugged as I untied the ribbon, though I could see he was trying not to smile.

Inside, impossibly, was a *bikini*. Purple, with black stripes, that matched my cast perfectly.

I threw my head back and laughed, the best laugh I'd had since the accident, and maybe even in weeks. Carter's face exploded into a smile about as bright as the Mexico sun was going to be. "How did you *find* this?"

"You don't want to know." I did, actually. Still grinning, he said, "I *might* have convinced a few sales girls into checking the stock rooms for me." On Christmas Eve, no less. Good lord, his powers of charm knew no limits.

I leaned forward and kissed him squarely on the mouth. "I love it. Thank you."

He laughed. "Even though it's purple?"

"Yes. Even then."

"I," he said, "love *you*. Merry Christmas."

"Happy Birthday," I repeated. And it was.

Circumstance and a few missed days of my beach holiday aside, at that moment I was so happy just to be alive and with the boy I loved. In fact, in some ways, it was the best-worst Christmas I'd ever had.

ALONG WITH A renewed appreciation for life, I returned from winter break with a few other things: the cast I'd done a poor job not getting sandy; what was sure to be an awkward tan; a new card from Senator Astor to add to my collection, wishing me well and a quick recovery; and, finally, a terrible feeling I'd forgotten something important, something I'd been thinking just before the car crash.

Amy returned from break with a pet.

"Isn't he pretty?" She petted the leaves of the potted fern as if "he" were a dog.

"Um." As far as plants went, I actually thought it was pretty *ugly,* like a plant having a bad hair day. It has wispy fronds that looked soft but seemed to stick in every direction. At least the green of the leaves went with our color scheme.

She narrowed her eyes, patting the plant protectively. "Don't insult Ferny!"

"Ferny?"

"Listen, Young, I've never had so much as a goldfish before now, so don't kill my joy, okay? Ferny's mine and I love him."

I laughed. "Okay. I love him, too. But where did you even get him?" Despite what she said, he was *not* a pretty plant. Amy wouldn't have chosen him on her own.

"One of my dad's nurses thought his office needed more color. She couldn't know that he kills, basically, every living thing besides patients. We have a landscaper for a reason. Anyway, she grew him this plant for, like, a year, from a baby plant cutting from her great-grandmother's prize fern or something. So it wasn't like he could keep it and let her watch him kill great-grandma's fern progeny, so he gave it to me. Told her it was going to be my favorite Christmas present ever. Which was a lie, because my favorite present ever was totally my Acura, but I *do* love him. I *want* to take care of something. Ferny seems like a good place to start. Less commitment than a fish. And he could be a lifetime companion!" She looked at her plant again, stroking one of the stray fronds. "You'll always listen and never leave me or cheat on me or want to watch just one more football game, right baby?"

Ferny didn't disagree.

He received a pedestal of honor near the window, and the more I looked at him, the more I realized he was like a bulldog. Adorable for his ugliness. He was, in fact, a good listener, and never complained about Amy's or my choice of music, and never blushed like I did whenever Amy asked him a personal question.

And Ferny never would cheat on her. Amy'd been joking when she'd said that, but her fear was there, and the more I listened to her talk to her plant, the more I worried about just how off things were between her and Caleb. They were fighting more and more. They'd always fought, because that was Amy, and that was Caleb too, but the fights weren't real. It was flirting, or foreplay.

Lately though, they were real. And though I'd never have thought it possible a few months ago, the prospect of Caleb cheating was real too. I knew because I saw it.

THEY WERE IN a great study corner of the library, one with a window and lots of privacy. It was a week after we'd gotten back from break. I wondered if he always did his tutoring there, or if it was only with Mandi Worthington. Usually I wouldn't even go by there during work hours, but when I ran out of things to do early, the librarian sent me around to check for stray books. I didn't have my cart, which always announced my presence, so they didn't hear me coming. I had my music on, so I didn't hear them either. But I saw them.

When I saw how *close* they were, I ducked to the side of the study carrels and watched. They were studying, in that they had books spread on the table and pencils poised over notebooks, but it really looked more like organized flirting. Mandi leaned over to look at Caleb's work, letting her shoulder brush his, her pretty blond hair falling on his arm until he laughed and brushed it away. She touched his arm and pointed to her own work, and his fingers seemed to glance against hers as he nudged his pencil across the page.

Part of me wanted to cry, the other part to go kick Caleb right in the tutors, but I was frozen. When someone else stepped out of the elevator and drew their attention, I disappeared. I didn't know what to do, but I *didn't* want them to know I'd been watching.

I told Carter. I had to tell someone, do *something,* and Amy wasn't the right choice. Plus, a check of my watch told me she was at Physics Club, and even though *she'd* definitely think this was an emergency, I wasn't about to drag potential relationship problems out in front of all her science nerd friends. I loitered in the library pretending to do my homework until it was closing time at the bookstore.

"It wasn't him," Carter said.

I looked over in his direction. We were sitting in front of the fireplace with the store lights off. The flames threw alluring shadows across his features, but it didn't look like he was joking. "It was him. I *saw* it, Carter. Contrary to what the song told you, that excuse doesn't work. I know Caleb's your friend and all, but the guy solidarity—"

"No." He squeezed my hand. "I mean, it wasn't…it's not *him*. It's her. She's doing it."

"You sure about that?"

"Well, maybe it's a *little* him. He's got to be attracted to her. But I swear, it's *her*. A Siren…they can make you lose your mind. I tried to warn him, as much as I could."

I sighed. I hated to admit what I said next, but it was true. "Sometimes I think Amy makes him lose his mind."

Carter didn't even hesitate. "It's part of why he loves her," he said. And he was right.

"But it's getting worse. You've seen it. Don't you think this is part of it? They're just…off, and now I see him with Mandi and I don't know. I never thought he'd do this to Amy."

"He's *not*. Lane, I swear. She's doing it." Softly, he added, "She got sent here from Webber not to be closer to Alexis but because there was some kind of issue there."

I was half surprised and half nodding like I'd expected him to say something like that. I knew she was trouble, and I wasn't surprised she'd been *in* trouble, whatever it was. I only wished they'd told me; as her dorm representative, it would have been nice to know. Which made me wonder how Carter did. "Did your uncle tell you that or something?"

"No." He looked away, probably to cover his guilty expression. "Her cousin did."

Wow. Apparently it was boyfriend-screw-up night. I extracted my fingers from his and folded my arms across my chest. "So she really *does* need physics help every Wednesday night, huh? I thought I was joking about that. Just how much time do you spend talking with her?"

I was being that girlfriend I hated to be, but it was *Alexis*. He knew better. He *should have* known better.

He ran his now-free hand through his caramel waves. "Fuck, Lane. Now I'm under suspicion too?"

Oh, it was on. "Should you be?"

"Christ. *No*. I help her with physics. In the bookstore lounge, in front of *everyone,* all of whom can see that *nothing* is or ever will be going on between us because, in case you haven't noticed, I am a thousand lifetimes in love with *you*. Sometimes she talks to me like a friend, because her other friends are shitty. The end." He was standing by the time he got to those last words.

Just like that, my anger rushed out of me. *I* felt like the one who was shitty. What the hell was wrong with me? With *us*. Everything felt so unstable. First Caleb and Amy, and now I was picking fights with Carter.

I dropped my head, hair falling over my shoulders to cover my warm cheeks, and apologized. "I'm sorry."

He sighed and sat back down, brushing away those tendrils so he could see my face. "No, I am. *I'm* sorry. I shouldn't have gotten so angry. I...I probably shouldn't help her, talk to her at all, but, I don't know. She's not perfect, but maybe everyone deserves a chance to make up for it."

And then it all made sense. He empathized with Alexis. Sometimes I felt like Carter trusted *everyone* and I trusted *no one* and I wasn't even sure how we got that way. I could never tell if he was blind to the bad or chose to focus on the good in people. And when had I become so suspicious? Maybe because I'd spent so much of my childhood by myself. It was a self-reliance thing. Carter wanted *not* to be alone in things, and I wasn't sure anyone but myself could get things done.

But Carter and I needed to be in this together.

I leaned my head on his shoulder. "Did you mean all those other things you said?"

He put his arm around me, pulling me closer and adding a kiss to my forehead. "Yes. Most of Alex's other friends are shitty."

I laughed and our fight was over. "Except Brooke."

"Except Brooke," he agreed. "And," he added, voice lowered and lips close to my ear, "I *am* that in love with you. Don't forget it."

THE NEXT DAY I practically sprinted from class after last bell and managed to catch Brooke just as she was leaving the Arts building. We walked together to volleyball. As co-captain, I still dutifully attended every practice, cheering from the sidelines or helping retrieve errant balls. I was allowed to run, so I ran with them. But it wasn't volleyball advice I needed from her today.

Exactly like I hoped, no one joined us on the way to the gym. Besides some of the team, we had basically zero friends in common, being as we were technically on opposite sides of Northbrook's great divide—Alexis Morrow. But Brooke was cool. She didn't hold it against me that I was Alex's enemy, and I didn't hold it against her that she was Alex's long-time friend, so we got along great. When we saw each other.

"God, it feels like I never get to talk to you this year," she lamented as we started up the hill from mid-campus. It was a clear day, but cold, and everyone was hurrying from place to place. Several inches of new snow had fallen in the last few days and frozen solid, forcing everyone to traverse the acres of campus only on the cleared walkways.

"I know," I replied. "We need to start our breakfast dates again, now that swimming and Push are over."

"Ugh, Push. I'm so not looking forward to it next year."

"I'm pretty sure they make it so bad on purpose, so we know what it feels like when we get to college."

"Seriously. I think Lex didn't sleep all week, right?"

"That's kind of what I wanted to talk to you about…"

She gave her delightful laugh that I envied so badly. "About sleeping with Lex, or *not* sleeping with her? Because I think that honor is reserved for a kid from Hotchkiss right now."

You'd think Alexis would've been the kind of girl who always had a boyfriend, but she didn't. She had boy*friends,* a rotating collection of expensive ones who'd drive up to visit from Manhattan or schools like Andover and Choate with their luxury cars and shiny hair. The closest she'd had to a relationship since I'd known her had been the few weeks after last year's disastrous Winter Ball when she'd kept up her fling with a senior I'd sort of dated before Carter. That had ended as horribly (for him) as I'd worried it would. I realized now she was still holding out for *my* boyfriend.

"Um, no. No no no," I said, laughing too, before I dropped my voice and got to the point. "Actually, it's about her cousin, Mandi. Do you spend much time with her?"

Brooke made a noise that wasn't nearly as pretty as her laugh. "What was it you just said, 'Um, no, no no no?' 'Cause that's about what I think of Mandi. She's insufferable. I mean, I feel bad for her, but I can't stand her."

I nodded. I knew what she meant. There were days *I* thought it was hard being a teenager, and I couldn't imagine being a teenager while trying to control a gift that basically made your hormones, and everyone's around you, go crazy. But still. "I think she's worse than Alex."

Brooke agreed. "Times ten. I know Lex can be a bitch, but she's *really* not all bad. Mandi's just…off in the head or something. It's not all because of the gift. But, so, what was it you wanted to ask about her? I might not know, but ask anyway."

We were almost to the gym, just passing the Chapel, so even though it was freezing out, I pulled her around the side of building. "Okay, I hate to ask, but…do you think you could, um, *eavesdrop* on her?"

Brooke looked curious. She knew what I meant. "This is serious, huh? I mean, I don't really like to know what a Siren's wanting basically ever, right? But for you, okay. What's she up to?"

"That's the thing. I don't know, exactly. But remember what you said to me after the SATs?"

"You think it's her?"

"Maybe. She's, well, she's flirting with Caleb Sullivan. Hard."

"Oh yeah." She nodded. "I know. Her little confrontation with Amy didn't help either."

I grimaced. "I know. I guess I want to know why. Why him? It's more than that though she—"

But I never finished that sentence because that's about when I heard Mandi's laugh. Speak of the devil. Brooke and I both turned in that direction. My cheeks flushed, more even than from the cold, and I'm sure I looked exactly like I'd just been talking about her. Mandi came around from the back of the building and paused when she saw us huddled by the wall in the snow. She looked happy to see us.

"Wow. Hey, Brooke! And Lainey. Are you guys waiting for a turn in the Cove? It's empty…now." She giggled again and flounced past us before I could even say anything. I looked over at Brooke and just caught her eyes flashing as Mandi went by. Before she could tell me what she learned, a second person emerged from behind the building.

Caleb appeared next, head down and walking toward the gym. He didn't see us.

"Holy shit," Brooke said.

I was almost too pissed for words, but I managed one.

"Caleb!" I shouted and he froze. He turned to look at me and his expression shifted through a number of things—surprise, confusion, anger. But also, guilt.

Beside me, Brooke muttered, "Yeah, I'll let coach know you're going to be late." Before she took off, she gave my elbow a light squeeze and whispered, "I'm not sure it's what it looks like. She *wanted* someone to see this."

For Caleb's sake, I hoped she was right. In my rage, it crossed my mind that I might kill him. And unfortunately for him, I had the power. I was glad I was wearing gloves.

I stormed over, shouting whatever words decided to come from my lips. "You're kidding me, right? Out here, in the middle of the day? How *could* you? And she's in eighth grade!" I didn't know why her age was a big deal, but in my head apparently it was. Mandi was still a kid to me, though I was pretty sure she was less innocent than I was. I should have been concerned that people were probably watching, but I wasn't thinking about that. All I could think about was Amy.

Caleb's eyes grew wider the closer I got. "Whoa, Lane, what do you think I *did?*"

"What *did* you do?" I shot back.

He ran his hand through his hair, another habit he picked up from Carter. Or maybe all boys did that and I'd just never spent enough concentrated time with them to notice before. Whatever it was, it meant he was uncomfortable. "Obviously you know I just canceled on Amy."

"So you could visit the Cove with fucking Mandi Worthington?!"

"What?" He looked stricken by my accusation, but there was still…something. We were just about the same height, so he had to look me in the eyes. And I saw that flickering of guilt. "I…no. Why would you even think that?"

I laughed a truly humorless laugh. "Why would I think that? Because I just saw you come out from behind the Chapel together! And Mandi practically told me as much."

"Lainey, I *swear* I didn't. I have no idea what she said, but I was walking from Marquise up the back path and Mandi caught up with me. We *walked* together for a little ways. She went ahead when I stopped to find my phone." His phone was in his hand and he waved it at me. "And two sophomores from the debate team just snuck out of there when I passed."

I stared at him. Was he lying? Caleb didn't have a lot of guile in him, while I knew Mandi did. She hadn't said *they'd* just been the ones to vacate the Cove. Canceling something with Amy was bad, but not bad enough for the expression on his face when I called his name. Like he'd been *caught* at something. "Then why do you look so guilty? Tell me the truth."

He dropped his head. "Because I *thought about it,* okay? We were walking and almost to the back of the Chapel and I thought about what it would be like. I'm sorry. Amy's being crazy and, God, Mandi's pretty and when I'm with her, sometimes things I swear I'd never think otherwise seem like a really good idea." He looked at me again. "I'm sorry. I love Amy, you *know* I love Amy, but sometimes…I don't know."

No, he didn't know. But *I* knew. I wanted to cry, like this was all my fault. Like I was protecting Sententia secrets when I *should have* been protecting my friends. Sententia or not, one of my dorm girls or not, I *should* have warned him. "Oh, Caleb." I touched the back of his hand that was gripping his phone too tightly. "Listen to me. I should have said this before now, but you have to be careful of Mandi. She's…got history."

"I know all about it," he said, nodding, but I knew that couldn't possibly be true. "I feel bad for her." I opened my mouth to say something, but he held up his hand. "I *know* Amy wants me to stop working with her, and maybe she'd be less crazy but…" He shrugged. "I guess I like it. She actually tries to do the work. And then when she says how much she likes working with *me* because I don't try to flirt with her, I guess I feel bad handing her off to someone else. Which might be kind of pathetic, considering what I just admitted I was thinking."

I wondered just what kind of story Mandi had told Caleb about her past, but then, I *didn't* know the whole story either. "Maybe you should think about letting them reassign her anyway," I suggested. "Maybe to a girl. Just think about it, okay? Working with her might be good for her, but it doesn't seem to be good for *you.*"

"Yeah, I…yeah." He leaned his shoulders against the wall of the Chapel and looked dejected. The tip of his nose was red from the cold. I knew I should have been shivering by now, too, but I was too worked up to feel it. "First Amy, now you too. Jesus, Lane, this is frustrating. I didn't think I was the kind of guy who'd think…things about a girl who wasn't Amy. But then she started to treat me like I was, and now I guess she's right. Will you tell her?"

I leaned up on the wall next to him and let my shoulder touch his. "I don't think so," I said. "But maybe you should. Maybe you should *really* talk about this."

"Yeah."

"And for the record, I *don't* think you're the kind of guy you're starting to think you are. *That's* what I'm going to tell Amy. Just…don't let Mandi get under your skin either. She's not as sweet as she seems. Trust me on that. Try to think of her as your little sister."

He made a noise that was some sad combination of a laugh and a sigh. "Carter said sort of the same thing to me a while ago. Except, you know, I don't *have* a little sister." With another tug of his hair he said, "I wish I hadn't thought that, earlier. Or I could scrub it out of my memory or something. But it's too late, right? How do you kill a memory once it's already there?"

Kill a memory.

Kill a memory that's already there.

Before I responded, he'd pushed off the wall, standing up straight and slipping his bag back over one shoulder. "I've got to go. I'm late for practice. So are you, I guess. Thanks for…" He shook his head, like he wasn't sure which things to thank me for. "Just, thanks," he repeated and took off for the gym while I still stood, mind whirling with the strangest sense of déjà vu. Where had I heard that before?

How do you kill a memory that's already there?

Chapter Fifteen

I actually skipped practice completely and went to my room, where I was unsurprised to find Amy crying on her bed. She was surprised to see me, though, and sat up quickly, scrubbing tears from her eyes while stuttering.

"I...just...um. Shit." She flopped back down onto her mountain of pillows. They were all different from last year's but there were no fewer of them. "What are you doing here?"

"I live here, remember?" I joked, but my heart wasn't really in it. I went and laid down next to her on her bed. It was a tight fit, but she moved over to make room for me. "I skipped practice," I admitted.

"Why?"

"Because I ran into Caleb on the way in." She squeezed her eyes shut but didn't say anything. "I thought my roommate might need a cheerleader more than the volleyball team right now."

"What'd he say?"

I'd promised I wouldn't tell her what I'd seen or, worse, *thought* I'd seen, or, worst of all, what Caleb had admitted, but I could tell her *something*. "He said nothing surprising: he loves you but sometimes you make him crazy."

She rolled over onto her side, facing the wall while she hugged a pillow to her chest. "He makes me crazy too, you know."

"I know." I rubbed circles on her back.

"He canceled on me tonight. So, I'll be here. Sorry."

"It's not a big deal."

"Yeah it is."

"It's not a big deal *to me.*"

She giggled and glanced over her shoulder at me. "Carter will probably mind a little."

"He'll survive."

It was supposed to be, as Amy liked to call it, "date night." I knew it was silly that I kept risking getting caught sneaking Carter into my room when we could really do whatever we wanted at his apartment, but I just couldn't handle the fact that his aunt and uncle lived there too. They felt too much like parents and I felt weird when we even closed the door to his bedroom, whether we were fooling around or not. I was sure they knew what was going on when Carter came to my dorm, but that weirded me out less than them knowing it was going on at their house.

She sighed again. "Caleb didn't even want to this afternoon."

"Ame, geez."

"That's not like him. He always wants to." And that was probably true. Actually, that was probably true of most guys, but Caleb and Amy were the couple who were *always* fooling around. All our friends joked about it. Hell, all of *campus* joked about it. When they'd gotten together last year, the bonfire they were *supposed* to be tending had almost burned out of control. Usually Amy joked about it too.

I tried to lighten the mood. "Maybe he *is* tired, Ame. You're a lot to keep up with."

And it backfired completely. She started sniffling again. "I know I'm not as skinny as other girls, okay? I get it."

"That's not…Ame." I touched her shoulder and when that failed to elicit a response, I just went ahead and hugged her. "You *know* that's not what I meant."

"It's true though. I'm not. I don't think I'll ever be. I can't be skinny like you and Alexis and…and Mandi."

There it was. I wasn't going to say her name but I knew Amy would bring it up eventually. Alexis and I weren't really the problem. Amy "hated" the two of us for our long legs and skinny asses all the time. I mean, she hated Alexis for plenty of things, but not, actually, because she was beautiful.

With Mandi, it was different. Mandi was Amy's opposite, and all the things Amy sometimes wished she could be. Mandi was maybe close to Amy's height, but where Amy bought a medium or sometimes a large, Mandi was an extra-small. She had straight blond hair and blue eyes and probably could get away with not wearing a bra.

Most of the time I thought Amy knew how gorgeous she was. She joked how guys loved her for her boobs and her laugh, and she was never afraid to flaunt either. But when she felt bad, she felt all wrong. We all had those moments. Amy felt fat. And like her pretty brown curls were frizzy, and her perfect eyebrows were too Italian, and her D+ cup breasts were the *only* thing guys liked about her. Comparing herself to Mandi just amplified all of those feelings.

"No one wants you to look like me, or Mandi."

"No? Then why did my boyfriend turn down—"

"Jesus! Ame. I *don't* need the details. And I may not know much, but I know if you think a guy loves you only for how you look or what you *do* for him, *he doesn't love you!* Caleb loves *you,* all of you. Give him a little credit. Give you a little credit too."

"God," she sniffed. "What's wrong with me? When did I become this girl?"

"You're *not* this girl. This isn't you, and I, for one, would like *you* back. So would Caleb. Maybe start by trusting him."

She disentangled herself from my arms then and we sat up. "You're right," she said, rubbing her eyes and taking a few deep breaths. "You're right. And I think I *do* trust Caleb. I do. I just don't trust Mandi Worthington."

"That's okay. I don't trust her either. She's bad news, even though I'm not supposed to say that about my mentees. But you still have to trust Caleb."

"You're right," she repeated and gave me one more swift hug. "Thank you for skipping practice."

With a tug of one of her curls and a smile, I got up from the bed. "Any time."

Behind me, she flopped backward on her pillows again and rolled in my direction, watching me. "There are days, Lane, I mean, look at you—why can't I be attracted to *you?* It would be so much simpler. We could push our beds together and never have to sneak anywhere."

"Date night every night?" I laughed.

"Exactly!"

"I'm not so easy to cuddle with this monstrous cast on."

She made a face and rubbed a spot on her ribs. "I know. I think you left a bruise. But it's perfect for clubbing our enemies!" We laughed together, and for that minute, it felt like everything was perfect. When we stopped, Amy sobered. "Seriously though, thank you. And I was only half joking. You're hot, and I really do wonder sometimes if the boys are worth it."

Did I ever understand that. "I hope they are."

DINNER LATER WAS an odd affair, with Amy and Caleb in an unresolved fight that basically no one knew about. They were themselves, but strained, not looking at each other when they laughed at jokes. I don't know if anyone else noticed, but to me it was like there were feet of space between them though they sat right next to each other. Their shoulders didn't touch, and neither stole anything from the other's plate.

Finally, when we were all just about ready to leave, Caleb leaned over and whispered in Amy's ear. She stiffened, then nodded. They left together and I watched them go, trying not to look as worried as I was. But as they were walking out the dining hall doors, Caleb slipped his hand into Amy's and her whole face brightened. Maybe this would be a *good* talk.

Her text came in just before the curfew bells started to ring.

be back late. staying here for a while tonight. just to sleep. xoxo

I was glad. I thought sleeping together without *sleeping together* would be good for them. Just being close to each other. It meant Carter could have come over, and I could still have called him, but I thought I could use the time alone. To think.

I pushed my notebook away and tilted back in my chair, staring at the cracked plaster of the old building's high ceiling.

It seemed like as soon as I solved one problem another was ready to slip into its place. Now that my looming death was no longer looming, or at least on hold, my best friend was basically on the verge of a breakdown or, for her maybe worse, a break *up*. And part of me felt like I'd let her get there.

I felt totally trapped. Between my two worlds, between everything. This was exactly why I'd wanted to get away from the Sententia in the first place and I was beginning to fear I never would. Hell, lately I'd been considering getting even *deeper* into Sententia business. Not for the first time, I thought about how the only thing keeping me involved was Carter. How maybe no man was worth this trouble.

But the problem with that line of thinking was my heart didn't believe it.

On the shelf above my desk, a paperback copy of *Love's Labour's Lost* slid out of its place, teetered on the edge, and fell with a soft thump onto the books scattered in front of me. Carter Penrose, the comedian. He did that sometimes, sent me little signs that he was thinking about me. Sometimes they scared the crap out of me, and then sometimes it was like he just knew when *I'd* been thinking about *him*.

I always thought it would have been cool if he could make messages appear in my notebook with my pen, but that was beyond even his abilities. He could make them appear on my phone, though. It buzzed from somewhere under all the books.

still studying?

sort of. but not really. more like on a break

how's moretti?

gone actually. they're making up.

So, want some company?

I was tempted. Really tempted. I'd already considered it. But a night alone was what I planned and I still had something else I hadn't really had a chance to think about: memories. What Caleb had said that afternoon kept coming back to me.

Yes…but I really do have to study.

I could help.

You don't help.

Just to say goodnight?

I'm about to get in the shower.

Which was true.

Even better.

Damn him.

Amy could come back any minute.

It'll only take a minute.

That doesn't sound fun for me.

That was when the phone rang, and I answered it to the sound of Carter laughing. "You really won't let me come say goodnight?"

"You're incorrigible."

"No, you're beautiful, and I haven't seen you all day."

I was also an easy mark. I sighed. And smiled, but he couldn't see that part. "Fine. But I'll meet you *outside*. Under the tree in half an hour."

When I came out of the bathroom after my shower, he was lying on my bed, grinning exactly like the Cheshire Cat. I'd have screamed, but I was only moderately surprised to see him.

"You really are incorrigible," I said as I pulled the towel off my head. My hair fell down with a heavy thunk, dampening the back and shoulders of my robe.

His grin didn't diminish a bit. "And you," he said, "are late." He tapped my alarm clock, which of course read more than half an hour after I told him to meet me. Crap. "Plus it's freezing out, and your hair is wet."

The great, and not so great, depending on the day, thing about dating Carter was he could easily sneak in with no help from me. Our quirky old building featured a beautiful window conveniently placed in the first floor landing of the back stairwell. It was locked, of course, as was *my door,* but that was a minor impediment to most Thought Movers, and none at all to Carter. Once he'd seen the locks, he could get in without opening any doors that would either set off the fire alarm or require him to pass Ms. Kim's apartment.

Now that he was here, it wasn't like I was disappointed to see him. I laid down next to him and snuggled into his open arms. "Thank you for thinking about me."

"I'm *always* thinking about you."

MORE THAN A minute later, as he played with my hair that was drying in tangles, Carter said, "So, when are you going to ask me?"

"To go home? I didn't exactly invite you in the first place."

"You were late on purpose," he said and tickled my nose with one of my tangles.

"You're delusional."

"You could have kicked me out," he countered.

With a pronounced sigh, I elbowed him in the ribs and got up to fix the mess on my head he was only making worse. "When am I going to ask you...?"

"To the Winter Ball."

My hands stilled in their brushing. The Winter Ball. The Winter *Debacle,* as I thought of it. I didn't exactly have fond memories of it. This year, it had the added bonus of being held *on* my birthday. I didn't want to go.

"Who said I was going to?" I joked, except I wasn't joking.

He tipped his head to the side, as if he knew I wasn't playing around. "You had another date in mind?"

"Yes." I told him the truth. "None."

He stood then, turning his perfect bare back and, well, *everything* to me while looking for various pieces of clothing, and I lost all cognitive abilities. "...stag? I'll miss wearing the tux, but okay."

I shook my head. "Wait, what? No." He was mostly dressed and I was thinking again. "You think I'd go *without* you? I meant I don't want to go at *all.*"

He looked up from tying his shoes. "Seriously?"

"Seriously."

"It's your senior year. And your birthday. You should go. *We* should go."

"So all I can do the whole time is think about last year? No thanks. Ugh!" I concluded, pulling too hard on my brush.

Carter came and sat on the ottoman across from the divan, where I was fighting with my hair. And, really, my feelings. "Hey." He gently removed the brush from my hands and held them. "It's not last year. That's all in the past."

True. "But what about the future?" I wasn't sure what came over me, but every one of my worries, from the real to the insignificant, poured out of me. "Everything just feels so messed up. Amy and Caleb fighting, and I'm afraid she's not going to get elected to the court this year but *I* will, and I still can't see what's going to *happen* with you and me, and I'll still be wearing this ugly thing." I held up my cast, another thing making my life more difficult than it should have been. "And I don't even have a *dress*—"

Carter leaned forward and kissed me, stopping any other complaints I might have come up with. Kisses had their own language, and this one said *shhhh. Relax* it told me, and *I'm here.* It spoke to my heart, rather than other places, and my heart thumped in response. When he pulled back, I took a deep breath and let it out slowly while I tipped my head against his chest. He scooped me onto his lap and held me even closer. It would have made more sense to sit on the couch, where I'd been, but still. It was nice.

"*Nothing's* going to happen to you, remember?" he whispered, hugging me so tightly I almost felt safe.

"You don't know that," I whispered back.

"I *do* know," he said. "Because you do too. What you saw once, fate realized wasn't for us." We sat together like that until my tension of moments ago started to ebb.

"As for the rest of it," Carter went on, "you can't fix Amy and Caleb's problems. *They* have to do that." When I started to interrupt, he stopped me, lightly kissing my forehead. "Just listen, okay? Turn off the worry machine for a few minutes. Next, who cares who gets elected to the court? You've both already been nominated and you can't do anything more now. Besides, you'll probably be *Queen,* not just on the court."

God I hoped not. Alexis already hated me enough. "That's not helping."

"But it's true. I mean, my girlfriend's going to be prom queen. How sweet is that?"

"Not if I don't go."

"You can wear a dress you already have and we'll get some sparkles or something for your cast." He knocked on it for emphasis. "No one cares about that."

"I'm not the kind of girl who bedazzles her cast. The purple is bad enough." I kind of hated whoever let that happen. I assumed it had been the doctor or a nurse who chose it, thinking I'd like it, but I a little bit suspected it was Carter, who thought it would be funny. Short of coloring it entirely black, I got my aunt to do some art on it with a black Sharpie after I'd gotten to Mexico.

Carter snickered. "Fine. I'll get you a corsage that covers it."

"I'm not the kind of girl who wears wrist corsages either."

"No. You're the kind of girl who has to make everything difficult."

He tickled me then, and I shoved him, and about when we fell off the ottoman is when Amy opened the door.

"OH, God." She shut it quickly behind her. "Seriously? And why can't Penrose be the one wearing a robe that's showing, like, everything."

We got up, Carter laughing, and me hiding my blushing face behind his shoulder. "Hey," I squeaked. I cleared my throat. "Hey. You're back kind of early."

"I'm not, really." She dropped her bag by her desk and went about getting ready for bed like Carter wasn't even there. "You just obviously haven't looked at a clock in a while." She ducked into the bathroom while I did what I obviously hadn't done in a while. She was right. It was later than I realized. "And also," she continued, voice floating out the open door, "you could have texted. Or put out the ribbon you insisted we needed."

Carter interjected, "I take it the coast is clear now?"

"Ah, good," Amy said, the words garbled by her toothbrush. She poked her head back into the room. "So you're actually on your way out. At least that explains why your shoes are still on. I was a little worried. Night, Penrose." She shut the door behind her.

"Night, Penrose," I echoed and he kissed me.

"I love you, Young." Just before he slipped out, he turned his head back and said, "And pick a nice dress, okay?"

"I'm not going," I replied, but he'd already shut the door.

Chapter Sixteen

The morning of my eighteenth birthday started with a surprise. At the beginning of second hour, I was summoned to the Administration building. I hoped it was something about reviewing my increased permissions, now that I was technically a legal adult. Some other seniors could leave campus on weekends and I thought that would be nice.

But it was actually something much bigger for which I found myself in Headmaster Stewart's office for the first time since the beginning of the school year. Dr. Stewart and I saw each other, of course, at Honor Board meetings and other things around campus, but you didn't usually come to her office unless you were in trouble. Practically all of the staff wished me a happy birthday as I climbed the stairs, and Dr. Stewart met me at the door to her suite.

"Happy birthday, Ms. Young," she said as she ushered me inside. It was a lot warmer than the way she might have said it the year before. She gestured for me to help myself to coffee from the service waiting on her sideboard.

From her collection, I picked a cup patterned with wide cobalt stripes and pewter flowers. Every time I visited the office I used a different one. If I could be said to have a favorite thing about Dr. Stewart, it would be the stacks of antique teacups that were just one of the ways she embraced Northbrook's old-world charm. She asked me about college as I stirred in my cream.

"Well, I haven't gotten my acceptances yet. It's still a little early for those."

The headmaster regarded me with an expression that seemed to say only with great effort was she containing a sigh. "Elaine, really. I admire your humility, but you must know your acceptance at nearly any school worth attending is guaranteed. Your performance here has been exemplary, as are your references. Senator Astor's name alone is enough to ensure your admittance, and I'm well aware of the personal interest he has in your success."

As always, I had to remind myself to stand up straight when I was around Dr. Stewart. Even her praise could be as intimidating as her scrutiny. "Thank you," I said, trying not to stammer. "I guess if everything goes okay, I'm probably going to choose between Baltimore and Boston, but maybe New York. They were always my favorites."

She nodded, unsurprised. "I'm sure Senator Astor will be pleased to hear it, and that you'll make the best choice." After a brief pause she continued in a softer voice. "You could do great things, Lainey. I think you will."

I barely knew what to say to that, so once more I told her, "Thank you." I hoped I didn't disappoint her, disappoint *everyone*. The truth was, I didn't *want* to be great. Maybe I lacked ambition or drive or my life was too easy or whatever. But what I wanted was to have a small life, be a good person, and be happy. Deal in antiques and then, someday, get married, maybe have kids or at least be a really good aunt to Amy's.

Dr. Stewart interrupted my thoughts by saying, "Well, now, let's not keep your guest waiting."

"Guest?"

She almost, just barely smiled as she opened the door to her inner office and stepped away. Behind it was my Uncle Martin. *He* was wearing an enormous smile along with his typical suit and tie, and when he opened his arms for me, I flew into them.

"What are you doing here?!" I said into his shoulder. I couldn't believe he hadn't told me he was coming. Much like my aunt, "Uncle" Martin wasn't technically my uncle at all. But he was family. Before the accident, he'd been my father's financial manager and, more importantly, his friend.

"I thought it would be fun to surprise you," he replied. "Happy birthday, Lainey. It's so nice to see you." He stepped back to look at me and gently inspected my cast. "I see Tessa's gotten a hold of this."

"For sure the *only* thing I'll miss about it when it's gone is the art."

My uncle chuckled. "I like the purple on you, though I don't suppose you do. I hope you've chosen a lovely dress to coordinate with it for this evening."

"I guess Dr. Stewart told you about the Winter Ball," I said. She'd left the office for our privacy, but I dropped my voice for the next part anyway. "But, well...I didn't actually want to go this year anyway, so now that you're here, we don't have to! Carter and I will take you to dinner!"

Uncle Martin led me over to the chairs in front of the headmaster's desk while I rambled. This was perfect. Now I *didn't* have to go to the Ball. Carter would be disappointed, and probably Amy too, but I knew they'd understand. Plus, Carter would love spending time with my uncle.

But that wasn't what was going to happen. "My dear," Uncle Martin said. "I have no intention of keeping you from your Winter Ball. It's your senior year—you should enjoy all the events that come with it." When I started to protest, he held up a hand. "And though I am here to wish you a wonderful birthday, there's more than that—there's business, too. You're eighteen today, Lainey. An adult. My time as executor of your trust has officially come to an end."

Wow. That hadn't even occurred to me. "I…" didn't really know what to say.

In truth, I didn't think a lot about money. For one, thanks to my parents, I was lucky enough not to have to. My allowance had always been generous, maybe even extravagant, and more than enough for pretty much anything I wanted or needed. I'd never spent much time thinking about this day, when *all* the money in reserve for me would become unrestrictedly mine. I couldn't say I'd looked forward to it; I'd surely have given it all up to have my parents here to celebrate with me.

But they weren't, and my life was what it was. Uncle Martin reached for my hand.

"Would that it were different," he said, echoing my thoughts, "and your father himself were here instead of me in his place, but congratulations, Lainey, you're an heiress."

I still didn't know what to say, so I leaned over and hugged him again. When I finally found a response, it was simply, "I'm just glad you came."

"Just doing my job," he joked and I squeezed him tighter.

From there, it was oddly formal, and easy to think of as distant and apart from myself. This thing I was doing, signing papers and initialing clauses and accepting a card printed with access codes. It was business. It was me retaining one Martin Schearer as my personal financial manager at nothing less than his usual rates.

Dr. Stewart joined us to serve as witness, along with the effusive woman from the front desk who usually served me tea but was also the school's notary. It amazed me that someone who worked with teenagers and Dr. Stewart all day could always be so jubilant, and I liked her even more for it. She seemed charmed by my uncle as she stamped and sealed our documents, which was hardly surprising. He was polite and polished, the very definition of dapper, an educated, wealthy, and, also, gay man closer to sixty than fifty. He charmed *everyone,* especially women over forty. I adored him.

When the business was concluded, I was excused from the rest of the already abbreviated day of classes. I took my financial manager to lunch. It was early enough, so we went to Dad's. Breakfast was their specialty, but during the week they served sandwiches with soup, chips, and a pickle too. I knew Uncle Martin would love it there, and that Mercy would love him as much as everyone else.

"E-laine!" she cried when we came through the door, using my full name and an extra-heavy accent for effect. The dining room was about half-full and split between people having late breakfast or early lunch. "I know you ain't skipping classes because it's the very day of the dance, but what're you doing here?"

I laughed. "I take it Carter came in this morning?" He also had a rare day off today—and tomorrow too.

"He did." She bustled over to hug me. "But it's good to see you too. And who've you brought this time?" she added, eying my uncle, and his suit, with interest. Possibly no patron ever had worn a suit like my uncle's to Dad's Diner.

"Martin Schearer," my uncle interjected, taking Mercy's hand into his own for a warm shake. "Lainey's uncle of sorts, and also, though I know she'll protest, the man here to take her to lunch for her birthday. It's a pleasure to meet you; I've heard so much."

Mercy eyed him even more. "Well aren't *you* a delight. First the senator, now you. Our Elaine certainly brings the best dates to the diner." She turned her scrutiny on me. "And I *wondered* if you'd mention the birthday. Thank you, but don't worry, Mr. Martin Schearer. Lunch will be on the house, birthday girl."

From the back, Dad called, "Order UP! And happy birthday, Lainey!"

All things considered, this hadn't been the worst of my birthdays so far. I couldn't stop smiling as we chose an empty table in the back, actually the same table I'd shared with Senator Astor what felt like both forever and no time at all ago. I told my uncle as much as we sat down.

"Speaking of," he said. "I have an envelope for you he asked me to pass along. I momentarily forgot about it during all our business this morning." When I looked at him with surprise, he said, "Have I told you how Dan's persuaded me to join the board of the Astor Arts program?"

"Uh, no, you didn't mention it. Sounds perfect for you, though." It felt slightly strange, or ironic maybe, that the man I'd always considered my uncle was now on a first name basis, and joining the boards of charities, with the man who was *actually* my uncle. Aunt Tessa had introduced them, of course.

But I really couldn't think of someone better to help direct the Astor Arts charity than Uncle Martin. They funded youth arts programs across the country and provided grants for working artists early in their careers. Aunt Tessa had told Dan and me during our dinner in Baltimore how she'd actually been preparing to apply for a grant before my parents' accident. After a moment of mulling it over, I told my uncle, "You know what? I'd like to make a donation. That can be your first official act as my financial manager."

"Consider it done," he said. After a pause he added, "He looks quite like your father you know, the senator."

"I know." Boy, did I know.

"I'd seen him before, glimpses in the political news, but even with Tessa's warning, seeing him in person was…a bit like meeting a ghost. One I miss very much."

"Oh, Uncle…" I covered his hand with mine and squeezed.

He patted our joined hands with his free one before saying, "Just a fond moment for an old man, nothing to worry about."

"You're not old!"

"Not at heart, no, my dear. And never when I'm with you." God, I loved Uncle Martin and the way he always made me—*everyone*—feel special. After another pause and a last squeeze of hands, he said, "It *is* a surprising likeness though."

"Did you, uh, mention it to him? What did he say?" I was sure my aunt had by now, but I didn't want to put ideas into Dan's head. If I ever told him who I was, I wanted it to come from me.

My uncle shook his head. "No. It didn't seem necessary. They're different men, after all. But I enjoy having a new friend who reminds me of my old one. How interesting it would have been for them to meet, don't you think?"

We had a great lunch after that, the perfect kind of birthday afternoon I wished would never end. Uncle Martin's surprise visit was only for the day, so we lingered until closing over discussions of antiques and my aunt, investments and charities, new friends and old, and, also, my future. Unsurprisingly, my uncle heavily favored my return to Baltimore.

"Your time at the Academy has been so good for you, with the stability and the rigorous academics," Uncle Martin explained, and sometimes I smiled at him just because who else said things like *stability and rigorous academics* seriously? But he did. He was a good salesman too. He went on, "I can't help but believe a similar environment that's also close to your family wouldn't be equally healthy or better."

Though his argument for "coming home," as he called it, was practical, I knew it was mostly that he wanted the chance to live close to me and my aunt for the first time in my remembered life. His enthusiasm, along with Aunt Tessa's more subdued encouragement, was hard to ignore.

"I'm strongly considering it," I promised him as we pulled back through the gates at school. Campus was busy with Winter Ball prep, students scurrying and cars coming and going. We pulled up to my building, only to find a limo already there and my roommate pacing around outside it.

"Lainey!" She was calling before I'd even finished opening my door. "Oh, finally! C'mon! We're so late!"

Uncle Martin stepped out of the car and I officially introduced them. Amy did her best rapid-fire conversation as she ran around to my side of the car. "Hi, Mr. Schearer, it's so nice to meet you! Are you staying? I hope so, because I'd love to talk to you some more and maybe you could tell me embarrassing stories about my friend, but Lainey and I *have* to go!" She tugged on my arm, like an excited little kid.

Uncle Martin was clearly amused. He'd never seen me with my friends before and he indulged my roommate's whimsy with all the excitement of a favorite uncle. "A delight to meet you too, dear. And if you *have* to go, I mustn't keep you!" His eyes sparkled and I knew Amy loved him instantly. I managed only a quick hug and goodbye before Amy dragged me into the limo.

We waved to him as we started away and Amy gushed, "Wow, he's *adorable.*"

"He is. I miss him already. And I don't think I'm *that* late?" I was maybe a little behind schedule, but not enough to warrant the fretting and rushing my roommate was doing.

"You *are,*" she insisted. "Because I have a surprise! Happy birthday!" She was grinning and practically vibrating and that's when I realized:

"Have you had some champagne?"

"Maybe just a little." She shrugged and before I could say anything, she went on, *"Anyway,* I know you said you didn't want any presents blah-blah-blah, but you *need* this. It's perfect for you and I don't know why I never thought of it sooner. No protests. Drink this"—she handed me a bottle of water from a little cooler—"and thank me profusely later."

What she got me, it turned out, was a massage.

I'D HAD MASSAGES before, mostly to help with my "migraines" before coming to Northbrook solved that problem for me. It was the only treatment I ever liked, but none of them compared to the one Amy got me. The salon, really a *spa,* where we had our hair and nail appointments, was the fanciest one in the area. You had to make Winter Ball appointments a whole year in advance, and now I understood why.

After a magical ninety minutes of hot stone massage followed by a private, million-nozzle steam shower, I felt amazing. Relaxed, limber, and practically weightless. Amy was right—a massage was *exactly* what I needed. Actually, she'd probably argue that I needed them *more often,* but today's at least was the perfect present. I didn't care that I only had time to get my nails *or* my hair done. I chose nails, because my roommate was pretty handy with a hairbrush. I felt so good, I was even looking forward to the dance.

When I finally got back to our room, Amy looked amazing and had polished off nearly an entire bottle of champagne, all with no help from me. Because of the combination of those things, she wasn't nearly as concerned about the state of my readiness as she should have been.

"You've got a *lot* to do, miss, and not much time to do it," she admonished me and thrust my own glass of champagne into my hand. "Starting with *this."*

"This didn't go so well for me last year," I told her, but I took a sip anyway. It was just as bubbly and sweet as I remembered it.

"No," she countered. *"This* is exactly what you need to keep yourself from reverting to your natural state of stressing. Drink up, and let's get you done."

We talked while she fussed over me, doing my makeup and helping braid my hair in a sort of crown I used to practice on myself during my frequent hours of alone time before Northbrook. It was nice just to be with my roommate without drama. I sipped the champagne—slowly—and let her cheer fill me up better than the drink ever could.

"Why is it such a big deal here, the Ball?" I asked, eyes closed while she worked her magic on my hair. Almost everyone who could go—sophomores, juniors, and seniors—went. Freshmen were allowed as dates, but no students from the lower school. I'd have thought more people would skip it, would be too cool or not want to go alone or whatever. But they didn't.

"Well, it's tradition. Everybody goes. That's what you hear from your first day here, so by the time it's your turn, you *want* to go. It's a chance, well, three chances, to get dressed up and have fun and show off and be out way past curfew with all your friends."

"Everybody has prom though, and they don't all go."

"Yeah, but a lot of them do. My friends from home all go and they have a million other things they could do. But us? We have campus and the bookstore. Curfew, like I said. The Ball *is* the thing we get to do. So"—she pulled my head back with the brush and I opened my eyes to see her wicked grin—"we fucking *do* it."

Amy had pitched a fit when I confessed I *didn't* want to go, and between her and Carter, I'd caved easily. How could I disappoint both of them like that? And how could it possibly be worse than last year? That was probably a dangerous question, but I was pretty sure last year couldn't be topped. Now I was feeling so relaxed about, just, *everything,*

I was determined to make this year's dance great. Or at least not a debacle.

Amy had also pitched a fit when my dress came in the mail at the last minute, mostly because I hadn't let her choose for me, but I knew it was perfect when I saw it online. And I was right. I kept looking at where it hung on the back of the bathroom door. The silk was deep emerald and the skirt flowed all the way to my feet, but the top had a low V in the front and tiny straps that slipped up my arms and over my shoulders to keep it in place, leaving my back completely bare to the waist. It was a dress I could imagine my mother would have worn, sexy but relaxed and with some mystery, and I couldn't wait to put it on.

When Amy finished her work, she playfully turned my head from side to side while we watched in the mirror. "You know I like your hair down best, but this hairdo is going to look awesome when they crown you."

"Ugh. Would you stop with that? It's not going to happen."

"You wait. It is." Before I could protest, she wrapped her arms around my shoulders from behind in a fierce hug. "I love you, Young, you know that, right? I can't even imagine what it would be like without you anymore. Happy birthday."

"Love you too, babe." We stayed like that for a few moments. Then I bit her on the forearm and she jumped away with a squeal.

"Bitch!" she yelled, giggling. "I'm going to return your birthday present."

"Too late!" I gave a languid stretch of my arms over my head. "And it was awesome. Thank you. Again. Even though I asked you not to get me anything."

"You didn't ask me to get your *other* present either…"

"What?!"

She reclined on her bed, carefully spreading the fluttery tiers of her skirt, and patted an overnight bag I hadn't noticed next to it on the floor. "I'll be gone tonight, so you, you know, have the place to your-self."

I laughed. "You know what? It *does* feel like last year all over again."

"Not really. This time *I'm* wearing black and I know you'll actually take advantage of an empty room." She *was* wearing black, a color she rarely chose, so it made her look extra dramatic. Her halter dress en-hanced her already sizable assets, and had an asymmetrical skirt of chiffon ruffles that made it fun instead of severe. I'd missed dress shopping with her this year, but she never needed my help anyway. "Plus," she added, "I mean I'll be gone *all* night."

"What? How?"

Very fast, as if all one word and with at least two exclamation points, she said, *"Wegotaroomatthehotel!!"*

"What? How?" I repeated, just like an owl.

"Caleb's leaving in the morning for a college trip and he got per-mission."

There was still something missing. Knowing Amy as I did, she should have been talking about this for weeks. Instead, she was spring-ing it on me now, moments before we were leaving. I knew some other students got rooms; their parents gave permission and they took cars or cabs home in the morning. But Amy's parents weren't the kind who'd do that.

Bingo.

"What about *your* permission?"

Amy tapped her perfectly painted nails—they were black with sparkly silver stripes and I wanted to copy them immediately—on the wall and cleared her throat. I wondered if she thought by telling me at the last minute, I might not ask. "Who's going to notice?"

"Ame…" I started and she sighed dramatically, but I continued. "I know, I know, but it's not a good idea. Just stay there for a while and come back before morning. Is it really worth the risk?"

"For an *entire* night and the chance to wake up together for, like, the first time ever? Yeah. Besides, there's no risk."

"That's not—"

"Lane," she said and her tone told me there was no convincing her otherwise. "I'll see you in the morning sometime. Drink your champagne and relax, okay? Now it *does* feel like last year again," she added and giggled, our moment of disagreement was forgotten. I knew anything I said would be wasting my breath, so I finished my champagne like she suggested. I wouldn't, however, let her pour me another glass.

THE BALLROOM WAS just as beautiful as last year, though entirely different, in a color scheme of royal blue and cream with tiny hints of maroon in some lights and decorations. Naturally then, Alexis was in a dress of vibrant red that shined as if she'd been spotlit. The satin hugged her like skin, with a sweetheart neckline and a long skirt that looked impossible to move in but so sophisticated. In comparison, my simple green dress suddenly felt plain.

"Wow, over-the-top much?" Amy said when she saw where I was looking and I squeezed her hand in solidarity.

From behind me, Carter whispered in my ear, "Not even half as beautiful as you."

"Besides, I bet she can't even dance in that thing!" Amy added.

"You guys are the best." Sometimes a girl didn't mind a few little white lies.

Alexis was a sure standout, but Brooke's short dress was probably the best one in the whole room. It looked almost vintage, with a fitted strapless top that made her waist look impossibly small and a flouncy skirt that didn't quite hit her knees. Under the top layers of the skirt was a bohemian sort of pattern that was so unique and all Brooke. The gold sparkles matched the amber in her eyes.

When Dr. Stewart made her way to the podium to announce Winter Queen my stomach began to flutter. I realized I was repeatedly smoothing my dress across my legs and stopped. Amy caught my eye and gave me a thumbs up.

"Dork," I muttered, but her goofy grin made me laugh. A year ago, I wouldn't have thought it possible that I could even be a candidate. But tonight, I might *win*. A lot of me *didn't* want that, but I'd be a liar if I said it was all of me. Carter squeezed my hand as we waited.

Next to us, Caleb said, "Where's the crown?"

Exactly what I was thinking, but pretending not to. Something was up. Last year, someone had carried the little tiara onto the stage behind the headmaster. In her best headmaster voice, Dr. Stewart welcomed us and thanked us and commented on the long tradition of the Winter Ball and after not very long it all sounded to me exactly like radio static. I just wanted her to get it over with and announce my name or not.

Finally, *finally* she said, "And it seems that this year, for the first time in the Ball's long history, we have no Winter Queen." Gasps and murmurs filled the air and my stomach plummeted. Alexis's jaw dropped perilously close to her knees. After a pause long enough to make us all uncomfortable, she said, "We have *two.*"

Two sophomores carried two matching tiaras up to the front, while Dr. Stewart called, "A return queen, Miss Alexis Morrow, and new queen Miss Elaine Young," and my whole face became one huge grin. I'd never have guessed the headmaster had any sort of flair for the dramatic, but boy did she.

"Shit," Amy muttered, but I wasn't even trying to hide my delight. A tie! I'd sort of won! But I hadn't completely taken the crown from Alexis and she cared *way* more than I did.

"Please congratulate them both," Dr. Stewart continued, "and also, wish Miss Young a happy birthday!" It dawned on me that she'd probably known about this all day. My visit to her office seemed so long ago.

"Guess I really should have voted for myself," I mused as I started toward the front. I could hear Amy groaning behind me. But then she had to get up and follow, because despite her worries and mine, she was elected to the court too. When they called Brooke's name, I was even more thrilled.

The only person *not* thrilled was Alexis. I could see it in the stretch of her smile and the shine of her eyes. She was proud and beautiful, waiting for her crown, but also disappointed. I took my place next to her on the little stage and whispered, "I voted for you. Just so you know."

She was surprised. More surprised than the tie. I didn't think it crossed her mind that her competition might support her. After a longer pause than even Dr. Stewart's she said, "Thanks. I guess I wouldn't be up here if it wasn't for you."

"Not really," I said. "It's not like I cast *all* the votes. And I voted for the girl who I thought made the best queen."

After she'd leaned down to receive her crown and I'd done the same, during the whoops and applause of our classmates, Alexis surprised *me*. "Just by saying that you proved yourself wrong. But thank you anyway. This"—she cleared her throat—"means a lot to me."

"I know," I said, and to both our continued shock, I hugged her. A stiff second later she hugged me back. But not for too long.

"Your cast is giving me a bruise," she said and pulled away. I smiled, because that was Alexis.

After that, we danced. And laughed, and shouted along to the music, and partied, and by the end, hugged and cried. It was the Winter Ball of our senior year and it was *amazing*. Everything I'd hoped it would be. It felt like nothing bad could possibly happen, tonight or ever again, and I realized I'd been wrong earlier: last year actually *could* be topped, except in a *good* way. A whole night dancing in the warm safety of Carter's arms, surrounded by friends and even a few enemies who were having just as much fun as me—it was so perfect it didn't seem real. But it *was*.

Before it ended, Amy and Caleb were ready to sneak upstairs, and I gave them each a last hug goodbye. "Be careful, and don't be *too* late," I told Amy.

"You be careful," she said, laughing. "'Night, Lane. Night, Penrose. I love you guys." She gave her dress one more twirl before she slipped out the door.

Carter was standing behind me, arms around my waist, while I leaned into him and swayed to the music. "They were happy tonight," he said and I nodded my head against his chest.

"It was a great night."

"No. It was *perfect.*"

I smiled and tilted my head way back so he could see me looking up at him. "It kind of was, wasn't it?"

He leaned down to kiss me, lightly, once on the lips. Silly and awkward, it was the best kiss of the evening. So far.

"You know what's even better?" I asked.

"What?"

"The night's not over yet."

Chapter Seventeen

In the morning, I slept late—way late—and lounged in bed for a long time. There was no reason not to; Carter was long gone and I had nothing I had to do. I felt like the longer I stayed there, the longer it was still part of the night before. Amy wasn't back yet, which would have worried me if I was letting myself worry about a single thing.

My lips tightened into a surely pouty line across my face. I envied Amy, I realized. I *could* have gotten off-campus privileges for the night if only I'd thought to ask. But I could still get them *today*. I decided to call Carter, knowing he'd be up even though he wasn't working, and have him take me to Dad's.

As I reached for the phone, my Winter Queen crown caught my eye and brought back my smile. I plucked it off my bedside table and balanced it on my messy hair. Hidden underneath it, half poking out from under my alarm clock—which Amy said was archaic and I should just use my phone like everyone else—was something that didn't belong there. An envelope.

The edge of a bright green sticky note was just visible. On it was my name in Ms. Kim's handwriting. *A birthday card,* I thought. *Yay!* She must have given it to Amy when I was still at the spa, and Amy promptly forgot about it.

But under the sticky note was a message scrawled by Uncle Martin about how I'd been rushed away before he could give this to me. It was a birthday *something,* just not from Ms. Kim. This was the envelope from Daniel Astor. Inside was a handful of pages, topped with a note.

Dear Lainey,

A very happy birthday along with my gift to you. I saw no reason for you to wait for these. I look forward to learning what you choose.

Best,

D.A.

Folded underneath were personal acceptance letters from all of my top colleges.

THE LETTERS SLID from my hands and I watched my future scatter across the floor while my heart began to race. When I bent to retrieve the papers, my silly tiara toppled off my head and one of the rhinestones popped loose. I kicked it, sending it to sparkle alone under my bed.

Hands shaking, I picked up the letters, one by one, and read them again. And again. They said nothing remarkable, *Congratulations on your acceptance to…We look forward to seeing you in the fall…,* but they were here, *all* of them, and it was only February. It's not that I wasn't expecting to be accepted, but…what? Why was this bothering me so much?

It wasn't because of excitement that my hands shook. It was something else.

For a while now, Uncle Dan had been mentally penciled onto my short list of pleasant thoughts. It was hard not to be caught up in his mystique, flattered by the attention he showed me. How many girls could count a U.S. senator among the people taking an active interest in her life? And that wasn't even considering all the *other* things he was. I'd been clinging to the idea that he was a *positive* in my life when it had felt like literally every other thing was fucked up.

But lately, everything else *hadn't* been so bad at all. The vision wasn't looming, my friends were mostly happy, and the future seemed like a real possibility again. Maybe that gave me the perspective I'd previously lacked, or purposefully ignored.

If I'd told Amy, or any one of my friends, about the senator's notes, they'd have told me it was strange. Maybe even creepy. The only one who'd understand was Alexis, and she wasn't my friend.

I'd never taken the time to think about how odd it was that the notes had found me at personal moments. I'd accepted it as part of the senator's charm that he preferred hand-written gestures, and thought the strange delivery of them was just further proof of that charm. A minute ago, when I'd unfolded the thick pages of stationery from my four favorite schools, signed personally by the presidents of each and delivered by my own uncle, I'd been awed.

But more than that, I'd been freaked.

It was like my brain flipped a switch. Just like that, I went from fantasy to reality. Just like in the woods with Carter the day I'd visited the cemetery. One second I'd thought one thing, the next I knew the truth.

I'd convinced myself Dan wasn't pressuring me to join them, to take up the Marwood family's mantel. He was giving me solid arguments to help make a difficult decision; he was making my life *easier*. He was my uncle, this blood relative that only I knew about. Someday I'd have the courage to tell him that, and then he'd love me and I'd have a family, a *real* family even more than the one I had now.

These were, I realized, my fantasies.

The notes, the acceptances, everything—it wasn't evidence of Senator Astor's charm and thoughtfulness; it was his power and its reach. It went all the way into the deepest parts of my personal life. I'd spent most of the year feeling unsure who to trust, not even myself or Carter, and thinking that maybe Dan could be the one I did.

And now, I wasn't unsure at all. I was certain I'd been wrong.

Restless, and no longer hungry, I abandoned the plan to call Carter. Instead, I threw on my cold weather gear and snuck off campus. What I *really* wanted to do was go to the shooting range, except for a few more days my right hand was still in a cast. But what I wanted most was the feeling of concentration and exhilaration that came with the shooting. A long run on a clear winter day would be a close approximation.

The cool quiet of the forest welcomed me. At first, I counted my steps, like sheep, like it would lull me into a place where all I could hear were the thumps of my stride and the numbers that ticked off my progress. It worked. With every step, I concentrated a little harder on what I was doing and a little less on the rest of my life. By my second mile, I was in a groove, running fast and watching my footfalls on the packed snow.

No room for the million concerns I'd let creep back into my head. No tingling feeling from any of my supernatural senses. No dawning realization that when my hands shook after I opened Dan Astor's letter it was because I was scared, not pleased. And most of all, no unwelcome and uncomfortable feeling in my stomach that said I was still missing something. I just ran.

Eventually what happened was I thought about running. How I didn't love running, not in the way Carter did. I was halfway decent at it, but because I didn't love it, I didn't push myself to excel. For Carter, running was more like an *extension* of himself. If he couldn't run, it would be like killing a part of him, part of his very *essence*.

And that was it.

The word *essence.*

It was such a pretty word, sibilant and soft, but vital too. Powerful. It was what made things what they were. Made us who *we* were. It was the *heart* of who we were.

Essence. Heart. Essence heart essence heart. In my mind, the two words reverberated with each footfall, faster and faster until I was gasping, crashing to a halt and grabbing a tree to hold me up before my lungs or legs gave out.

When I caught my breath and the stars dancing in front of my eyes began to fade, I slid to a seat at the base of the tree and forced myself to be still. I'd come out here to outrun my mind, but my mind had other ideas. It had run in a different direction and I needed to listen to it. To think, *really* think, about all the ideas I'd been chasing in incomplete circles since the beginning of the year.

I had this great, big puzzle I was trying to solve, with all these different components, but instead of lining up the edges and filling in the middle, I'd been throwing the pieces on the table and watching them scatter. Chasing them around without any real effort. Kind of like running. If I pushed myself, I *could* do better. If I forced myself, I *would* figure this out.

I went back to Jill. She was a piece of the puzzle I'd left dangling at the edge of the table, trying not to examine too closely. But by accident, I'd just found where she fit. It was those two words, *heart* and *essence.*

When she'd been revived, she'd lost not just her life but her Sententia gift as well. Only one of them had been temporary. We'd restored the mechanical piece of heart pumping blood and oxygen and animating the body. But she couldn't get back her *essence.* Thought, capital T, had killed that part of her that made her Sententia. A gene or a tiny piece of her brain or whatever our magic was, a connection to

God or the greater life consciousness. Something. I didn't know where it came from, this essential Sententia piece of ourselves. There was something beyond science about what we were, and I had taken it from Jillian. One gift had expelled another.

I hadn't meant to. I hadn't *intended* to, I realized was the better word. That was the third key to this puzzle: intent. Carter had used it so long ago to describe Thought Moving. Intention. Changing the intention of things. When I'd turned my gift on Jill, I hadn't known how to use it, how it would work, what it would do except stop hearts because that's what I'd been told. My intention when I'd made the desperate Thought was to save myself. To let Jill die in my place. It had been good enough to work, and it took everything from her.

But why couldn't I be more specific? I used intention in my Diviner gift all the time and it listened. I focused on future or past, on seeking details and seeing the clues. Why couldn't I focus my Hangman ability in the same way, to use intention to hone its effect?

All the other wisps of ideas, the scattered pieces began to coalesce. Everything had a sort of heart, didn't it? An essence? If I could focus on essences, get to the *heart of something,* what could I do?

I thought about the tree behind me, supporting my back with its wide, old trunk. The tree was so many things all working together. The roots, the branches that in the springtime would fill with leaves, the strong body holding it all together. In a way, each piece had its own heart, its own essence or little piece of life, didn't it? Jill had proved I could do more than stop a literal heart.

Ever since the day I'd been sparked, I'd done two things: touched basically every object in Carter's apartment to see if I could learn more about his father's death and touched every living thing I came into contact with until I could feel its life, like I first had in Carter.

I stood and turned, looking up at the canopy of the great tree, its bare skeleton arms clacking together in the winter breeze. I took off my glove and rested my hand against it. The bark was rough under my skin, but when I opened my senses, I could feel the tingling pulse of life, warmer and more pleasant than the buzz from any object with a death story, but slower and bigger than the sense I'd get from a person. I stood there for a long time, trying to follow the connections, to trace the path from the roots to the branches with my mind. I wished it had leaves so I could try to feel those too.

I wondered how Thought would or could affect it. I'd hoped a sort of map would appear if I concentrated hard enough, but that would have been too easy. My visions were only for the dead. Life, I had to feel. And I *could* feel it, all connected, each little piece making up the whole.

Maybe all I really needed was intention. Mental focus and my own ability to visualize. Or maybe I was just crazy.

But somehow this felt like the right kind of crazy.

THAT'S HOW I began my new hobby of killing things. I added it to my other hobbies of antiquing, keeping secrets, and worrying.

I couldn't bring myself to harm the oak tree. It was old and strong and beautiful. Also, I couldn't easily observe it. I needed to try something smaller and closer to home, preferably with leaves. I'd once told myself I couldn't practice my Hangman gift, but I was wrong. I *wouldn't* practice it. I didn't see a need to or even how. Now I did.

The spark had shown me I could feel the life in everything. Surely I could extinguish it, too. This was research, I told myself. Science. I had to do some things I didn't necessarily want to in order to understand the scope of my gift. Plants would be my sacrifice.

My hypothesis wasn't just that I could kill one, but that I could affect it in pieces. There was more to my theory, but this is where I would start. Could I kill a single off-shoot? A single leaf? I understood now, long after the fact, that when I'd tried to kill the rose on the day of my spark, I was too late. It was already dead. It looked alive, but it wasn't, not really. It was just in the beginning process of fading.

While the simplest and least guilt-inducing thing to do would have been to buy a series of plants and experiment on them in an orderly way, I didn't have that luxury. There was no way I could bring a bunch of plants to anywhere on campus without explaining myself to some-one, and that was the thing I couldn't do. How did you explain to people, even other Sententia, you were systematically practicing killing things? Dr. Stewart had basically forbidden me from ever using my *Carnifex* gift on campus, and who could blame her. So instead, I had to seek out plants of convenience.

At Marquise, on a small table between the entry and Ms. Kim's door, was a poinsettia plant that was not fading at all. Since they were pretty and also essentially non-denominational, campus was covered with them at the holidays. The dorm attendants, the adults anyway, had a yearly contest to see who could keep theirs alive the longest. It was silly, since most of them died during winter break or sooner, but some of the staff took it seriously. Ms. Kim had won last year, and I was pretty sure she'd already won this year too. I hoped so, because I felt like shit for what I was about to do.

When I finally got back, without giving myself any more time to think about it, I closed the door behind me, swallowed my guilt, and touched the plant stem near the dirt. I felt the life-tingle as soon as I opened my senses and without further ado, I extinguished it.

It was quick, the sensation of the Thought rushing up and then dis-sipating. What replaced it was interesting. I expected maybe there'd be nothing, no feeling, no more vibrations of any kind. But instead, there was a new buzzing, the kind that told me the plant had a death story to tell. I supposed, in a way, it was my signature.

Out of a sense of duty, as well as curiosity, I watched it. Given the opportunity, I imagined any other Grim Diviner could see it too. I was glad there were no others on campus. I couldn't use any of my gifts on myself, but the plant, even though it was my victim, gave up its vision easily. I felt strangely detached from the image of myself gripping the stem. It looked like nothing, a girl touching a plant for a few scant seconds, though I knew it was more than that; even if I hadn't just done the deed, my gift told me otherwise. The girl had done it—she was the killer.

I ran up the stairs, trying hard not to cry from the shame, reminding myself it had already had a much longer life than average. The knowledge did not comfort me. I knew it was only a plant, and I probably hadn't ruined Ms. Kim's contest, but I still hated myself for harming it. Intentionally harming it. Maybe the problem was I hated myself for *being able* to harm things.

But I had to know. I had to know what I could do and the extent of my powers, because they were the best defenses I'd ever have and right now I needed to feel like I had any defenses at all. Plus, if my theories proved true, maybe someday I could use my gifts in a way even I could accept.

What awaited me in my room was a mess of another nature.

Chapter Eighteen

Amy got caught.

That's what I gathered when I found her pacing in the middle of our room with eyes red from crying. She stopped and looked at me when I opened the door, meeting my eyes for just a second before looking down and starting to pace again. I didn't say anything right away. On my desk was a large coffee from Anderson's which I was, frankly, more happy to see than my roommate right then.

After I picked it up and took a long sip—she'd gotten pretty good at my preferred level of cream and sugar—I stated the obvious. "You got caught."

She stopped again and looked back at me, nodding. She looked like crap, tired and worried, with bedraggled curls and unevenly removed eyeliner smudged even worse from crying. I knew before getting caught had ruined everything, she'd probably looked post-dance-bliss cute in a rumpled way. She hadn't brushed her hair on purpose.

Her eyes told how upset she was, pleading with me for something, I didn't know what. To help, to make the problem go away, to not be mad at her. Except I was. I was mad at her. I was sweaty and exhausted, physically and mentally, and had bigger problems fighting for space on an already too-full plate of them. I'd just killed a freaking defenseless poinsettia plant, for God's sake.

I sighed, took another sip of my coffee. Looked at her for another few seconds. "I told you," I said. It was a shitty thing to say, but the truth.

Amy swallowed, and the look on her face made clear how bitter that was going down. "No shit, Lane. I should have listened. Obviously."

"*Obviously,*" I snapped back. I could tell Mount St. Amy was brewing, her temper always quick to boil and erupt, but for once, I didn't feel like stopping it. She could get as pissed at me as she wanted, because this was a problem all her own. What I really wanted to do was take a shower at least as long as yesterday's, but I drank my coffee and listened instead. "Tell me what happened. And thank you, for this," I added, shaking my cup. We were both angry, but I shouldn't be rude.

She flopped on my bed, because she'd haphazardly unpacked half her bag on hers, and picked at threads unraveling from the hem of her sweatshirt. Actually, Caleb's sweatshirt. It was gray, with UMASS across the chest in a kind of funny script. The first time I'd seen it, I'd thought it said WASS, and couldn't figure out what that meant. Everyone had laughed at me and now whenever I was being daft, Amy'd say, "You're such a *wass,* Lane." Thinking about that made me a tiny bit less angry.

"It was perfect," she said, softly. "Wasn't it? The dance." From my nightstand, she picked up my crown and tilted it a few times, watching the sparkles.

"Yeah, it was."

"I told *you,*" she said, shaking the crown in my direction.

"I guess we were both right."

"I wish you weren't so freaking noble all the time and had voted for yourself."

"I don't. It worked out perfectly."

She grimaced. "You had to share. With her."

"I didn't mind," I said, shrugging. "And...I didn't hate it. Being queen." Maybe a piece of me had even loved it, and the look Amy gave me told me she knew just how much I didn't hate it.

"It was perfect," Amy repeated. "Why did Stewart have to be wandering around campus this morning, huh? I mean, where does she even *live?* Does she sleep in her office? I swear she just haunts this place twenty-four seven."

Ouch. And of all the people to catch her. The headmaster lived in a house on the bookstore side of Main Street, close enough to walk to campus, but outside the bounds of where students could go without permission. Everyone knew that, including Amy. But it really did seem like she was always somewhere on campus. I also wanted to point out that it was afternoon now, but that wouldn't make things any better.

"It should have been *fine,*" Amy continued. "I had the car drop me off by Anderson's and if anyone saw me I could just say I came to get coffee. The cups would be proof when I came back through the gates."

"You *look* like you haven't been home."

"That's what Dr. Stewart said." She sat up, hugging her knees to her chest.

"And you were carrying your bag."

"I can carry a bag whenever I want!" Her temper was rising again. "It's not like I was still wearing my dress or something. Besides, I thought she was *joking* with me. It sounded like she was trying to be funny."

Uh oh. "What did you say? No, what did *she* say?"

"She said, 'Just getting back, Ms. Moretti?' but I *swear* she sounded like she was joking."

For real uh oh. "Seriously? When is she *ever* joking? What did *you* say?"

"I said, 'Of course not!' and I laughed, because…I thought…" The extent of her error was starting to become apparent.

"You *lied* to her?! Amy! You know better!"

She spun on the bed to look at me. "What the hell was I supposed to say? It was just being funny. Except then she didn't laugh back."

I groaned. "You *can't* lie to her."

"I wasn't lying!"

"Yeah, you were."

"I didn't mean to! I was, like, joking." Amy got up and started pacing again, face a little pink from her frustration. "How does she even *know?* I bet she kills at poker. Who can bluff her?"

She had no idea. I held my tongue from saying that and asked, "So now what?" Amy shook her head. "Just a warning maybe? I mean, it was the Winter Ball." Infractions were practically expected. Plus Amy was good, never in any trouble. She was the freaking Valedictorian, or would be soon enough. When she didn't answer right away, just shrugged and looked down, I knew something more was wrong. "Ame?"

"Maybe I already had my warning," she said to her feet.

I sat up straighter in my desk chair and set down my nearly empty coffee. "Sorry, what?"

She cleared her throat and looked at me, meeting my eyes for about a millisecond before glancing away. "I already had a warning."

"You already had a warning." That was news to me.

"Two warnings," she basically whispered before she dropped back onto my bed and buried her face in my pillow.

Two warnings. Two strikes and I didn't know about either of them. I stared at her in silence until she lifted her head to look at me. "You've gotten two warnings, which you didn't tell me about." Now *I* was pissed. Maybe it was a little irrational, because I kept a *lot* of secrets, but whatever. She had two warnings and had just lied to Dr. Stewart. This was Honor Board territory. "Are you fucking kidding me?"

"You don't have to curse," she said and I cursed again. I swore all the time, just never at her, and she flinched.

"Sorry, but this is cursing serious. Of which you are perfectly aware." She made a face but I persisted. Like so many times, I was the mom between the two of us. Usually it was something we laughed at, but like her run-in with the headmaster, this was no joke. "What were the first two?"

She sighed and sat up, letting her feet dangle over the side. My already messy bed was even more of a mess from her. "I cut final hour too many times and then someone saw me on the way back from Caleb's a week or two ago."

The only thing I could do was curse again.

"I know, okay, I know."

"Do you? Really?" She was upset, yeah, but also…defiant. Maybe that meant she was *really* upset, but at the same time, she'd broken curfew for the Ball *knowing* she had two warnings. And she hadn't just broken curfew; she'd meandered back onto campus after freaking *noon*. I was pushing her, but she needed it. Or I wanted to do it. Either way, it forced the eruption.

"Yeah, Lane, I do!" She launched herself off the bed and kicked one of the lounge pillows in the middle of the rug. "But it's my senior year and everything's fucked up. You almost died, but you're always with your boyfriend or, like, wrapped up in yourself or some other world, and I'm trying not to *lose* my boyfriend, so I'm just *whatever*.

Having fun or trying to keep all my shit together, with basically no help from you. Thanks St. Elaine, for taking a few seconds from shining your halo to give me your *super* helpful commentary."

I gaped at her back as she angrily dumped the rest of her things out of her bag and put them away with unnecessary force. She made sure not to look at me as she moved around her half of the room. In a way, she was right. I wasn't being helpful. I was hurt. Maybe I wasn't a perfect friend, but neither was she. If I was the angel she was implying, I would have done something helpful. I probably *should* have, apologized or I didn't know what.

But I wasn't an angel, no matter what she said, so I didn't do any of those things. "See you at the Honor Board hearing," is what I said, right before I slammed the door to the bathroom behind me.

As usual whenever I didn't know what to do, I ran to Carter. Amy was gone when I came out of the shower. It felt strange and terrible not to have a text or a note on our board telling me where to come find her. Not that I would have.

I went into the bookstore first, instead of going straight upstairs, thinking I might actually talk to Melinda before I found her nephew. She was so good at listening and girl problems, but she was nowhere to be seen. Instead, even though he wasn't supposed to be working, Carter was there. He sat behind the counter on his stool, a newspaper in front of him even on his day off. It must have been obvious something wasn't right, because as soon as he saw me, he flipped the newspaper closed and opened the counter hatch to come through.

"Hey. What's wrong?" In only a few strides, Carter had enveloped me in his strong arms.

I'd come to talk to Melinda, but I'd take this in exchange. I never felt safer or more comfortable than I did with him. Loving Carter was the one thing that scared me in a good way. It had thrilled me long before the vision and after and, no matter what happened, I suspected it always would. So I held him there in the middle of the bookstore, soaking up the sense of safety and belonging that was like breathing in and out. A lounge full of underclassmen watched us, but I didn't care.

"Hey," he repeated, pulling back to search my face with his eyes. "What's up?"

"I had a fight with Amy." It was only one of my problems, but it was the only one I felt ready to tell him.

"Do you want to talk about it?"

"Not really," I admitted. "It was stupid."

"Stupid enough to make you cry?"

"I'm not crying!" I *was* upset about it though. I looked up at him. "She just, she said some things…and maybe they weren't all wrong." He hugged me again but didn't press for more details. I decided to change the subject. "What are you even doing down here? You're supposed to be off."

Carter pulled back and smiled, grabbing my hand to lead me over to the counter. "I wasn't really working. Either job," he added softly, after I made a face and eyed the newspaper he'd been reading. I didn't really believe him until I got close enough to see the paper's front page.

"Real Estate? What's this?" Besides a good distraction.

"Just…looking," he said and I examined the paper more closely.

"This is from the D.C. area."

"Yeah," he admitted. "But there are more." He moved it aside and underneath was one covering Boston/Cambridge and one for Southern Connecticut. "I thought…maybe you'd look at them with me? Tonight, if you want."

"You're buying a house?!"

"Probably just a condo, but yeah."

We'd never talked about this before. In fact, since the dinners and tours his uncle had arranged for us in the fall, we'd barely talked about college or next year at all. For a while, he'd been too worried about the vision and, regardless, I insisted on waiting for my acceptances until I made any serious decisions. Those acceptances were now tucked in my desk drawer. I wondered if Carter had a stack in his drawer as well.

"You never said anything."

He bumped me with his shoulder. "Neither did you. But you have to live somewhere, wherever you choose, don't you? So do I."

I guessed that was true. There was so much about next year I hadn't considered, for so many reasons. Also, I was, simply, scared. Not just about my possible lack of future, but about having one too. I was comfortable at Northbrook, settled for the first time in my whole life, and one way or another, I'd have to give that up. I wondered if I was the only girl in the whole senior class who *didn't* want to graduate.

But there was nothing else I wanted to do tonight, so why not talk about the future? I pulled up a second stool and sat next to him. It wouldn't be long until the store closed and all the students would have to go down to Anderson's Cafe or back to campus and Carter and I could claim the couch in front of the fireplace. Mandi Worthington sat there now, and I could feel her watching us.

When I looked in her direction, she smirked and I had to fight my instinct to stick my tongue out or go slap her. Maybe I did want to graduate after all. I turned back to Carter's newspapers.

"You know, normal people just look at this stuff online. What did you do, special order these, old man?" I knew full well he preferred print because of his *Lumen* gift—it was easier to remember pages than scrolling computer screens—but I still liked to tease him.

He kissed the side of my head and smiled, ignoring my commentary. "I got some for you too." From under the counter, he pulled out a second stack and handed them to me.

I quickly scanned the D.C. one on top. "This is different from yours?"

"Babe, your *budget* is different from mine."

To his credit, it wasn't bitter or embarrassed the way he said it. He took it in stride that I was wealthy, though he was always more conscious of it than I was. For the first time, I realized that was probably annoying about me. That I forgot about the money, in the way only the truly wealthy can. Before Northbrook, my life with my aunt moved so quickly, I never had time to compare myself, and at Northbrook, I was surrounded by students with comparable bank accounts.

I blushed. "Sorry," I said and resolved, going forward, not to be so thoughtless. About *everything*, I added to my resolution, thinking back to what Amy had said earlier. Occasionally legitimate or not, maybe I did spend too much time wrapped up in myself.

Carter pushed the stack closer to me and put an arm around my shoulder. "You don't have to apologize. Just buy yourself a nice place that I can come visit."

We sat in companionable silence for a while, perusing the various papers while we waited for closing time. It was kind of thrilling, looking at the listings and imagining myself there. I'd never considered *buying* somewhere to live. It wasn't a typical concern for someone my age. Of course, neither was antique furniture, and I had a ton of that just waiting to furnish my own place. Whenever I let myself think about after graduation, I always figured I'd bounce around between my family and Amy's before living in a dorm. I could still do that. I even might.

"Why not just rent?" I asked Carter. I knew he'd never choose a dorm or to have roommates, because that's just how he was, but renting seemed simpler.

He glanced over. "I thought about it. But I've been saving for years…it feels like a waste just to spend it on rent and get nothing back. Real estate's a good investment."

That was true. Uncle Martin said so all the time; in fact, he'd encouraged me to consider it once before. And I knew Carter wasn't a pauper or anything. Between the bookstore, his Perceptum income, and a college fund he didn't really need for tuition, he had savings far greater than a lot of people, especially guys his age. Now that I was thinking about it, buying a place seemed like a natural step for him.

The more listings I looked at, the more exciting the idea seemed to me too. A little while ago, I'd been sad about leaving Northbrook, a place I'd finally experienced the feeling of being *settled*. I still had to leave Northbrook, but I realized I could make my *own* place to feel settled. I didn't have to be a wayfarer. I'd already experienced that. I could travel whenever I wanted, but putting down roots took time to grow. There was no reason I couldn't start now. The real question was, where did I want those roots?

"Where?" I blurted, my thoughts slipping from my mind to my tongue. The students all gone and the doors locked, Carter and I were performing the nightly ritual, wiping the tables and pushing in chairs.

Carter looked up. "That chair? Wherever. Either of those tables."

"No, I meant…I was thinking out loud. I meant where should I choose?" I gestured toward the papers we'd left on the couch by the fireplace. "Where do *you* want to go?"

"Wherever you want," he said, wiping the last table and stowing the cleaning supplies in their cabinet. "I like them all." As a non-answer, that stressed me out and I told him so. After a hesitation, he said, "I promise I'll choose wherever I want most."

"But?"

"I like *you* best, Lane."

I sat on the couch, tucking my knees up on the seat, and Carter joined me after stoking the fire. "I don't want you to go somewhere just because I'll be nearby. My aunt thinks you're crazy."

"She's right." He winked at me as he unfolded a paper to a page with a few listings he'd circled. I huffed and he put the paper down, finally serious. "This is different for me. I don't *have* to go to college. I want to, for fun, but I have a career. I have this"—he gestured around the room—"and I *love* it. I've never wanted to do anything else. I *am* crazy, just like your aunt thinks. I'm twenty years old and already as content as the old man you joke about me being. I want to *study,* but there are so many places I can be happy doing that. All of the places I've looked at, and none of them are going to change my life. I *have* a life. What will make me happiest right now is being close to you."

He was looking right at me by the end and I couldn't do anything but stare back. My heart swelled and plummeted and did whoop-di-whoops in my chest. As he spoke, I saw it. I saw my whole future right there in front of me. And it was a *happy* one. After college, we'd move back here and I'd start my own antiques gallery just like I'd always wanted, and it would be perfect. Eventually we'd get married just like Amy predicted and everything *would. Be. Perfect.* If there was a such a thing as fate, I felt like I'd just seen mine, *without* the help of a Sententia gift.

"Do you believe in fate?" I asked.

At my unexpected question, he tilted his head just to the left. He was so beautiful it was almost painful and I couldn't help myself from leaning forward to kiss him, quickly on the lips. His whole face brightened with a smile.

"What was that for?"

"I think it was fate," I said. "If you believe in that kind of thing."

That bright grin shifted toward the mischievous, my only warning before he reached forward and grabbed me tight around the waist.

Papers fluttered to the floor around us as he pulled me onto his lap and held me there. I made a halfhearted squeak of protest but ruined it by giggling when his breath tickled my neck. "I do," he said, and his tone told me he took my question seriously. He always did. "Believe in fate. How could I not? I'm holding a Diviner in my arms. You deal in fate every day."

"That feels more like…chaos."

He kissed the skin behind my ear and made me shiver. I wished I was looking at him but I didn't want to ruin the perfection of the moment by trying to turn around. His closeness was a warm blanket and I snuggled deeper into it. "It is," he agreed. "Chaos is part of the process."

"Then how can it be fate? How can that be the same thing?"

"You've really thought about this, huh?" he teased and I bumped him with my head. Of course I had, and I knew he had too. While he continued, I traced his fingers with mine. "Why can't it be the same thing? Fate's not this one fixed, immutable thing. Fate's the future. It's ever-shifting. Some of it shifts more than others."

"That's not fate at all then."

"Isn't it?"

I didn't know.

"Fate's what happens in the end," he went on. "What good would God, or whatever you call what connects us, be if our decisions and actions meant nothing?" The question hung there in the room with us, the fire crackling and the air sparking with something that might have been the elusive fate I was trying to define. Always more concerned than I was, Carter asked at last, "Is this about the vision? Has something changed?"

"No," I said. "Our fate is currently wide open." On a whim, or in a choice made by my heart without strict permission from my head, I told him, "And I think…I want it to be in Boston next year. I think I want to go to Boston."

As soon as I said it, the vision returned.

Chapter Nineteen

I was shocked, almost literally.

As soon as I'd said Boston, the hum of recognition rose up between us, vibrating subtly at every point where we touched. It was different from the quiet, barely discernible sense that came from his birth, from his mother's death. I had to work to notice that at all. This was a new feeling, insistent but somehow erratic. I'd grown used to the idea that it was gone, a defunct possible future and no longer on our worry list.

Carter squeezed me tight, oblivious to the continued coming and going of his role in my death, while I tried to control my breathing. "Harvard. Nice."

There were still no details—just my face, cold, white, and lifeless, along with the irrefutable knowledge that Carter had made it that way—but I knew I was dead. Really dead. Or I would be, and soon, if I went through with the decision I'd just made.

I wasn't sure what made me say that, about Boston. I thought I *hadn't* decided yet, especially after just seeing my uncle. Was *that* it? Had I been unconsciously leaning toward Boston all along and something about going *there* would bring about my death?

So, I changed my mind.

"No, wait! That wasn't final. Baltimore…the others are still definitely on the table."

The vision faded away.

That was it. Fate was that facile. One decision, made with conviction, could change everything in the matter of a few heartbeats. I was safe again, for now. Just as quickly as it came, the hum disappeared.

My pulse began to slow and breaths come easier. If Carter sensed the moment of anxiety, he didn't comment, likely writing it off to the decision I was struggling to make. I knew I should tell him what just happened but for some reason I couldn't bring myself to say it. A few minutes ago, I wished I could see him, but now I was glad he was behind me and couldn't see *my* face. Why Boston?

"So what you're saying is I can recycle the New York papers?"

"No. I might be into this real estate thing."

"But not NYU?"

I tested fate. "Not NYU."

Still no vision. New York was my clear third choice, so with no vision when I eliminated it, I kept it off the list. Baltimore, not Boston.

"Good," he said, and I could feel him smiling. "I knew we'd be on the same page. I wasn't really sure I wanted to buy a place in New Haven anyway."

Interesting. Did our changing fate have something to do with *his* favored destination? The thought made my breath catch again. "Do…do you *really* want to go to D.C.? Is that what *you* want?"

"No," he said. "Not necessarily." It *sounded* genuine. He shifted me off his lap and back onto the couch, making me work hard to control my expressions. "Yale was just my least favorite of a bunch of great options. I wouldn't have minded it, though I meant it that I might not have bought a place in New Haven. I'd *like* D.C., but I'd like Boston, too. *I'd* even like California," he added and poked me in the ribs.

"I'm not sure either of us could afford a place out there anyway," I joked, but it wasn't very convincing.

"Hey. What's up? Do you really *not* want D.C.? Did you just say that because you thought I did?"

"No. I don't know what I want." Just that I want to live. "This is harder than I thought it would be."

"Planning the future usually is."

Is it? I didn't know that either. "It never was before. We moved where the art took us, and then Northbrook fell in my lap. Now I have to…to make a *commitment*. Amy would tell you I'm afraid of that." I'd half forgotten about my fight with my roommate.

"She'd be wrong," Carter said. "You're afraid of *deciding*. The commitment part you do with your whole heart."

ON THE WAY out of the dorm the next morning, I took a moment to observe the poinsettia. It was a little wilted from yesterday, but a brief touch of one of the leaves told me it didn't just need water. There was no hum of life to it; I'd definitely killed it, even if it would be days before it truly showed the signs of what I'd done.

Amy and I still hadn't spoken, and I didn't think either of us was ready to apologize. We'd both returned right at curfew last night, and I'd left this morning before she got up. On Sunday mornings, I didn't have anywhere I had to be; I just didn't want to be there. I grabbed my real estate papers and went to the dining hall for caffeine. At breakfast, I found Brooke. Thank God for having one friend who was a morning person.

"Hey early riser," I said and slumped down into the seat across from her.

She smiled. "Hey yourself…though you're not quite yourself this morning. Usually you *like* being up this early. Still tired from Friday?"

"Something like that." Actually, I'd just killed one of the plants that sat on the table with the silverware and plates, but I didn't mention that. After a sip of coffee, I finally managed a smile for her.

"It was pretty awesome, the Ball, wasn't it? I had more fun than last year."

"Not me," I said and we laughed.

"Of course not!" She shook her head seriously. "Only one girl kissed your boyfriend, and it was *you*. Where's the fun in that?"

"You know…" I said, and I told her about how Alexis had actually been the first girl besides me to kiss him last year. I wasn't sure why I decided to tell her, if it was because I was feeling a little less at odds with Alex now so I could laugh about it, or if I was actually feeling really bitchy because of Amy and wanted to spill someone's secret.

"Wow," Brooke said, her lips hanging in a perfect *O* shape. "And not only did you vote for her this year—she told me what you said— you seemed thrilled when you both won."

"I was!" I said, and we laughed again.

"If I weren't actually your friend, I think I'd probably hate you for being so frustratingly goodie-goodie."

And that hit a little too close to home, after what Amy had said. I didn't mean it to, but my smile disappeared and I pushed some bites of breakfast around my plate.

"Hey." Brooke reached across the table to knock on my cast with the back of her fork. "I was just kidding. You're a sweetheart and, I mean, you were Winter Queen. Everybody *the opposite of* hates you."

Now I was getting a pity party, and that just made me feel worse. "Sorry," I said. "That's not—I wasn't fishing for compliments or whatever. It's just…" a lot of things. The problem was that *I* was an- gry, with Amy, with myself, and basically with everything. I'd gotten one night—*one freaking night*—where everything seemed great, and now

I was bitter. Maybe I shouldn't have gone to the dance after all. It was only making me unhappy now. "I'm *really* not perfect," is what I said.

Brooke took a bite of rye toast—I swore she was the only girl in the whole school who ate rye toast—and chewed thoughtfully while I stirred my coffee. I realized how much I was going to miss her next year, and if last night's discussion with Carter had made it apparent, this breakfast emphasized how soon "next year" really was. Supposing I made it to next year, anyway. Brooke would still be here, and I'd be...I wanted to say in Boston, I realized, but that was dangerous.

Wherever I was, I'd have to find someone new to get up early and have *real* conversations with me. That was the great thing about our friendship—we almost never hung out together other than volleyball, which meant we didn't share drama. She had her friends and I had mine, and together we could just sort of *be*. Plus being up early, especially on weekends, hardly anyone else was around. Here was a little bubble of comfort no one had managed to take from me yet, but in a few weeks, one way or another, I'd still lose it anyway.

After a moment, she said, "I wasn't kidding that you're not yourself this morning. And I'm super tempted to check what you want right now, but I promise I won't. Do you want to tell me though? What's up?"

"I want..." I wanted to tell, everything, all my secrets, if just to tell *anyone,* but I couldn't. So instead I told her, "I want permission to conduct these dates via telephone next year, that's what I want. Promise you'll let me call you when I'm up on Sunday morning and just want someone to have coffee with me and cheer me up?"

She smiled, then picked up her own coffee mug and clinked it against mine. "Promise."

"Thank you."

"Hey, we can even do a video call. Just prop me up across from you, and I'll even get you your own cup of mediocre dining hall coffee. It'll be like you never left."

"Perfect."

We both went to refill our mediocre cups of coffee and our impromptu date turned into a long one. By the time we finally got up to leave, the students who actually make it to breakfast hours on Sundays had all come and gone around us, while I clung to my tiny life raft of sanity for as long as I could. In some ways, that breakfast felt like an encapsulation of my whole year. I was jumping from stone to precious stone while a river of secrets and fears surged around me. For the few seconds I managed to stay out of the water, it was a relief to feel dry.

But breakfast was over, and when we stopped inside the glass doors to watch a light snow that had started to fall, Brooke gave me a helpful push back into the rapids. "Hey, speaking of wants…I've been trying to get to the bottom of, um, the Mandi issue."

I pictured her smirking at me last night. I was supremely glad lower school students weren't allowed to attend the Ball or no doubt she and her smirk would have been there. "Any idea what she's up to? I mean, is it more than the obvious?"

Brooke spoke in undertones, with a look of concentration on her face I recognized. It was similar to the one I wore when I tried to explain a vision, to put into words the impossible things our gifts could let us know and feel in our minds.

"It's…confusing." No doubt it was. "I think *she's* confused. But, I don't know, maybe it *was* Mandi I sensed earlier in the year. I mean, sometimes she just wants, like, a candy bar—I wish reading people was always as easy as those simple things. But when it's not, well, you know. For Mandi, it's like she's got some crusade going, something about family. She wants Lex to win, whatever that means, and she wants to help. She wants *recognition* for helping. And it's like, wanting

Lex to win, she wants you to lose. It's like that's the same thing. And maybe it was for the Winter Queen, but…it *feels* bigger than that. I'm not sure I can explain it right."

"No, I think I get it." Another student rushed through the door to try to catch the end of breakfast and we went through it into fluttering crystal flakes. It was nice snow, the kind that wasn't too cold and made you want to go play in it, though tonight it would probably freeze and make for a slippery walk to class in the morning. There was a chance it could be the last snow of the year.

When we were outside, Brooke continued, "I know you don't have to believe this, but I don't think Lex put Mandi up to whatever she's doing. Lex isn't stopping her, but I don't think she's responsible. This is Mandi's own thing, for whatever reason."

"Actually, I do believe it. And thank you, for trying to figure this out."

Brooke nodded. "For what it's worth, I told her to leave Caleb alone, and it seems like maybe she has? I kind of think she does like him, but obviously she was messing with him and Amy on purpose too. I still think it's more about you. What'd you do to her, anyway? Something terrible, like steal her flatiron?"

LATER, AT THE library making up my work hours from the day before, naturally I saw her. I wasn't sure why I had such trouble believing in fate when every time I spoke of the devil he—or she—always appeared. Mandi waltzed through the main floor, toward the elevator, just as I finished loading my cart. I don't know why, maybe to see what would happen, maybe to torture myself, but instead of hanging back, I pushed a little faster to make the elevator with her.

"Hey, Mandi," I said as the doors closed behind me. "How are you?" Whatever was really going on with her and my friends, I was still her dorm rep.

"How's *Amy?*" is how she answered. "Heard she got caught."

Taken aback, I stared at her for a moment. I *shouldn't* have been surprised at the blatant antagonism, but for some reason it always caught me off guard. She played with a strand of blond hair while looking innocent and bored. "Did you have something to do with that?" I asked and she shrugged.

"Not this time, but, I mean, she *was* breaking the rules."

Not this time. Another time then? Was she the reason Amy got caught on the grounds after curfew? At this point, I wasn't sure it mattered. Amy'd set herself up plenty for getting caught all on her own.

"She was, you're right." I leaned on my cart, pushing it toward Mandi and forcing her closer to the wall. I'd followed her into the notoriously slow elevator and I was blocking her exit. "You wouldn't know anything about rule-breaking, would you?" I asked.

The elevator dinged and the doors behind us started to slide open. "This is my floor," Mandi said. She tried to squeeze past, but the cars were tiny.

"Oh, sorry." I gave a halfhearted tug on the cart before the doors started to close again. "I guess you'll have to ride up with me." She glared her best glare, and I was tired of playing nice. "Why were you chasing Caleb Sullivan so hard?"

"Why do you think *I'm* chasing *him?*"

"Because I know Caleb. And I know you."

"You *don't* know me," she huffed. "That's one of your problems."

She was right, too. I *didn't* know her that well. She wouldn't let me and, also, I didn't really want to. "Fine. I know you *enough.* But Caleb is my friend, and he's not a prize or some game you can win, okay?" The elevator was chugging to a halt, so I had only a little time left to say what needed to be said. "Hurting him, and hurting Amy, won't help you. Or Alexis. Leave them alone. Please."

Her eyes widened a little and then narrowed. "You don't know anything, Lainey. You really don't. Want to know your other problem?"

The elevator finally dinged and the door slid open behind me. I wondered when I started losing this confrontation. Maybe since I'd manufactured it, I'd lost before it even began. I couldn't believe Mandi's gall, but despite a perverse curiosity to hear what she'd say, I refused to take her bait. I backed out of the elevator without response, but she told me anyway.

"You know that phrase some general said, 'Lead, follow, or get out of the way?' Your problem is you don't *really* want to do any of them." She leaned forward and put her hand on the door to keep it from closing. "You like being the center of attention too much to choose."

With a toss of her hair and a dare in her eyes that seemed way too old for an eighth grader, Mandi let the door close between us while I stood gaping.

Chapter Twenty

The Honor Board convened on Monday after final hour. We had regular monthly meetings and situational meetings. Today's was the latter, and for the first time, *I* was part of the situation.

I wasn't exactly on the block, but I was an accessory. And even if I hadn't been, I wasn't impartial in the proceedings, so I couldn't vote. I wasn't even supposed to be part of the discussion, and I felt very impotent sitting there, a spectator unless spoken to.

The best part of Honor Board was the meeting space, a richly appointed dining-turned-conference room in the Administration building, with floor-to-ceiling windows, damask draperies, and a huge solid oak table surrounded by—my favorite part—a completely mismatched set of antique swivel chairs. Northbrook was my kind of place in more ways than one. Even if I hadn't ended up Sententia, I'd have loved it here.

Ms. Kim was our faculty advisor. With her subtle gift for questions—if she asked, people wanted to answer—she was a natural choice for the position; there were no prohibitions against *teachers* using their Sententia abilities, so students under review were a little less reluctant in their responses. And if Dr. Stewart was attending, we were assured we were hearing the truth.

I'd learned pretty quickly about Northbrook—probably all schools—that student groups divided naturally down expected lines. Honor Board, however, being a faculty-nominated group not voted on by other students, had an interesting mix of representatives. There were thirteen of us, because, if anything, Northbrook *embraced* superstitions, and at least one student from every grade but seventh.

We had one eighth and ninth grader, two sophomores, and the rest were juniors and seniors. The only thing we had in common is that we were, of course, all Sententia. Three faculty members were always in attendance, Ms. Kim and a rotating group of others. Dr. Stewart had ultimate veto power but she'd never used it. If there was ever some kind of tie, she solved that too.

Our youngest member was actually our toughest. If Amy's punishment were up to her, I knew she'd be expelled. That was a scary word. Northbrook's conduct standards were tough and *expulsion* was an actual possibility. Three strikes and you could be out. I didn't think it would come to that, though.

The good news for Amy was her strikes weren't *that* bad. Breaking a few curfews and skipping classes wasn't a huge deal when you were still academically performing at the top of your class. And she was popular. A lot of kids at the school and sitting around our table liked her. The bad news was Alexis Morrow was also popular and she had a long and well-known history of *not* liking my roommate.

Amy sat at the front of the room looking pale, tired, and resigned. Usually I'd try to smile or encourage her in some way, but I wasn't feeling especially charitable and, also, I really couldn't help her. Caleb could have been made to attend, being an accessory like myself, but he wasn't back yet. I wondered if he would have been, if he already had warnings too from Amy's previous infractions. Somehow I doubted it though. More likely was that he didn't know about Amy's warnings either. He was least likely of all of us to jeopardize his time at Northbrook, because he couldn't afford it. Literally. The sad truth was that money lessened problems, even here.

Ms. Kim started the meeting and laid out the facts. It was exactly how every meeting started, except that additionally, as happened from time to time, she recused herself from voting because of her close relationship with the student as her dorm attendant. I'd have been expected to do the same if I weren't already part of the violation. The "case" was pretty straightforward, the kind where it would take us longer to get everyone together and called to order than to go through the process. Amy answered a handful of questions dully, without resisting or arguing.

"And so you knew about this?" That was directed at me, from our plucky little eighth grader. I wanted to sigh, but also, I hoped she went to law school someday.

"Yes," I admitted, though it wasn't much of an admission. It was already established.

"Why didn't you stop her?"

"I tried."

At the front, Amy did sigh. "She strongly discouraged me from breaking curfew," she vouched. Dr. Stewart was at the back of the room, so everyone knew this was a true statement.

"But," the eighth grade esquire continued, "you didn't report her either."

"For serious?" one of the juniors said and we all tried not to laugh, most of us succeeding.

"Miss Young isn't really our concern today," came from the trigonometry teacher.

"She should at least get a warning though."

It was true, and everyone agreed, myself included. I was duly warned.

"Caleb, too."

Amy called out, "He thought I had permission!" But he was duly warned, too, in absentia. As discouragement for future incidents. Amy blanched. She might have been resigned to what happened to her, but I don't think she'd considered how it could affect Caleb.

Commentary bubbled up around the table.

"Harsh."

"No offense, Indira, but I'm glad I'm not your roommate."

"Or your boyfriend."

"Shut *up,* Sean!"

"Order, please." That was Ms. Kim.

The question then was what to do with Amy. There were plenty of options, all of which were brought up. Indira did indeed remind us the rules allowed for expulsion. With three warnings in just one semester, it was even warranted.

Groans flew from all over the table, and I even saw, out of the corner of my eye, Dr. Stewart's lips twitch with a hint amusement. I knew probably better than anyone at the table how she wasn't *quite* as heartless as she seemed. She liked the students, and she enjoyed the Honor Board process of our debating appropriate punishments for our peers.

Commensurate punishments, she called them. What fit the incident as well as the student. It was why there were few set guidelines for what would happen if you broke a rule. One of the perks, or downsides, of private school, depending on what side of the table you were on. And because of that, there was serious talk of stripping Amy's academic honors.

One of the most brutal parts of the Honor Board process was that you actually *stayed* while your punishment was determined. Amy was doing her best to be still and blank, but her anguish was apparent to me. This wouldn't ruin her future or anything, but it would hurt. A lot. Short of kicking her out, it was probably the worst we could do. It wasn't an inappropriate punishment either, not really.

"It's conduct unbecoming. If this was basketball, I'd lose team captain."

"You're *not* team captain."

"It's a *metaphor.*"

"She's right."

Alexis had been surprisingly quiet through the whole meeting. I assumed she was relishing the slow torture of her longtime nemesis, so it was with great shock to basically the entire table when she finally said, "Oh, come on. Are we really considering this?"

Amy's head shot up to look at her, and even Alexis seemed a little surprised at herself. She wasn't looking at Amy, though. She glanced, instead, at me. We usually sat next to each other—keep your enemies close—but I was at the end of the table near the headmaster today, out of the way. At least they hadn't made me sit at a desk of shame as well.

"What do you propose as an alternative?" Ms. Kim prompted.

Alex fussed with her hair and cleared her throat. She usually loved being the center of attention, unless it was for unexpectedly defending a girl we all assumed she'd happily let roast. "Listen, I get your arguments, but seriously? She broke curfew. It was the *Ball.* And we're supposed to discourage it from happening again. So give her probation—*strict* probation—and let's go to rehearsal or whatever the rest of you are supposed to be doing right now. Okay?"

From behind me, Dr. Stewart interjected, "Very reasonable, Miss Morrow." She rarely said anything during the meetings, so when she *did,* we listened.

Amy was placed on strict—*strict*—probation and that was that. Meeting adjourned.

I followed Alexis out of the room and just before we turned in different directions I said softly, "Thanks."

She nodded and we went our own ways, one kindness repaid with another.

DAYS TICKED AWAY too fast. At times the pace seemed glacial—like when my roommate and I were alone together—but in barely more than a blink, I found myself weeks closer to graduation and more unmoored than ever.

Things for Amy, in a word, sucked. And that meant the rest of us were feeling it too. I wished we could just talk about it, but we weren't talking. Not really. I was no longer sure who needed to say sorry more, but I hadn't forgotten why we needed to say it, and I still didn't want to do it. Neither did she. Even worse, her relationship with Caleb was deteriorating at a rapid pace, more rapid than before winter break.

"Aaron wants me to come visit for my birthday, for the whole weekend," Caleb said as he sat at our lunch table about halfway through the hour. He was grinning like he'd just hung up the phone with him—Caleb loved his older brother, his whole family actually. I admired them.

Amy speared a carrot and looked at it, not him. "Good for you."

I watched them both as I pushed my salad around my plate. Caleb was trying, *really trying*. His fingers tightened on his fork. But he took a deep breath and said, "So why don't we see if you can come with me."

"Which word don't you understand, *strict* or *probation?*" Amy bit off half her carrot and put the rest down.

Caleb, too, put his fork down. It clattered against his tray like a warning and I wished Amy would heed it. "Do you not want to go?"

"That's not the point."

"So why don't we ask your parents? They can't force you to stay here if your parents are letting you leave."

Amy shoved her tray away. "You actually think my parents are going to let me go with you to a college campus for a weekend?"

Caleb rubbed his eyes. "It's worth asking, isn't it?"

"Not when I know the answer."

Before long, everyone else at the table had—smartly—taken off, and I was the only other one left. I didn't even know why I stayed, except to torture myself with the rest of their argument. It was painful to watch on so many different levels but I couldn't shake the feeling that it was all partially, maybe mostly, my fault. But I didn't know how to fix it either. Carter had told me I *couldn't* and he was probably right.

"Okay, fine," Caleb said. Angry red splotches were developing on his usually adorable baby cheeks. *"I'll* ask them, if you want. Or don't even try. Whatever."

Amy flicked her fingers. "Just go, if that's what you want. Have fun with your brother. You know where to find me if you want to hang out with *me.*"

"Hasn't this whole conversation said I *do* want to hang out with you? *You're* the one—God, whatever. I'll let him know you can't make it."

She looked down at her still-full plate. "So you're going."

"Yeah. I'm going."

"Great. Happy birthday." She twirled her finger in a sarcastic *woo-hoo* circle and that was when Caleb gave up.

He grabbed his tray and stood. "Thanks. I'm done. Later."

"Wait!" Amy reached for his hand, but seriously, she should have done that a long time ago. Caleb let her take it but he didn't really hold hers back. "Are you coming to the bookstore later?" The bookstore being the *only* place Amy could go that felt the least bit like having fun.

"I have tutoring," he said and walked away.

She made a fist with her hand that he'd just dropped. "UGH!" she ground out, but I honestly thought she was more mad at herself, which seemed valid to me. She glanced at me, the silent witness on the other side of the table. "Are you going to be there?"

I shook my head. "I have therapy. Sorry," I added, and I picked up my tray and left too.

In the weeks since the vision returned, instead of focusing on a number of important things I was running out of time to do, like make necessary decisions about the future, or work harder to solve the still-hanging mystery of Mark Penrose, or reconcile with my best friend, I'd thrown myself into physical therapy and killing things.

I practiced planticide with the same passion I'd devoted to practicing my volleyball serves over the summer, approaching my theory as scientifically as I could and working up to my end goal. I started with the poinsettia, killing whole plants. I killed plants from all angles, by touching the stem, touching the leaves, touching the tiniest, slimmest piece I could find. Where I touched the plant didn't matter; they all died with ease. I tried touching just the dirt, but that had no effect.

Next I moved on to the first true test of my theory—I killed just one *part* of the plant. The first few attempts failed, and the whole plant died. I was too nervous and didn't have the right focus for my Thought. I had to hold the intention in my mind and concentrate until I felt the energy, the essence of just the *piece,* not the whole.

In a major breakthrough, I managed to kill a branch of a large plant in the entryway to the Auditorium. Under the pretense of visiting Aunt Tessa's installation, I watched it carefully to see if killing the branch eventually killed the entire plant. But it didn't; the branch withered as if I'd snapped it off, but the rest of the plant continued to vibrate with life.

After that, confident I could affect a reasonably large piece of a whole, I moved on to the huge, beautiful umbrella tree—I'd asked one day what it was called—outside Dr. Stewart's office suite. I made ex- cuses to visit, including but not limited to requesting off-campus privileges, seeking advice on the merits of my favorite schools, and updating her on my progress in physical therapy, and had killed fully half the leaves before the entire plant began to die. If she thought my sudden reappearance in her daily life was strange, or noticed the slow demise of her waxy-leaved plant, she said nothing.

In fact, if anyone noticed my new interest in horticulture, they didn't mention it. I'd tried to be discreet, which wasn't hard, because it took no more than a passing touch for me to wield my gift and take a plant's life. The more I practiced killing in segments, the faster I became at that skill as well.

The more I practiced, the more I scared myself.

In fact, I scared myself so much, I gained a new understanding of the Perceptum, which scared me even more.

There *were* people whose Sententia abilities were so profoundly dangerous their very existence was a danger. I was one of them. I *epitomized* them. I hadn't truly understood it before. The one time I'd used my gift, it had been a moment of wild desperation. Almost a fluke. I hadn't even been sure it would *work*. Now I was using it regularly, and just like with practicing my Diviner half, I was getting better at it. It took less concentration every time, became more of a reflex. That was my goal—I *needed* that level of control if my theory had even a chance of working—but it was a frightening goal.

I knew I'd never turn the *full* power of my gift on another person, not unless it was literally life or death—that's why I was practicing. But I recognized the substantial level of trust it would take for someone else to believe that. I knew, too, that there were plenty of people not deserving of that trust, who *would* use their gifts not just for personal gain, but for the detriment of others. I understood, deeply, why Senator Astor had sworn off using his gift at all.

I understood why Carter hid.

I understood why all of Sententia hid.

Most of all, I understood why the Perceptum wanted me.

There was even a moment when I really thought I'd join them. I understood. Finally. But I wasn't ready. I wouldn't play executioner, no matter how horrible the person was.

When the next note arrived, it was a big surprise, as big as the first one had been. The headmaster handed it to me, right after I finished killing her plant completely and just before I headed out of her office to be driven to my twice-weekly physical therapy. It was a ridiculous contrivance and waste of Academy funds, forcing me to be chauffeured to the doctor's and back, but the seeming one iron-clad rule of the Northbrook academic year was no cars for students, and though mine was parked behind the bookstore, it may as well not have existed.

I clutched the note between my hands until we were out of the gates and past the bookstore, as if somehow, someone might see me and ask questions I wasn't ready to answer. The further we got from the Academy, the safer it felt to open it, as if being off the grounds would make it less real.

I'd stopped expecting them, the notes. I'd never *expected* them, but for a while they'd been thrilling, so I anticipated them in a not unpleasant way. Now that they'd come to feel sinister, I was surprised again. Afraid. Almost as much as I was afraid of the future, or myself. I finally opened it slowly, the way you opened a door when you were afraid something dangerous was behind it.

It was short and to the point, and like the others, wasn't overtly threatening. Anyone else looking at it would think it sweet, maybe a joke. It's just that I was reading it with new eyes.

Lainey, he wrote,

We're all waiting on you. Don't keep us in suspense.

-D.A.

The notes were the only direct contact we had, Dan and I, and were only one way. I'd never replied, not personally. While I had the means to contact him directly, if necessary, it hadn't seemed expected. Not yet.

But if the calendar I marked off every morning didn't remind me, the note in my hand was an alarm sounding a clear warning I was running out of time.

I WAS STILL thinking about the note later, and what Mandi had said to me, while I stared at Ferny, who sat unobtrusively and content in the sunny corner of our room.

I was afraid Mandi was right, that secretly I liked the attention. So much seemed to revolve around me right now and maybe I *wasn't* trying hard enough to make that stop. Carter had said I was afraid of deciding, and that was true, but *was* it because at least part of me didn't want the decision-making attention to go away? I thought I hated it, but love and hate were such close cousins.

Whether I wanted the attention or not, my time to have it was almost up. I had to make choices. And I still wasn't ready. I actually did hate what I was about to do, but I couldn't put it off any longer. The most perfect test subject had sat in my room since the New Year, a comforting green presence that recently seemed more Amy's friend than I was.

Since I'd decided to use Ferny, I'd spent some time only touching him, stroking his spiky fronds, and feeling out his energy. And mentally apologizing for making him an innocent victim. A nice plant in the wrong place at the right time.

I gripped one slender leaf, barely a hairsbreadth wide, and Thought.

Then I touched another one and Thought again. And again. And again.

One by one, as I touched them, the tiny pieces lost their spark. Some fell off immediately and I collected them. It wasn't an accident. I hadn't tugged too hard and pulled them loose. Each one told the story of how I killed it.

Close. I was getting close to what I thought I could do. If I could discern such a small, truly *tiny,* leaf of the fern, out of I couldn't even guess how many thousands of leaves, *maybe* I really could—

And that was when my phone rang and changed *everything.*

Chapter Twenty-One

D o you think you could bring my watch back when you come over later?"

"I'm sorry, what?"

"My watch," Carter repeated. "I left it there after the Ball. Thanks to your roommate's antics, I haven't been back since."

I'd have laughed at the bitter tone in his voice, if I hadn't just been killing things and he hadn't caught me by surprise. Carter's watch. It was in my room. The watch I'd surreptitiously been *looking for,* in *his* room, since the Ball.

"Anyway," he continued, "I guess you didn't notice it? In your nightstand?"

I pulled open the drawer I pretty much never used unless Carter was visiting, and sure enough, there it was. Carter's watch.

Except the thing was, this *particular* watch wasn't just his—it was his *father's* first.

Carter wore it only for special occasions, though it wasn't very fancy. At the Ball was the first time I'd ever given it a second look. When I'd joked about getting him a new one for his birthday, he told me whose it was. It was the kind of watch his father had worn every day.

The watch Mark Penrose had likely been wearing the day he died.

"S—sure. I'll bring it over."

"Thanks." When I didn't say anything more, he added. "You okay? You seem a little distracted."

That was an understatement. "Um, yeah. Sorry. I was…in the middle of some pretty intense homework. I'll see you later, okay?"

I barely waited for him to say goodbye before I hung up.

Here it was, the clue I'd been waiting for, I'd *looked* for, hiding in my room.

The watch and I stared it out for a little while. I was afraid to pick it up. I didn't *know* what it might show me, but I already knew the end was not a happy one. Taking a deep breath, I plucked the watch out of the drawer and closed my eyes.

Of course, it was even worse than I imagined.

I didn't need more than a few seconds to see all I needed to see, every heartbreaking detail. Like all death-connected objects I'd touched since the spark, the tingling sensation that told me there was *something* about this watch was there. It was different from the others, from the couch that constantly buzzed in my room, but similar. More painful, not in strength but emotion. I knew I'd learn to understand the subtle differences in the electric hums over time, but today all I could feel was devastation.

Tears rolled down my cheeks as I rubbed my fingers across the smooth metal links of the band. The watch seemed warm to the touch, maybe because I was gripping it so hard, and under different circumstances, I'd have pretended it was because Carter had just taken it off. I wanted to associate this piece of jewelry with *good* memories, but that would never happen again. In fact, I wasn't sure how I'd ever be able to see him wear it without crying.

Mark Penrose had poisoned himself.

I watched him do it: pouring tea into the mug I'd broken at the beginning of the year. Mixing in a spoon of sugar and a splash of milk. Going to his room—the room that now belonged to Melinda and Jeff—for the small bottle of poison hidden in his nightstand and emptying its contents into the mug too.

He sat down at the kitchen table as if it was any other day, as if he hadn't just done the thing that would kill him by morning.

And sitting across from him was Daniel Astor.

DANIEL ASTOR HAD made Mark Penrose do it. Had Thought him to it.

The whole story was there in a series of images, a silent movie for me to decipher. There were Mark and Dan in a heated argument. There was Dan hugging a younger and thinner, and sobbing, Carter, hugging him like he was the most precious thing in the world. There was Mark in a new-agey apothecary I actually recognized, a local place, still in business, chatting familiarly with the owner and carrying a bag out to the car. There was Dan smiling and chatting with the same woman. There was Carter again, younger still, talking to Dan and nodding, rapt at whatever his uncle was saying. There was, interestingly, Mark Penrose sobbing over his wife's grave. It was snowy and on a few nearby stones I saw wreaths. I wondered if it was Christmas.

I stopped there. I'd watch the vision again later, really study it, but I needed some time to recover, to keep myself from completely breaking down. My migraine problem was officially cured, but that didn't stop my head from throbbing for different reasons. Shock. Anger. Fear.

Daniel Astor was a murderer.

Carter's hero, *my* uncle, was a murderer.

Just thinking the words made me want to retch. I'd dined with him, talked with him, granted him influence over my future, given him the opportunity to ingratiate himself with my *family*, and, if I was being honest, let the idea of him worm more than a little ways into my heart. I had even entertained the idea that I might someday be ready to join the Perceptum. And that was only about *me*. He was practically like *Carter's* second father.

This would *ruin* Carter. Ruin him. I didn't know how I could ever tell him what I saw, nor even if I should. And I knew now what had happened with my vision. It was no impending accident, no fortuitous shifting of fate, nothing we thwarted or changed or managed to evade at all. With this final, damning piece of evidence, it all made perfect sense.

Daniel Astor had an idea to kill me.

And to use Carter to do it.

This explained why I could never read any details and why the vision seemed to come and go—it was just an idea. A very real idea, but not a definite one. Carter had been exactly right when he'd said it was our *potential* fate. Before now, before I'd discovered this very ugly secret, I wouldn't have known why, precisely, he'd want me dead. At first, it was probably because of Jill. Perhaps the moment I first had the vision was when he learned her gift was gone. Maybe killing me had been one potential way of dealing with what I'd done.

But now? Now I knew the *potential* was even greater than it had been before. It was probably closer to inevitable, and would likely hinge on what *I* did.

But why involve Carter? It seemed cruel. I already knew he was cruel, but he *loved* Carter. Maybe it was convenient. I'm sure he could easily have poisoned Mark Penrose himself, but it was neater not to get his hands dirty. To make it look like something Mark had done, if the question ever arose. To make it *be* something Mark had done, I realized. That was why touching *Dan* had never produced a vision. He was ultimately, but *indirectly,* responsible. I wondered what he'd made Mark *Think* the poison was.

I wondered what he'd make Carter *Think* happened to me.

Daniel Astor was a murderer, past and future, and I didn't know why or what to do. One thing was certain though—I couldn't do anything if I was dead.

ALL THE WAY across the street I repeated the mantra *I will not cry, I will not cry, I will not cry, I will NOT…*and it worked. For a few minutes anyway. Carter's watch was in my bag, wrapped in a silk scarf to protect it and so I wouldn't have to touch it again.

I went in the back door, just in case. I'd calmed down and cleaned myself up to the point that I looked not *good,* but not like I'd just had a major breakdown or uncovered a murder. The refrain in my head was helping me stay that way and the dim back rooms of Penrose Books would help disguise me further. Plus if I couldn't hold it together, I didn't want to be standing in front of the whole school. There was even a chance my roommate was here, and I really didn't want to see her like this.

Instead, I saw Carter. And Melinda and Jeff.

The entire family was there.

Melinda leaned her back on the counter, talking over her shoulder to her nephew while he laughed. Seeing the two of them together, with all the features that would re-create Mark Penrose's face between them, I couldn't help but cry for them once more. Jeff stood just off to Melinda's side, watching her with an expression that broadcast devotion. They were nothing short of beautiful together, and I loved them all. My mantra crumbled like wet paper.

Carter must have heard me because he turned around. He smiled when he saw me peeking from the shadows of the back room and stepped into the doorway. "Okay, *this* time you're crying."

It was a sweet joke, and I loved him desperately for it, but all I could do was cry harder. When he realized this had to be serious, he immediately switched gears. "Hey, hey. You're *really* crying. What is it? What can I do?"

"I have to tell you something."

"Okay. It's okay." He pulled me to a seat on the dusty floral couch and I buried my face in his chest. I'd glimpsed Melinda hovering in the doorway and Carter's helpless expression, telling her he didn't know if he needed her or not. "Did something happen? Did you and Amy fight again?"

"No, it's not that. I..."

I almost told him. I faltered, the confession on the brink of spilling from my tongue, before huge, racking sobs choked it back.

I couldn't do it. Not yet, and not here. Not while he was at work, in the middle of a bookstore full of students. It was just too terrible. Last year, I'd been a brilliant actress after the *Jillian Incident,* never once crying or slipping up, but I didn't think anyone in the world was a good enough actress for *this* secret.

In between rubbing my back and hugging me tightly enough to stop the shaking, Carter said, "Can you tell me why you're crying?"

"I don't know if I'm making the right decision."

"There's not a *wrong* decision here, Lainey," he soothed. He thought I was still talking about the future, when really it was the past crushing me now, sitting on my throat so that I couldn't take a deep breath and squeezing my heart so that it hurt to beat. It was almost like last year, like I could feel Jill on top of me, choking my life away. "Trust me. Wherever you choose, we'll *make* it the right one."

I stayed there, holding Carter and wishing today had never happened, until I started to calm down. "Deep breaths, there you go. Yoga in, yoga out." I tried not to laugh at that, afraid it would set me crying again, but a ridiculous snort-sob escaped and Carter smiled down at me. "Perfect," he pronounced and I did it again.

I shouldn't have been laughing, or close to it, but that was the thing about life. I'd learned it last year and was relearning it again now. Something happens, something that changes you, changes *everything*, but life still goes on. You feel like the world should stop for the weight of what just happened, but it doesn't. Life doesn't even slow. You laugh again, sometimes even when you shouldn't. You have things you still have to do, like finish your homework and stop putting off choosing a college.

I wasn't sure if I was going to make it there, but I knew where I wanted to go. I even knew what was going to happen the moment I made the decision.

"Carter?" My voice was rough and muffled by his shirt.

"Still here, babe."

"I want to go to Boston. For real this time."

I could feel the smile in his lips when they brushed the top of my head. "Perfect," he repeated. "And see? That wasn't so bad. The world didn't even end."

But he was wrong. As soon as I said it, and meant it, the vision returned.

Except this time it was complete.

Chapter Twenty-Two

I was surprisingly used to watching people die. I had no choice. I saw them all the time.

They just weren't usually *me*.

More terrible than *knowing* you're going to die, than even knowing someone you love will have a part in it, was watching it happen. A tragic silent movie of the worst possible horrors, starring a heroine unwilling, a hero unwitting, and a villain hidden safely off-screen.

I'd seen how I was going to die. I knew where, I knew how, and thanks to a lucky tidbit of information from Carter, I even knew when.

There was no time stamp on my visions, which would have made this gift/curse of mine so much more useful, but just before I left for curfew, after Carter gave me one final, reluctant kiss goodbye, he said, "Hey, did I tell you my uncle's coming to graduation this year? It's supposed to be a surprise, but I figured he wouldn't mind if I told you."

Actually, he probably would.

I could have guessed anyway, but it was helpful to have confirmation. Since the beginning of the year, even if it was unspoken, I'd known the deadline for my answer—join the Perceptum or not—coincided with graduation.

Now I was pretty sure I wouldn't even make it *to* graduation.

The thing I couldn't figure out was *why*. I mean, the fact that I knew the secret of Mark Penrose was probably good enough reason for Senator Astor to decide once and for all to eliminate me too, but I didn't think that was it. He didn't know I knew, and I'd decided not to tell. Not yet. My gift would have told me the moment I touched Carter whether just the *knowledge* of his father's murder would lead to mine. But it didn't.

The vision hadn't returned until I'd definitively chosen Boston.

What was so important about Boston? And why was the vision complete this time? I couldn't understand the nuances of what I'd done or hadn't done that brought me to this. Maybe because knowing what I knew, I was also certain I'd *never* join the Perceptum. That made some sense. If that was it, I wondered a little why my refusal to work for the Perceptum hadn't maintained the vision all along. Maybe before now I hadn't believed it enough. Maybe Senator Astor didn't.

Ultimately, though, whatever it was, the *why* didn't matter. I didn't understand this compulsion, why he'd want to kill anyone, including me, and I might never. All that mattered was this:

I was going to die, and I had a plan to save myself.

I had a lot of work to do before graduation and not a lot of time.

SOME OF THAT work was to make things right with my best friend. I was angry at her, and at myself, but most of all, I missed her. But I'd never been in a fight like this before and I had no idea how to end it.

So I did it by accident. I came into our room to find my once perpetually happy roommate sobbing at her desk.

"Hey," I said gently, rushing over and ignoring the fact that we weren't speaking. Her head was down, face buried in her folded arms, and her body shook with crying. I brushed my fingers through her soft curls without thinking. It always made me feel better when Carter did that to me. "What's the matter?"

She stiffened when I touched her but then only sobbed harder before finally wailing, "I hate Iowa!"

Er. Iowa? It wasn't the answer I expected for her level of sorrow. I'd barely ever thought about Iowa, let alone generated any emotion over it, but I'd go with it. This was probably the most we'd said to each other in weeks. "What has Iowa done to make you hate it so much you're crying?" I probably should have known the answer.

"Caleb is going to Iowa for college. *Iowa!* Where the population ratio is forty cornstalks to one. I thought…I thought he'd go to UMass."

I thought he would too. They'd been recruiting him for the baseball team and his brother was there. The main campus wasn't that far from Northbrook, actually. But more importantly, it was only a few hours from Boston. Iowa, on the other hand…well, I wasn't even sure there were daily flights to Iowa. I hadn't realized he was seriously considering it.

Once Amy started talking, she didn't want to stop. Her eyes were swollen and red, ringed by pools of mascara, and her clothes truly did not fit. She'd lost even more weight without my noticing. I stepped back and sat quietly on my bed to listen while she moved as she rambled, pulling at her hair and kicking pillows. "It's my fault, I know it. If it weren't for, just, *everything,* he wouldn't have…he wouldn't…I mean, Iowa. I-oh-wa. It's nowhere. It's, it's a freaking *red* state—"

"Actually, I think it's a swing—"

"—and I don't understand how he could *go* there. Without me," she added very, very softly before she slumped onto her own bed.

She paused long enough for me to ask, "Why *is* he going there?"

"Full scholarship." Her voice was barely louder than before and she tossed one of her smaller pillows up and down over her head.

"And baseball?" She nodded and her pillow thumped into the wall. "Well…that sounds hard to turn down."

She sighed. "I think…I think I should just break up with him."

"*What?*"

"It's, just, it'll hurt less now, I think. Be easier. Iowa is so far and I…I can't even deal with him being around a freaking eighth grader while I'm *here*. I don't think I can do it, long distance, and I don't want to wait until summer."

"You're *crazy*."

I'd forgotten for a moment we were still in a fight, that anything I said would cut deeper than usual. But Amy hadn't. She exploded, sitting up on her bed and spearing me with narrowed eyes that filled with angry tears. *"I'm* crazy? What the hell would you know about it, you and your perfect relationship? Your boyfriend is ready to follow you *anywhere*. You have no idea, Lane. *No idea."*

No idea? Who the hell was *she?* I had *every* idea and then some. Amy was shouting, her words no doubt echoing through the building, and I should have known better. I should have stopped myself and not let her get to me and been the bigger person. Whatever. I should have done a million other things besides what I did next.

"Perfect relationship?!" I shouted back. *"You've* got the perfect relationship and don't even realize it! I'd *love* your new biggest problem— your boyfriend's going to be a few hours' plane ride away. Oh, how tough. You poor thing. At least he's not going to *kill you*. Try dealing with that!"

Amy's sniffling stopped abruptly. "What?"

Oh. Shit. "Nothing. I was just joking."

"No you weren't."

"I—"

"You're the worst liar in the world, Lane. Your cheeks give you away every time. What the hell are you talking about? You said *kill you.*"

"You're right. I did say that."

She'd shifted on the bed and sat on the edge, looking at me with a baldly worried expression—completely the opposite of only a few seconds ago. "Someone...someone's. Is someone *threatening* you? What's going on?!"

I was so sick of everything. Of lying, of discretion, of choosing between my *friends* and my heredity and having it be my *heredity* that was winning. Sick of secrets. The only person I trusted more than Amy was Carter, and he was scheduled to kill me.

To hell with it all.

With a sigh, I said, "Are you sitting down?" despite that I was looking right at her. When I realized I was standing, I sat down myself.

Her eyes were wide and dry now. "If I could sit down any more than I am, I get the impression I probably should. *Is* someone threatening you, Lane? Is it—is it *Carter*? Is he...is *that* why you always seem so secret-secret together? Why you, no offense, kind of look like shit lately?"

"No!" I whipped my head back and forth. "It's—No. Carter's not...you'll understand in a second. And no one's threatening me. No, wait. That's not even true. Mandi Worthington"—Amy's eyes narrowed again—"is sort of threatening me, but she—" *doesn't even matter,* I was going to stay, which wasn't just insensitive, it was wrong. Completely, utterly wrong.

It finally dawned on me what Mandi was *really* doing and she did matter. A whole lot. She was ruining Amy's relationship. On purpose. *On purpose* on purpose. Not just because she was a Siren, but because it was also destabilizing me and *our* relationship. Alienating me and my best friend and pushing me toward making a choice. In a flash, I remembered the art unveiling, pictured the arm around her shoulder and her beaming smile up at her family's old friend.

Jesus. Where did the manipulations end? Everything Brooke had said made sense now.

"Lane? I'm getting scared here. I need you to talk to me."

"You're right," I said, looking straight into her pretty brown eyes, which were round with fear but still determined. "I'm so sorry," is how I started.

And then I told her.

SHE LISTENED. I have no idea how long I talked, but it was a long time. By the end, I'd wrapped pieces of my hair around my finger enough times that it was curling. My throat was dry and I wished I had a glass of water. And a shot of something stronger. I was exhausted by the telling, but felt better, *lighter* than I had in…a really long time. Possibly since the day so long ago when I first glimpsed Ashley Thayer's death.

After some creative cursing, some scientific questions I really couldn't answer, and a few assurances that no, I wasn't kidding, she said, "So let me get this straight: Carter Penrose is, somehow, going to kill you, and you're still not only dating him, but sleeping with him on a regular basis. He's either the best lover ever or you're crazy."

"It can't be both?"

"Yeah, actually, it can totally be both. Wow. This is like…Romeo and Juliet, who I thought were idiots, except *you're* the idiot."

"Thanks."

"No, seriously."

"It's not as simple as leaving him. Besides which, I don't want to."

"I rest my case."

I didn't tell her *everything*, not about Senator Astor or Mark Penrose or the specifics of my impending death, but pretty much everything else. It was a lot to take in, far more than I'd had to deal with, but, "You're really taking this...well. Like, unnaturally well."

Amy came to sit next to me. "Honestly Lane, I've always known you're different, and this school and Carter were...something else, so. This maybe isn't as surprising as you think. Plus, you forget I'm amazing."

I looked at her for a moment and then, tentatively, hugged her. When she embraced me back, I told her, "I never forgot."

"I'm sorry, too," she replied.

We stayed like that for a while, hanging on to each other and letting the wounds we'd caused heal themselves. After a while I said, "You kind of look like shit lately too, you know."

Amy drew back and *smiled* at me. Genuinely smiled at me. She did still look pretty bad, what with the crying and confessing and the burdensome story I'd just told her, but her smile was the nicest thing I'd seen in a while. "Yeah, I know. Finally lost ten pounds though! And you know what? I feel better now. I'm *not* crazy. That stupid little Sententia bi—"

"Don't say it out loud! Jesus, Amy."

"I say 'bitch' all the time."

"We're in enough trouble as it is, if Dr. Stewart ever finds out everything I just told you and she probably will!"

I stared at her until she relented. "Okay, I get it. Don't talk about Fight Club."

"Thank you."

"But seriously?" She got up and went to her dresser, picking up her hairbrush to run it slowly through her hair. "I wish you'd told me sooner."

I sighed. "So do I. But I...hope you understand. Why I didn't. I still shouldn't have."

"I know. 'Discretion is the better part of valor' or some shit. Prince Hal was kind of dink, you know? You should get a better motto."

"It wasn't my choice."

She brushed her hair a few more times and stopped. "I'm going to bust her pretty little nose."

"Please don't. Or wait until after graduation."

"She's probably with my boyfriend right now."

"I'm sorry." And I was. I told her how I'd warned him, and Carter had too, as best we could.

"He's such an idiot."

"He's human."

She paused to look at me. "Are you?"

"As far as I know. It's just genetics, plus a little bit of help from God or the Universe or whoever."

We were quiet for a few moments, me toying with the laces of my sneakers I still hadn't taken off and trying to figure out just how much trouble I would get in for this, Amy probably thinking about how gratifying it would feel to break Mandi Worthington's bones. When that got old, Amy grabbed her desk chair and sat backwards on it in front of me.

"Tell me again about the dying, if you would. Because I don't want that to happen."

I told her how soon it was, and Amy put her fingers to her lips and looked away. After a deep breath she said, "So why don't you just not do whatever it is that's going to make that happen? It must be some kind of accident, right? Cater would never…"

I shook my head. "It's more complex than that."

"You really think you can…change it? *When* it's happening?"

"We did it once before, over the summer." I told her the story.

"*Really?* When was that?"

"The day we went to the beach." Her expression told me what a terrible and obvious answer that was. I cleared my throat. "The night we almost…"

She laughed. "Ah ha. That explains the red cheeks. And the very un-Lainey-like recklessness you exhibited. Don't you wish you'd just, you know, done it then?"

No, I didn't wish that, not really. Well, kind of. But mostly: "It wasn't how I wanted it to happen, so, no."

After another while of sitting next to each other with the comfort we hadn't shared in weeks, Amy broke the silence again. "Lane?"

"Yeah?"

"So you did that to Ferny?" We both looked at the plant, who was denuded to an alarming degree and looked rather pathetic in his corner. Despite the damage I continued to inflict on him, he was still hanging on.

"I'm sorry," I said for about the thousandth time of the night, though I meant every one of them.

She nodded. "At least that wasn't my fault. I take care of my boy. But I thought maybe he was just…reflecting my mood." With barely a moment's hesitation, she held out her hand, letting it hang in the space between us. "Try it on me. Your idea. Instead of killing my plant some more and not *really* testing it."

"Amy—"

"Just do it, Lane. I trust you."

No matter what she'd said before, she *was* crazy. I didn't trust myself. Her *mind,* maybe her life, was at stake. I'd told her about my theory, even about how her relationship, Mandi's meddling and something Caleb had said, was instrumental in my figuring it out, but I *wasn't* ready to test it. I wasn't sure I—

She interrupted my thinking before I could hyperventilate. "Listen. I get the risks, but you need a human subject and *I trust you.* I *know* you, too. This is a thing you've never done before. You'll *never* try it unless I make you. Do it."

She shook her hand at me and I reached forward, grasping her around the wrist, where I could feel her pulse beating behind my fingers. I was shaking, but I held on.

It was the determination in Amy's eyes that did it. Excitement might have been a better word. She *wanted* to be part of this. I could see it. It was easy to forget that she was a genius, and a huge science nerd, and this was her passion. She was about to become a catalyst, Subject 1 in an experiment that had never been attempted before. And because it was Amy, I could *not* fail.

I licked my lips. "Ask me about a secret you'd like to know. *Any* secret."

She grinned wickedly before asking exactly what I knew she would and I told her.

A second later, I made her forget.

Chapter Twenty-Three

Unfortunately, it would take more than one Thought to undo all the damage between Amy and Caleb. I wasn't honestly sure they could. Amy was trying again, coming back to herself more every day. But it wasn't something that could happen overnight, and was made more difficult by the restrictions she was still under.

And also by the continued presence of Mandi Worthington. She had no interest in going away, and poor, beleaguered Caleb didn't necessarily want her to. He was under her spell, but worse, he'd fallen out of Amy's. It was a new game I played, keeping Amy away from Mandi with the threat of the Honor Board's warnings my constant refrain.

Spring break came and went, and Amy and Caleb didn't speak the entire time. My roommate was despondent by the time we returned to campus, sinking back into the bitter abyss she'd only recently started to pull herself out of.

"I'm telling him tomorrow," she announced. She lugged her bag of fresh laundry up the stairs in front of me, with her graduation dress in its garment bag thrown too casually on top of it.

"You can't."

"This isn't even my secret and it's ruining my life! I'm telling him."

We argued our way into our room, where I closed the door behind us and rounded on her. I wanted to tell her that one boy wasn't her whole life, but who was I to talk? Instead, I said, "That's not fair."

"Yeah?" Amy hung her dress in the closet with enough force to remove the wrinkles she'd created on the way from the car. "Well, *life's* not fair! Heard that one?"

I stared at her. "You're kidding me, right?" My life was, as she knew, approaching its possible end.

"Shit." She looked at her feet and took a deep breath. "I'm sorry. But I *have* to tell him. I can't let it end like this."

"It's *not over* yet."

But one way or another, it was about to be.

"LAINEY, I'M SORRY," Ms. Kim said. "We have to wrap this up. I have a session with Amanda right now."

"Oh, this late, huh?" I closed my notebook and capped my pen. "I think we're all set anyway."

At our dorm meeting, Ms. Kim had told us it was her last year in Marquise and asked if anyone would help her organize an end-of-year-and-goodbye party. I volunteered. Distractions were key to my sanity while I waited for graduation, and Daniel Astor, to arrive.

Amy thought I was crazy, that I should be *doing things*—whatever they were—to prevent what was going to happen, but I didn't want to explain that I couldn't. I needed to confront him, and I needed it to be a surprise, *my* surprise. So I told her I *was* doing things—I was *living*, for as long as I had left.

As soon as I picked up my bag to pack my things away, a message came in on my phone.

change of plans. caleb txted to meet him @ yost after tutoring. sorry.

Amy was supposed to meet me at the bookstore before dinner. Ms. Kim was still talking while I read her text. "…need so much help if she spent less time flirting in class, but I understand it's hard for her."

Wait a minute. "I'm sorry. Did you say Amanda? Amanda Worthington?"

"Yes. I thought she was one of your dorm girls?"

"Yeah, she is," I replied, but it was automatic. I wasn't thinking about what I was saying; I was thinking about how Ms. Kim's room was in Yost. And she was on her way there right now, along with Caleb and Mandi Worthington. And Amy. There was *no way* that was a coincidence. "You know what? I'll walk with you. If you don't mind."

"Not at all. Did you want to talk to Amanda?"

"Something like that."

Something was up and I knew it couldn't be good. I texted back:

not a good idea

But Amy didn't reply.

I forced myself to keep the same slow pace as my companion on the way to the class building. My legs wanted to run, to arrive before anyone else and stop whatever was about to happen before it had the chance to become a disaster. That's the only thing that could be brewing right now: a disaster. But despite my urgency, I had the feeling I needed to stick by Ms. Kim.

It felt like forever, though, walking the paths from our dorm to the lower school building situated near the back of campus. This was probably why Ms. Kim was moving out of Marquise and into the faculty residences—her campus commute would be cut in half. I tried to listen while she talked but I could barely concentrate.

I didn't know what we were walking into, so I didn't know what to do. Should I stall? Try to hurry? I considered pretending to trip, or telling Ms. Kim I had to use the bathroom and picking up the pace, but I was afraid whatever I chose would be the *wrong* thing and would ruin my opportunity to prevent or fix whatever was waiting.

All my prevaricating meant we arrived at the perfect moment. By which I meant exactly the moment Mandi was hoping for. We came in by the west end of the building, and as we approached the hallway for Ms. Kim's room, I could hear voices ahead of us.

"Sounds like Miss Worthington's early! What a rare treat."

"Yeah," I replied, but I was trying to listen. The hall lights were off now, this long after class hours. It wasn't exactly dark, but gloomy inside, the emptiness of the building making the voices echo and grow.

"…so *nervous,* Cay."

"You'll be fine. It's just a practice essay." Caleb, no, *Cay's*—the endearment made me want to be sick—voice was light, comfortable. Mandi was sugar and sweetness. I pictured her touching him, leaning on his arm and looking up at him while they waited outside Ms. Kim's door.

"You could help me, you know."

He laughed. "I'm definitely not the guy to help with English."

"No, but you could just be the guy. For me."

We were almost there, almost rounding the corner into the humanities wing. There was a pause. Caleb paused. He was thinking about it, or what to say, and I nearly ran ahead. Next to me, Ms. Kim frowned. She must have recognized Caleb's voice.

"Mand…" he started. Stopped. There was rustling and I *knew* they were touching now.

"You could," she said again and it was a tease, an invitation, a bomb about to go off.

We came around the corner at the far end of the hall, but we could see them there, embracing, Caleb's face lowering, slowly toward the upturned, expectant one of Mandi Worthington.

From behind them came a shriek of, "What the *HELL?!*"

"Oh, dear," Ms. Kim said and we, finally, hurried forward.

Amy was much closer than we were, at the east end of the hall. She was coming from her service hours, at Admissions, instead of the dorm, so of course she'd have come in on that side of the building.

Caleb and Mandi broke apart, Caleb moving as if waking from a dream to discover he was on fire.

Amy's face was white with rage. "You kissed her!!"

Did he? I couldn't be sure. Whatever had happened, it was far closer than it should have been. Close enough to send Amy stalking forward with steps that tapped out *danger*.

"I…" Caleb looked as stricken as Mandi looked smug. Triumphant. Like this was the moment she lived for.

"It was hardly the first time," Mandi preened and I couldn't tell you if she was lying or not.

But it didn't matter if it was the truth, because Amy hauled off and slapped her regardless. The sharp crack reverberated down the hall.

Mandi stumbled back while, without a moment's hesitation, I grabbed Ms. Kim's arm and Thought.

This was the moment Mandi had choreographed, had spent months working hard to achieve. She was counting on the perfect witness: faculty advisor for the Honor Board. She was counting on Caleb's weakness and Amy's wrath. She was counting on the perfect timing, close enough to Amy's other problems for it to look really bad and not so close to the end of the year that it could be quietly brushed aside. She was counting on triumph.

Except she didn't count on me.

It was mere seconds, or pieces of seconds, while my Thought did its work. In that blink of time, Amy lunged for Mandi again and I was afraid I'd failed anyway. I still held Ms. Kim's arm as if in shock, but I didn't think I could stop her memory a second time.

But Caleb caught Amy, holding her arms as she struggled and Mandi didn't step nearly as far away as she should have. "Ame, no!"

Finally Ms. Kim shook her head as if to clear it and shouted, "Hey! Everyone separate! NOW!" She might have been tiny, but damn if she wasn't commanding.

Amy and Caleb turned toward us with comically matching expressions of surprise; neither of them had any idea we were here. Mandi, on the other hand, turned on the dramatics. Tears shimmered in her eyes because, no matter that she wanted it to happen, it *had* to have hurt.

"Ms. Kim! Oh, did you see! She hit me!"

Ms. Kim absently touched her forehead. "Calm down, Miss Worthington."

"But...She—she *hit* me!"

"Miss Worthington, enough!"

Through all this, Amy was still taking deep, audible breaths, but her anger didn't stop her brain from working. She glanced at Mandi, then between Ms. Kim and me, at my fingers slipping from the teacher's arm. Her eyes met mine and I knew she understood.

"How could I have?" Amy countered. "Caleb's holding me." And he was, despite that she'd stopped struggling. Up until Amy said his name, he'd been essentially frozen.

Slowly, he dropped his arms, though his eyes stayed just as wide. "I...I didn't...I'm sorry...Ame—"

In the close contest for who was most confused, Mandi might actually have been winning. She took halting steps towards us, her eyes shining with those unshed tears and also growing frustration as her plan mysteriously unraveled. "She hit me! Right here!" She touched the spot on her cheek that was admittedly red, but Ms. Kim no longer remembered why. "You *saw* it!" Her anger was bleeding away her evidence, and red was *not* a flattering color on her.

"I saw no such thing. Calm *down*, Miss Worthington."

"Caleb, tell her," Mandi pleaded. She took a step in his direction, momentarily turning her back to us. He wavered, like he might actually go to her, and I couldn't believe she'd risk using her gift on a non-Sententia in front of Ms. Kim.

Amy, who'd gone statue—cool and under control compared to Mandi's simpering—uncrossed her arms, saying, "Nuh-uh, baby." She touched his hand and, once again, the spell was broken.

Caleb shook his head, looking a bit dazed and exactly like he wanted to hide in a hole. Right after someone explained to him what the hell was happening. He said the truest thing ever said: "I have no idea what's going on here."

Ms. Kim made a sound like a whale, air escaping through her nose in an exasperated rush. "I empathize, Mr. Sullivan. Maybe Miss Young and I were just too far away to be sure what happened. Did *you* see Miss Moretti strike Miss Worthington?"

Caleb shook his head and I could see it—he knew. *Knew* something was happening outside the bounds of what he could understand, and that I had done it. But he knew the right answer too. "She couldn't have, right?" he lied. It was a subtle lie, but he couldn't look at Ms. Kim while he did it, so he looked at me instead.

Mandi, finally, looked at me too. "You BITCH! *What did you do? You did something! How?!* Caleb—" She tugged at his arm but he backed away from all of us. It was as if Amy and Mandi had switched places, Mandi's former smugness sliding comfortably onto Amy's face while Mandi herself went from red to blotchy and shook with fury.

Shouting obscenities at another student wouldn't get you probation, but it would sure get you detention. "I said *enough,* Miss Worthington," Ms. Kim commanded. "Take your things and leave now while I file your detention slip. I'll see you in class tomorrow, and again after last hour to discuss this."

Mandi was crying now. Great, big, angry drops falling with plunks on her cheeks and to the floor. "I'm telling my father about this and Senator Astor!"

"See that you do. Good bye, Miss Worthington."

She ran from us, tears and blond hair flying behind her. At the end of the hall, she turned back just long enough to give me a final glare.

Ms. Kim didn't realize her threat was meant for me. And Mandi didn't realize that, at this point, it was too late. What she told anyone no longer mattered.

Amy and Caleb were alternately staring at each other and glancing in our direction. Ms. Kim rubbed her forehead again and took a deep breath in and out while I held mine. This was a teetering moment, and it could go either way. Amy was standing on a very fine line, and even though I'd managed to erase the worst of what she'd done, she could still be in trouble.

And if it was anyone other than Ms. Kim, she probably would have been. Finally, she said, "And Miss Moretti, I'm going to give you a break. You might not have struck Miss Worthington, but you did try. You'll owe me some service hours, but I won't submit your slip. And I won't be lenient if *anything* happens again." In softer tones, she added, "I want to see one of my girls at the podium at graduation, and despite a few frustrations lately, I think you deserve to be there."

"Th...thanks," Amy stammered. "Thank you. I'm sorry, Ms. Kim. Really."

"Well, Miss Young, I think that's enough dramatics for me today. I have a splitting headache." She opened the door to her classroom but stared down the hall where Mandi had disappeared. "Please make sure we don't end up with another emergency meeting."

"I will."

"Okay, everybody." She waved her hand in dismissal. "Disperse."

We turned to go, murmuring goodbyes and apologies, while Ms. Kim closed the door between us.

As soon as the three of us were around the corner Amy burst into tears, and Caleb, still wide-eyed and dazed, said, "What just happened? What in the fuck just *happened?*"

I, on the other hand, breathed a huge sigh of relief. At least *one* crisis was averted. It was a little messy, but totally salvageable. I counted it as a win. Now, just a few weeks and one more crisis to go. I only hoped my next one turned out as well.

I put my arms around both of them and led them away. "C'mon, guys. We've got a lot to talk about."

Chapter Twenty-Four

The day I was meant to die turned out to be beautiful. A perfect spring day of bright blue skies decorated with a handful of clouds, warm enough for short sleeves but not hot. It was the kind of day people lived for, that didn't feel like anything *bad* could happen. It was just too nice. After a long, gray New England winter, summer felt like a possibility again—not long now. For most of us, a lengthy summer of freedom was just a day away. Graduation. Tomorrow.

More than half the students were already gone, packed up and moved out as soon as their last final was over. Campus had been ringing with goodbyes and the crunch of car tires on gravel paths for days. Those of us left had plenty to occupy our time, with award nights and pictures, field trips and guests, and, of course, packing of our own. It was amazing how much stuff even I'd accumulated in just two years here.

This afternoon was the Northbrook Family Picnic, and tonight, the Senior Bonfire. From my window, I could already see them setting up for both. I was supposed to die before either of them. Though I'd been fairly certain my death was scheduled for *around* graduation, I hadn't been sure of the exact day until two days ago. That's when Carter had said, "Hey, let's go to the range on my morning off. One last time," and I'd agreed.

I knew we had to go there eventually, because that's where he was going to kill me.

At this point, I'd done everything I could. My family was already here, not wanting to miss the picnic today and other events. Not just Aunt Tessa and Uncle Martin, either. My grandparents—Aunt Tessa's parents—and her brother, my uncle, too, had come for something as big as my graduation, giving me a chance to hug them all and tell them I loved them at least one more time.

I'd added a few more great times with Amy and Caleb and our other friends to my memories. Amy knew what might be coming, but she hid it well, determined as I was to enjoy the end of our high school careers and believing without question my promise that I'd be okay. Every night before bed she'd ask me if she'd see me tomorrow and I always said yes. I'd had goodbyes with everyone who'd left, and had signed yearbooks with everyone else. My things were almost all packed and my life was, as much as it had ever been, in order.

I wasn't *ready,* but I was prepared.

WE TOOK MY car—my *new* car, since the old one had been totaled—because I just wanted to drive once more while I had the chance. I insisted on stopping at Dad's for breakfast, driving by the lake where we'd spent so many afternoons over the summer, and basically taking as much time as I thought we could afford. What would happen would happen whenever we got there. I hoped I kept the senator waiting.

Technically he wasn't scheduled to arrive until this evening, and officially I was sure he wouldn't. No one but me knew he was already here, somewhere. I even knew what he'd be wearing. In fact, I'd known what Carter would wear today, too, before I'd seen him, which was strange and disconcerting. I kept glancing at him with a weird sense of déjà vu.

For my own part, I'd intentionally picked out something different from what I'd predicted myself to be in. It was both a measure of control and a test. The first thing I'd done when I saw Carter this morning was re-check the vision. It reflected my change in attire.

My murder was still right on schedule.

Carter. He was the hardest part of the plan. As I pulled into the gun club's parking lot, I watched him out of the corner of my eye. His beautiful face was open, completely unaware, and totally relaxed. He tapped his fingers on the dash in time with the radio and then flexed his wrists back and forth, in anticipation of shooting. He caught me looking and smiled.

Not for the first time I considered simply turning around. Not going in. Saving us both from what was inside. I'd thought about it countless times before but the vision had never changed. And I knew why too. I'd *thought* about not showing up, but never actually believed I wouldn't come. If I didn't go through with this, it didn't mean I wouldn't die; it meant I might not be able to change it.

This was my best chance.

I was so sorry for what might happen, for Carter's part in it, but I had to believe he'd understand. He'd want me to take the chance, to do whatever I could to save myself. He'd said as much once before and I hoped it was true.

The slamming of our car doors was loud to me, a very final kind of sound not unlike a gunshot. I ran my fingers across the car's hood as my private goodbye while Carter picked up our gear bags, throwing them both over one shoulder. We fell in step next to each other as we headed toward the building. But before we went inside, before I never had the chance again, there was something I needed to say.

"Carter?"

I grabbed his hand so he'd stop and then tugged on it to make him come closer. I stepped right up to him, until we were touching, and he set down our bags to slip his arms around my waist. Perfect.

"What's up?"

"I have something to tell you."

He frowned and I forced myself to laugh, to lighten the seriousness I hadn't been able to keep from my voice. To make him think I was playing.

I leaned in close and whispered, "I love you."

With a grin, he bent to kiss me, just a light touch of his lips to mine. "Oh, yeah?"

"I'll *always* love you. You'll never forget that, right?"

He still thought I was playing. "Hm. I don't know. You'd better kiss me again to be sure."

So I did. There, in a parking lot in New Hampshire, I kissed him for all I was worth. I didn't care who saw. In fact, I hoped *everyone* saw this girl who loved this boy more than anyone had a right to, beyond reason and maybe even sanity, and they'd remember too.

When we finally pulled apart, Carter laughed. It was deep and filled with joy, and if it was the last sound I ever heard, I knew I'd be content. "That was pretty convincing." Grabbing our bags in one hand, he threw his other arm around my shoulder and led me toward the building, still smiling. "But you know," he added casually, "if you *really* want me to remember, all you have to do is write it down."

MY FIRST ROUND was terrible and the second wasn't much better. For pretty valid reasons, I couldn't concentrate. The private range was too quiet and too loud at the same time. The whir of the motorized target track wound into my skull and vibrated in time with my nerves. The muted thumps of each shot seemed like explosions, reverberating through my arms and causing stars to bloom behind my eyes. My pulse pounded just as loudly and my fingers shook, on the trigger and even worse when I stopped to reload.

I tried and failed not to look at the two-way mirror, hoping to see a shadow or hear a noise, any indication that the moment was near. Was Senator Astor there already? Had he been watching the entire time? There was a door into the observation room from our room, but there was a separate entrance into it from the club. He could come and go without our even knowing.

I became convinced the anticipation would kill me before anyone else had the chance.

Every time Carter spoke or moved even slightly in my direction, I flinched. And he noticed, both my crappy shooting and my tension. His rounds took about a third of the time of mine. He'd shoot, watch me finish, and then we'd reload together.

At the end of my third round, Carter joked, "Need help?" His voice was flirty and cute, and extra loud because he was still wearing sound gear, but I couldn't even smile. He reached up to pull back his ear protection. "Hey," he said. "Babe, relax."

Instead, I held my breath. He stepped away from his partition.

But it wasn't right. I realized his ear guards were still half on his head, only one ear exposed so he could hear me. In the vision, they weren't there. Were they? I began to forget the details or worry that they'd changed.

"Lainey," he coaxed, "just relax." He took another step, as if to come over to me, but instead turned to pick up his water bottle and take a drink. "It's hard right now, but you'll get the strength back. You're just out of practice."

I nodded, not trusting my voice. Of course he had no idea why I was so on edge.

"*Relax,*" he repeated, adding a smile—one more beautiful, genuine smile—that punched its way into my heart. No matter what happened,

I'd have that. I savored the image, letting it burn itself into my memory.

And that was when I made my mistake.

For a few seconds, my thoughts slipped from what I was doing, turned from what was going to happen to the last beautiful curve of Carter's lips. In the middle of my reloading, I fumbled. A bullet slipped from my grip and tumbled to the floor with a soft, pretty *plink*. Automatically, I bent to retrieve it.

Before I even stood, the sound of a round chambering echoed through the small space. I straightened to find Carter facing me and my vision complete.

The gun fired and I fell to the ground.

Chapter Twenty-Five

ove to the ground was probably a more accurate description of what I did.

I couldn't tell you which happened first, Carter pulling the trigger or me diving toward his feet, but I swear I'd never heard a sound louder than that gunshot. Even the air reverberated with it, shaking around me as my body slammed into the cool rubber floor and skidded toward my attacker.

The whistle of the bullet was the very noise of death, softly screaming just past my head, straight through the space where my heart had beat a second before, and into the wall of the shooting lane with a sickening thunk. A lock of hair, sheared from my pony tail, floated to the ground in front of me.

Propelling myself *toward* the gun was dangerous. *Crazy.* But backwards or sideways wouldn't have put me any closer to this: Carter, staring at the scene in front of him with mute horror. From my prone position, he was just a stretch away.

And if I didn't die trying, I *had* to get to him before his memories of what happened took any deeper a hold.

Or Daniel Astor tried again.

Carter was already in shock, eyes wide and glazed, and arms hanging at his sides. Just like in my vision, his ear guards were around his neck, and his cheeks were flushed. The gun dangled next to him, pointed at the floor, at *me*. I desperately reached my arm toward him before he could take another shot.

Finally, my fingers brushed skin, found purchase at his ankle, and I didn't hesitate. I Thought.

Even I was surprised by what happened next.

Carter looked down in confusion, as startled by my gentle touch as everything else. And then he collapsed to the ground, unconscious.

A GRIM DIVINER'S visions are interesting things. They're not movies. They're moments. Just moments, the series of which show you a death's *story* but not the entire picture. So I hadn't known exactly how I'd react to the moment of *my* death, how it would play out at all, until it happened. I'd reacted, not predicted, which is probably the only reason I was still alive. If I'd known any more, my own thoughts would surely have changed the future—and my vision—entirely. In which case, I'd probably be lying on the floor, bleeding to death in Carter's arms.

Instead, I was sitting on the floor, Carter's unconscious body cradled in *my* arms, when Daniel Astor stepped out of the observation room and quietly closed the door behind him.

He bent to retrieve Carter's gun from where it had landed, after skidding across the room to the base of the mirrored wall. I cursed my stupid self for not retrieving it. At the same time, I noticed the senator was wearing gloves, deep black expensive leather ones that fit and moved like second skin. My own gun was useless, half-loaded and unprepared, on the shelf in the booth above my head.

"I'd like to say that was incredibly lucky, but I'm sure there was no luck involved," he mused. "I must have underestimated your abilities."

While he spoke, he checked the gun with practiced hands, and finding it satisfactory, trained it on me.

I stared at him for a while, working through my emotions—anger, terror, disgust—and getting my breathing under control. My heart still pounded, painful beats crashing somewhere close to my throat, and I was afraid I might throw up. Here he was, my own personal villain, but it was difficult to see him that way. He looked like he did any other day, handsome and business casual, in a blue button-down and slacks.

He looked, I thought, like my father.

And he *was* my uncle. Maybe, if things had been different, this weekend I'd have told him. *You really are* my *Uncle Dan.*

He also, aside from the gun, wasn't behaving in typical villain fashion, whatever that was. Movies were my only villain education, but the senator wasn't sneering or ranting or recklessly brandishing his weapon while I devised a clever escape. In fact, he was calm and collected, as if we were just having a friendly chat, and I had no idea how I was going to get out of this. Finally I felt like I could speak without my voice shaking.

"You did underestimate me," I replied. "But I was still lucky."

He smiled his charming smile. "Perhaps. The more interesting question though is what have you done to my nephew? He's still breathing, so obviously you didn't kill him."

"I…" I started and then stopped. What the hell was I doing? I was about to tell the villain *my* secrets, which is the opposite of what I was supposed to do.

But what *was* I supposed to do? I was still pretty sure he was going to kill me, and besides, if he wanted to, he could use his own abilities to get me to tell him anyway. I was surprised he hadn't yet. Or maybe he had and I just didn't recognize it. Either way, I went on.

"I didn't kill him. I'd *never,*" I breathed. "I killed his memory of what just happened. It knocked him unconscious."

The unconscious part was unexpected. That hadn't happened before. Not with Ms. Kim and not with Amy. We'd practiced a dozen different times, Amy and I, and she admitted to a wicked headache after the fact, but the Thought had never knocked her out. My guess was that, in the same way I used to pass out all the time from resisting my gift, before I knew about the Sententia, Carter's brain had shut down in defense of the trauma.

Or, as I watched Senator Astor's eyes widen in disbelief, along with what I thought might have been a hint of delight, I realized maybe it was something else. Carter's memory had already *been* tampered with, and I had doubled the effect.

Softly Dan said, "Is that possibly true?"

I nodded. "You *really* underestimated me." I couldn't help but taunt him a little, even if it was stupid.

"It won't happen again. To be sure, it won't happen again." I was afraid that was the final threat, that he was going to kill me now, but instead he went on. "How?"

"I'm a Thought Mover, remember? You and Carter have been telling me that all along. I can kill thoughts too. Memories, after they happen but before they take hold. It's the opposite of what you do, when you plant a seed of forgetting."

"Why didn't Carter tell me you could do that?"

"He doesn't know."

"Interesting." He tapped the fingers of one hand on his leg absently, while the other kept the gun pointed steadily in our direction. "It appears you're keeping many secrets in that lovely head of yours."

"A few." As hard as it had been to keep things from Carter, anything he knew, his uncle eventually would too. Knowing what I did now, I suspected Carter developed his habit of telling Dan everything through Dan's unspoken encouragement. What I didn't understand was: why hadn't he just compelled the information from *me*?

"Share another with me then," he said. "Why aren't you surprised to see me?"

"I knew you'd be here somewhere."

"You foresaw that? Incredible."

I shrugged. "Why don't you share a secret with me too. Why do you want to kill me?"

He studied me for a long moment, and I shifted uncomfortably under his gaze and Carter's weight. I had no idea when Carter would wake up, but I hoped it wasn't soon. More than anything, I didn't want him to witness what was about to happen. I also hoped he didn't need immediate medical care. His breathing and heartbeat seemed regular, but I was unsure about the combined effects of *two* Thought Movers.

"I don't," Senator Astor finally replied. "Not really. You'd be a valuable asset, even more than I realized. The offer still stands for you to join us...though somehow, I don't think you will." I shook my head. "See, I knew that. And you're not the only asset I'd like to acquire. You're holding another one in front of you like a shield right now."

My fear for Carter increased tenfold. "What do you want with him?! How can you think of him as...as an *object* like that?"

"You're so young, Lainey," the senator said, leaning casually onto the wall next to him, though his gun hand remained poised. Not that I was going anywhere. "When you're older, and you understand ambition, you'll understand how people, even people you love, can be tools you can use to further your purposes." He paused and tilted his head. "Yes, I love Cartwright. Of course I do. He's my only nephew. You look as if you don't believe me, but it's true."

Even with his assurances, I still didn't believe him. I didn't think he was capable of love. No one who knew how to love could do the horrible things I knew he'd done. *This,* I thought. *This* is what happens when you want things and take them, no matter what.

I stared back at him before saying softly, "I guess you didn't love him enough to spare his father."

If I was hoping to take Senator Astor by surprise with that comment, I failed. He didn't even blink. In fact, he gave a small smile, which made my already nervous stomach clench even further in revulsion. "Your abilities must be truly astounding. But you don't understand much about *living* people. You're wrong. I did spare his father. From an already miserable existence, and from himself. And it's because I love Carter as if he were *my* own son that I did what had to be done. I spared Carter from the burden of a father who'd never get over the death of his wife nor amount to anything more than a simple bookseller—"

"That's it?!" I shouted at him. "You killed him because he was depressed? Because he wasn't *special* enough?" It made me sick to say it out loud. Tears began a slow path down my cheeks and I took one hand from where it had been gripping Carter's to swipe them away.

To my astonishment, Dan looked sad. "Of course not. You didn't let me finish. He insisted we had to tell the Council about his son's newly developed ability. He wasn't just afraid for him; he was afraid *of* him. I spared Carter from the father who'd *turn him in.*" The curious look returned to his face. "You really think I'd harm someone just because I could?"

"I think you'd do anything just because you could."

He laughed. "There is so much you don't understand yet. I only wish I could convince you to work with me, but I've known since Carter told me you've chosen Boston that it's not what you want."

"So that's why you want to kill me? Because you know I'll never work for the Perceptum? Or for you? But I'll never be able to do anything to…to…I don't know, *interfere* with you either." As my hysteria mounted, my breathing grew ragged and harsh, but Senator Astor remained as collected as ever. I understood why he was such an accomplished politician.

"But you *are* interfering. You'd be an incredible addition to the Perceptum, one we've been missing for far too long, but now you're a liability. A danger. If necessary, the Perceptum could be brought to a vote to eliminate you. I'm certain it would pass. But my nephew..." His eyes passed over Carter's slack body, and I tightened my arms around him in response. "Carter would never recover if the Council did that. He'd never work with the Council again. And with his devotion to you as it is, I don't believe he'll come work for *me* either, not now, when I need him most. He'd follow you to the ends of the Earth first. Your tragic accident will eliminate that problem, and give him a reason to need an escape from his comfortable life here at the Academy. For what it's worth, I'm sorry Lainey. But this is how it will have to be." He stood straight once again and gestured with the gun. "Stand please. Move away from Carter. Over to where you were."

I was crying in earnest now, but I did what I was told. If he was going to shoot me, I couldn't bear the idea that Carter might be in the way. I also wasn't opposed to begging. "Please don't do this," I pleaded. I stopped short of promising to help him. That I couldn't do, but I had one more desperate card I was willing to play. "Carter's going to figure out that you always seem to be there when he loses someone he loves. Or Melinda will see the pattern. It will change you, too, you know, if you shoot me. Any other Grim Diviner will be able to see what you are—a *murderer.*"

"I don't think anyone's gift will save you," he said, shaking his head. "And I don't plan to be here for long, nor officially arrive until long after your accident is discovered. But you know that. Now, tell me one more thing. I promise this will be quick and painless."

"Okay." Honestly, I was going to die. What was the point in being stubborn?

"How are you resisting me?"

That confused me. "I'm not." And I wasn't. I looked around. I was standing where he'd gestured, defenseless and waiting for him to take aim at me. I wasn't doing anything besides praying to God or whoever was out there that I still might live, somehow.

"You are," he insisted. "I've tried countless times to *Move* your thoughts with no effect. Can you use your gift to stop thoughts of your own, like you did on Carter?"

"No." I knew without a doubt I couldn't use my own gifts on myself. How many times had I tried to bring up a vision to clarify my impending death? It never worked.

He looked at me hard, an angry twist to his mouth. I flinched, ready to duck, or leap over the counter behind me—anything to keep from being shot. But instead of shooting me, he said, "I think you're telling the truth."

"I am. I don't know how I'm resisting you. That's the truth. Whatever it is, I'm not doing it intentionally."

"You truly are exceptional, Lainey. I'm sorry to lose you." The scholar in him came out. "It happens sometimes," he mused, "that some Sententia are naturally resistant to others' gifts. My father is the only other person I've known who could…" A shocked expression came over his face, and I knew he'd figured out my other secret. And I finally understood why he hadn't used his gift on me. He really couldn't. Because we were family. He actually faltered, his gun arm drooping an inch as he stared at me.

"Who are you?" he said, slowly and carefully enunciating each word.

I couldn't look at him, I hated what I had to say so much now. "I'm your niece," I whispered, staring down at the floor. I looked back up at him. "Now will you please not kill me?"

"How." That was all he said. It came out like a command, not a question.

"My father was your brother. Half-brother. Your father must have been his father."

"My father…" he started, then trailed off. "How do you know this?" he demanded.

"You look just like him. My dad, I mean. No one knows, officially, who his father was—he was adopted—but it's pretty obvious now."

Dan was looking in my direction but his eyes were blank, as if he wasn't really seeing what was around him anymore. I contemplated running for the door—it was only a few steps—but before I could move, his focus snapped back to me and the gun returned to position. "Your eyes," he said, and I knew what he meant. Though our likeness wasn't striking, I'd inherited most notably the *shape* of my father's eyes. Same as Daniel Astor's. "The last Marwood is my niece," he went on. "My niece. God, it makes so much sense now, Tessa's comments about resemblance. My nephew is in love with my niece, and I am about to…" he trailed off again. "Of all your considerable secrets, *that* is the one you were going to take to your grave? Why wouldn't you have told me?"

"I hate everything about you. I didn't want you to know. And I thought you'd just get me to tell you anyway, but I guess you can't."

"No, I can't," he mused, and I swear to you, tears shimmered in his eyes. "You have no idea how much I regret that. I was wrong before. You are beyond exceptional, Lainey. *You're* my heir. And now…"

And that was when Carter moved.

It was just a small movement, along with a sound, like a tiny grunt, but it was enough to save me. I froze. Dan froze.

I think he could still have done it, if he really wanted to. Carter's breathing had changed, become stronger the way a person's sometimes does when they're about to wake up from a bad dream, but for the moment he was still unconscious.

And of course, the bad dream was standing in front of me. I braced myself, but my uncle didn't shoot. Instead, he stared at me, considering. With matching eyes, I stared back.

"Perhaps," Dan said, "a third option has presented itself." He told me what he wanted me to do, knowing I would do it. When the other choice was death, what choice did I really have?

Though something inside me broke, I nodded, whispering, "Okay."

Dan inclined his head. "Thank you," he said and that was that. He turned to go.

"Wait!"

He stopped, and I could see the hopefulness in the way he stood, in the way his eyes shined when he looked back at me.

"Tell me. What he was meant to remember."

With a rueful smile, he did. It was a good story. Perfect, in fact. No one would have questioned it.

When he finished, Senator Astor placed the gun back where it had fallen and left out the same door by which he'd entered. It closed just as quietly as when he'd arrived.

I crumpled to my knees and sobbed until Carter woke up.

Chapter Twenty-Six

A fog.

That's what the rest of that day, and the next day, and possibly the rest of my life felt like. I was present. I smiled and spoke when spoken to. I took pictures and gave hugs and even, occasionally, laughed. But it was through a wall of gray that I did it all, behind which the real me watched my world fall apart and keep going all at the same time.

I honestly wasn't sure how I survived those days. Maybe all of me didn't. I'd cheated death once only to die slowly in a different way. Little pieces of the girl in the fog disintegrated, until I thought all I would ever be again was an appearance. A pretty outward shell filled with cold, gray nothing. What happened at the shooting range began to seem easy.

On the floor of the private gallery, I told Carter a story. A simple, perfect story that was almost true. I'm so clumsy, I told him. I dropped a bullet. It rolled away. You stepped backwards on it and fell. You hit your head. I was so scared.

I didn't tell him I'd nearly died. I didn't have to. He'd never know. He had no memory of what really happened. In my pocket, I'd hastily stuffed the piece of my hair he'd never know was gone. There was a new bullet hole in the range wall, but it was far from the first. No one would think anything of it, including Carter. He had no recollection of the single round he'd saved and fired at me.

It wasn't until much later I realized the gun Senator Astor had threatened me with was empty.

GRADUATION WAS BITTERSWEET. Unlike the sheer perfection of the day before, it was cloudy. Overcast, but not raining, and not hot as I sat near the end of the last row of the sea of polyester gowns on the soccer field. Even Northbrook couldn't improve graduation-wear, though I supposed the slick, shiny robes were a rite of passage and one I was distantly thrilled to pass. They were white, all of them white, like a hundred excited ghosts fidgeting in folding chairs.

Outward me cheered when they announced the Valedictorian and Amy took the stage. For the first time since almost the beginning of the year, she looked like herself. The real Amy. From his spot in front of me, I could see Caleb looking up at the girl he knew he loved without any unnatural influence. A few life-altering secrets went a long way toward smoothing things out between them. Inward me suppressed a pang of envy.

Amy's speech was everything I knew her to be: funny, intelligent, impassioned.

"Learning," she said. "We did a lot of that here. A *lot*. Right?" We all cheered, or booed, or whistled. "And it was good for us! We're wicked smart kids and we're going to do great things." She pronounced *wicked smaht* with her best Boston accent and everyone laughed. "I know we are, because Northbrook prepared us to. From up here, I'm looking at future doctors, and business owners, scientists and teachers. There's at least one future international rock star, and probably a few congresswomen and senators. I *might* even be looking at a future President of the United States"—cheers for the surprise guest, Senator Astor—"or maybe even two. How many people are lucky enough to say they sat next to a senator in detention? Well, at least one hundred and thirty two of you. Not that *I've* ever been in detention, of course.

"Do that thing," she instructed us, "that we're all going to do again in a few weeks, at orientation or basic training or any of the opportunities you're about to start. Look at the person to your left and right. In college, they're going to tell you one of those people won't be there in four years. It's supposed to scare you into working hard. But you know what? *Both* of those people you just looked at are *graduating right now,* and if we made it through here, we've got *nothing* to worry about next! We'll be out *kicking ass* in our new lives!

"I know you're all as eager as I am to get to that, but before we go, let's take a few minutes to be *sentimental.* All the studying we've done? That's no secret. But between all the learning, there's *more.* No one talks about it, and you may not realize, but you've been immersed in it the entire time you were here. Sure, up front, Northbrook's taught us what it takes to work hard and *learn.* We've got that. We could go pro at learning tomorrow. Straight from high school to the big leagues. But it took me six years to realize Northbrook was also doing one other thing."

Her dramatic pause, her whole last section, raised eyebrows, brought murmurs, would probably still get me in trouble somehow, and all around made me want to strangle her…but I couldn't deny, it was all Amy.

"Teaching us how to *live,"* she concluded.

"How to find our own way to dinner on time or not eat at all. How to do our own laundry, or, you know, at least how to schedule a laundry service. How to live with another person who doesn't have to like you because you're not related, or because you're different.

"How service to school and community is as important as grades.

"How to make decisions and live with the consequences.

"Northbrook has taught us how to use not only the powers of our minds but, also, the powers of our hearts and our wills. How to be leaders *and* collaborators, to be strong and independent and smart. Northbrook gave us friends, and loves, and occasional rivals, plus the strength of character to deal with them all. And finally, Northbrook gave us *futures*.

"Starting tomorrow, it's the future and it's going to be awesome. I'll see you all there."

Amy waved to us as she stepped from the podium, a goodbye to high school or hello to the future it was hard to say which, while the entire crowd erupted in ovation.

I wouldn't have wanted to follow that speech, and probably anyone else would have seemed boring in comparison. Except for Daniel Astor. He hadn't told me, but I knew what he was going to say in his speech. Pretty much everyone in the audience knew, even if Amy hadn't hinted at it. The media and television crews lined up along the back of the crowd knew too.

I tried not to watch or care, not even to listen. This speech hadn't been intended for my ears anyway. I tried to imagine it with the heartfelt memorial to me that would have led it off, if I hadn't been unexpectedly sitting in the audience. But even I, who had knowledge and reason more than anyone to hate the man striding up to the podium through a chorus of cheers and shouts, couldn't help myself. Inevitably, I was drawn in by his charisma and the visage of my father.

"From one sentimental to another," he began, and the whole crowd laughed, half because they were in on the joke and half because they weren't, "that was a hell of a speech…"

He had everyone rapt from the first words, and not for the first time, I wondered why he needed to resort to manipulations. And *mur-*

der. People would follow him anywhere just to see him smile and hear his smooth voice tell them what to do. Was it simply in the blood? Had my father inherited the same temptations? Had *I?* The ease and lack of guilt with which I'd changed Ms. Kim's memory suggested I had. Maybe I was more the man at the podium's heir than I wanted to admit.

Eventually, as the words clicked into place in my head, I realized his speech *was* for me. It was a reminder of what, in his eyes, I was failing to do, and also, what I'd *promised* to do. "As Miss Moretti so aptly described, for the last years here you've been practicing *living.* The next step, the one Northbrook has prepared you for, is living *up to your potential.* There's an enormous, possibly unfair amount of potential sitting before me, and the hope of everyone here is to see it fully realized. Recognize your potential, friends, and embrace it. You are here, so you are ready.

"You are also, as difficult as it may be, ready to leave Northbrook. Having been a student myself, I know how special your time at the Academy has been, how important are the relationships you've cultivated and the growth you've shown toward the men and women you find yourselves becoming. Some of those relationships will stay with you for a lifetime, others, though no less important, will likely end today. The important thing to remember is you're not leaving behind; you're *moving on.* It's time to fulfill your potential, or better yet, your *promise.* Your promising futures are just steps away. Take those steps. Don't be afraid.

"In fact, we'll take them together. Today is the day both you and I have looked forward to and from which there's no looking back."

It was then that he paused, and as if choreographed, planned down to the second and paid for, the sun broke through the clouds for the first time all day. It lit his hair to glowing gold and you'd have thought the universe was in tune with him, blessing his announcement. He glanced up at the new light and smiled unrestrainedly, delighted by the unexpected witness to his final words.

"So, friends, the answer is yes, the rumors are true—I am proud today to officially announce my candidacy for President of the United States, and even more proud to do it here, at my alma mater, in front of my *family,* and surrounded by our country's best and brightest future leaders. Thank you Northbrook, for your support, for the brilliant array of potential you've readied for the world, including the young men and women before me now, and for making me the man ready to lead our country into its brilliant future.

"The path is not promised to be easy, but join me, graduates, in finding the way."

If I thought Amy's ovation was loud, Senator Astor's was deafening, fueled by the shouts and questions from the media, all of which were met with a curt explanation that a full press conference would follow the ceremony. Then and only then would he speak to anyone but the graduates and their families. With that, one by one, we were called to the stage to shake hands with the future President.

It took a long time for my turn. Long enough for me to practice my yoga breathing and blank my mind. Outward me was ready to climb the steps, smile, and receive my diploma. I watched all my friends go first, and my not-friends too. Alexis crossed the stage like it was a catwalk, or her own personal red carpet, rolled out for her future. Her poise never faltered, and the crowd even cheered when Senator Astor kissed her on the cheek.

When my time finally came, the cheers from my family and Carter were as loud as those for students with far larger contingents of supporters. They were almost loud enough to drown out my thoughts and the comments from the senator and the headmaster.

"Congratulations, Miss Young," Dr. Stewart said, handing me my little black folder and holding it for a moment before sending me on.

"That was an interesting speech by Miss Moretti, didn't you think?" Sure I was blushing, I agreed. Clearly the headmaster knew I'd told at least some of our secret when I shouldn't have. "I've always wished she was one of us, you know. I was," she continued, "sorry to hear your decision as well. I'd hoped you'd join us."

I looked her in the eye when I replied. "It's the best choice for me. But I *am* sorry to disappoint you, headmaster. You know I mean it."

"Yes I do, Elaine." Her fingers released the diploma and I was free. "And I still think you'll be great."

Everyone had exchanged a few words with Dr. Stewart. Our conversation wasn't unusual, since there weren't that many of us and it was a close community. I was the only person who hugged her though.

"Thank you. For everything." She was so slim, my arms might have fit around her twice, but she was less stiff than I expected and she didn't rebuff me immediately.

She even patted my back, once, with a firm hand, "All right. Move along, Elaine. And you're welcome."

Past her, waiting with a smile, was Daniel Astor. I'd purposefully not been looking at him, but I had no choice except to stop. To take his extended hand and turn to the camera, baring my own teeth in an approximation of the expression on the senator's face. For one second, just one, I thought about how my bare fingers were touching his skin.

The flash dazzled after the mostly gray afternoon and I was still clearing my vision when Dan said, "No hug for your uncle?"

"No," I said through my teeth. I had to keep up the image of the smile. He put his arm around my shoulder anyway, and I couldn't stop him, not with everyone watching. I was surprised my skin didn't burn through my gown where the hand of the devil touched me.

He turned us slightly so we were facing the crowd. "You can still change your mind, you know. Come work for me. It'll be so simple,

Lainey." In the stands, he picked out Carter, my family next to him, and waved. They cheered again, along with more people around them. "You can have everything you want."

"It would all be a lie."

Dan glanced down at me. "You think how my nephew feels about you is a lie?"

I shook my head and though tears threatened, I didn't let them fall. "No," I repeated. "But the rest of my life would be."

"Then I'm sorry again." The next graduate was actually waiting now, forced to confer with Dr. Stewart while Dan and I spoke for what I hoped was the last time. "For both of you."

"I *hate* you," I hissed, still fake-smiling. "Stay away from my family." I finally looked him in the eye.

His smile never faltered. "Congratulations, Miss Young," he said, louder, a cue to the next in line that we were finishing up. "We'll miss you."

"CONGRATULATIONS!" CARTER ENVELOPED me as soon as the graduates and their families all met on the field, swinging me in a circle so my white robe billowed out behind us. As he set me down, he kissed me, for what he didn't know would be the last time. I lingered there, just for a moment, before turning away.

"My grandparents are watching," I murmured and he grinned a little wickedly.

"Then you shouldn't have kissed me back."

My aunt's turn was next. She couldn't pick me up, so she threw her arms around me and dragged us in a circle, imitating what Carter had just done. "I'm so proud of you, Lainey! So proud." She'd say it about a thousand times more throughout the night.

I hugged everyone, and I mean *everyone*. My family first, of course, but then the field became an impromptu festival of love, covered with shouting, laughing, and some crying. I found myself dragged from group to group, taking pictures, meeting people's families, and just generally being together, as seniors, for one last time. For a few minutes, I even had fun. I *would* miss Northbrook, for so many reasons. More than maybe anyone, I was sorry to say goodbye.

Later, after dinner while we finished coffees and they cleared away the remains of the graduation cake Melinda had arranged, Carter said, "I wish my uncle was here." It was a private comment, not meant for the whole table, since his Uncle Jeff *was* there, down at the end, talking to my Uncle Tommy. We were at the same restaurant we'd dined with Senator Astor, forever ago at the beginning of the year, when I'd thought everything was different.

Next to me, Aunt Tessa chuckled. "I think he's a little busy tonight. Even for this."

"What'd he say to you, on stage? You looked…" Carter trailed off, and I wondered what I *had* looked like.

"He said he wished I'd chosen Baltimore." Which is when, surrounded by my family and the boy whose heart I was about to break, I burst into tears. Conversation ceased and the sound of easy chatter was replaced by my weeping. We weren't alone in the restaurant, either. Other families and friends looked on as I, finally, broke down.

"Oh, honey." My aunt put her arm around my waist and led me from the table. "I think it's probably time to go." Carter, standing and looking bewildered, clearly wanted to follow, and Amy too—from the Morettis' and Sullivans' large table near ours, I caught a glimpse of her watching with concern—but Aunt Tessa waved them away. Thank God for her mother's intuition or whatever it was.

Outside, settled in the comfort and quiet of her rental car, my aunt said, "I bet everyone's inside fighting over who's going to pay the check."

Through my sniffles, I gave a little smile. "That's fine, because I already did it."

"What! You did not, young lady. *I* paid it."

We locked eyes and I shook my head. My smile grew to full size as I told her, "You only *thought* you did because I told them to let you. I arranged everything last week."

"Elaine Rachel! You sneaky brat!" Her own smile gleamed in the growing darkness. The clouds that had started to give way during the ceremony had grown even thinner, showing patches of deepening blue sky and a hint of stars. "Abuelo will be disappointed. And Martin. They've been looking forward to this argument for years."

"I bet they never thought I'd be graduating from a place like this."

"No…but you loved it here, huh?" I nodded, though the question was surely rhetorical. "Not many eighteen year old graduates out there arranging to pay for their own dinners."

"I think I'm not like many graduates." I turned to look out the window, counting the cars of people I knew.

Aunt Tessa reached over to take my hand. "No, sweetheart. You're definitely not." After a quiet pause, she said, "Do *you* wish you'd made a different choice?"

I took a deep breath and held it before I answered. Did I? What a difficult question. My heart was screaming, *yes, you idiot!* But my heart wasn't all of me. A different choice would have meant sacrificing a piece of my *soul.* So, "No, I don't. Do you?"

She opened her mouth, probably to deny it, but hesitated. "I can't say I didn't want you to come home. But even though I know it's hard, I think you made the right choice. For you. It's your turn now—you lived my crazy life with me for plenty of years."

"I liked your crazy life."

"Me too. But I think it's time for both of us to settle down…for a while, anyway."

"I'm scared."

"Me too, sweetie," she admitted, squeezing my hand. "But let's try it anyway, okay?"

When I told her what I was planning to do, she didn't even seem surprised.

Chapter Twenty-Seven

When Amy came home later, I was laying on my bed, still wearing my graduation dress while I stared at the ceiling and squeezed my stress ball. My stress avocado, as my roommate called it, which is really what it looked like. It was a multi-purpose avocado, good not only for stress but for strength-building after broken wrists. I was currently trying to build up the strength to walk across the street.

"Hey," Amy said gently. The door shut behind her and she slipped off her shoes before she sat on the end of my bed. Our room was as bare as I'd ever seen it, the majority of our things packed and ready to go if not already gone, which was compounding my sadness. "You okay?"

I shook my head. "I'm just…"

"Yeah, I know." She took a deep breath. "Last night here, huh?"

"I can't believe it."

"Me either. I'm…really going to miss this place."

"Yeah," I said. It came from low in my throat, sounding husky and soft. Amy leaned into me, until my knees were propping her up, and took it upon herself to fill the emptiness in our room with her good cheer, something she'd only just found again.

"I *love* that restaurant though, don't you? Caleb had never been before. Lobster Fricassee is, like, crazy delicious. My mom says it's passé but *whatever*. It's so good. I love this dress on you. You should wear white all the time, you know, it looks awesome on you. White and black, that's all you need. And no offense or anything, but your uncle is kind of hot." She sat up and turned a little to wink at me and I giggled.

"Uncle Tommy? Yeah, I guess he probably is." Actually, I was sure he was. So, too, was Uncle Tommy. He was younger than my aunt and just as pretty, but not so tiny, and had the most perfect white teeth. "He's a science teacher, you know—physics was his specialty."

"No way! Must be a lot of girls in class hot for Mr. Espinosa. I don't think I'd be able to concentrate if he'd been my teacher, and I *love* physics."

"I know." I tugged on one of her curls. "That's just his 'fun' career though, he says. He makes his 'real' living doing some modeling for advertisements. You noticed the teeth? I call him Tio Trouble because he always finds it. I think he's a bachelor 'til the end, which makes my grandparents sad. Between him and Aunt Tessa, they'll probably only get me as a grandkid."

"Your aunt could still surprise them."

"I hope so. I'd be an awesome big sister." Of course she could always adopt—she'd adopted *me*—but Aunt Tessa was just young enough to still have her own baby, and I knew she thought about it. I wondered if, maybe now that she was committed to staying in one place, she would.

"She seemed really friendly with another attractive bachelor...He's kind of old, but Senator Astor is—"

My little twin mattress rocked like a waterbed when I swung my legs over the side and stood up. Amy basically fell into the rumpled blankets without me to hold her up. "Hey!"

"Sorry. I'm…going over to Carter's."

"Nice!" She propped her head up on her elbow. "Why didn't you just say so? I won't wait up."

"No, you can, well, you don't have to, but…I'll be back."

"Seriously? Why come back? There's no curfew tonight, Lainey baby." She smiled as she stood and stretched. I knew the only reason Amy was staying in our room was because Caleb was already gone. With his brother's help, he'd been fully moved out before the ceremony.

"It's our last night."

"Psht. I mean, I know, but you're sleeping over at my house *tomorrow*. Do something reckless tonight."

Reckless? No. What I was about to do was horribly, terribly calculated. I pushed my feet into shoes I wasn't even sure matched and headed for the door. "Just…I'll be back."

It must have been the look on my face, or the catch in my voice, that tipped her off. Her eyes grew so wide I could see myself reflected in them. She knew. Maybe not exactly what was about to happen, but *something*.

"Lane?" she called but I was almost out the door. "What are you going to do? Lainey?!"

IT WAS ALMOST curfew, but as Amy had pointed out, that was inconsequential. I'd just graduated; they couldn't kick me out. They couldn't possibly do *anything* to me worse than what I was about to do. The first bells started to ring as I stood at the back door to the bookstore, shivering while I worked up the courage to climb the stairs.

For months Carter told me, over and over, how he'd never hurt me, and he believed it. For a long time, I'd believed it too. I knew he'd never harm me on purpose and he didn't think he was capable. But neither of us knew he'd do whatever our uncle wanted.

And it never once crossed his mind that *I'd* be the one to hurt *him*.

There was a moment, many moments, when I could have changed everything. Right up until this afternoon on the graduation stage. Probably even now, I could call Daniel Astor or walk to Dr. Stewart's and tell either of them I'd changed my mind. I could agree to work for the Perceptum.

But I was a coward. A selfish coward. I recognized at the end the other option Dan was offering me: the chance for escape. The cost was high, but not as high as my life, and I wasn't sure I wouldn't have to pay it anyway. This was the choice I hadn't seen I could take, the one I wouldn't have wanted to see anyway, because of the thing I'd been blind to all along—it *wasn't* all about me. I'd been guilty of that a lot this year, failing to see beyond myself. Maybe I deserved this.

Or was it a different kind of punishment? Twice now I'd tampered with fate, changed the future. Once was selfless, but the second time? I'd begged God, the Goddess, the Universe, whoever would help me, not to let me die. And they'd listened. But were they benevolent or malevolent? Had I unwittingly traded a terrible fate for a worse one? I didn't want to believe that, but right about now, it felt like it.

Because it was late, I knocked on the kitchen door before I opened it even though I wasn't really expected to anymore. Carter leaned out of his room at the sound and he smiled the most beautiful smile at the unexpected sight of me coming down the hall. "This surprise just made my night," he said. I was supremely glad to see he was wearing wind pants and a T-shirt, which meant he was still up reading or playing a video game. I'd delayed for so long, I was afraid he might already have been in bed. We were supposed to leave early tomorrow, which meant he'd get up even earlier to run.

When I got to his doorway, he embraced me. "Hey, beautiful." The stiffness in my posture was his first clue that all was not well. "I thought you said you were exhausted and we'd just see each other tomorrow. What's up?"

Behind me, I closed the door. I took one, two small steps into the room, afraid to move any further into his space or closer to him. "I'm sorry it's so late." I cleared my throat. "But I wanted to talk to you."

"Okay…" He looked around as if a little lost and then sat down on his chair, but not comfortably. He leaned forward with his elbows on his knees and waited for me to go on. Only one lamp was lit, and over his shoulder I could see a game, hockey maybe, on pause.

"I'm leaving in the morning."

"I know," he said. "I'll be there." He laughed, like I was being silly, and for half a second, he started to relax. But when I didn't smile, or move, or laugh along, he sat up straighter. Between us, his hand hovered in the air, beckoning me to come closer, but he dropped it after a while. I wasn't close enough to touch anyway, which contributed to the tension in the room. He knew there was something wrong even if he couldn't understand what.

I doubted he'd ever understand.

"By myself," I clarified and the confusion started to set in.

"You don't want me to drive with you?"

I swallowed, hard, and then met his eye. "I don't want you to come at all." I'd planned those words, practiced them in my head, and I'd meant them to sound hard, more determined. Instead, they sounded broken and unsure. But I said them.

"What?" He was standing now, coming closer.

"I'm sorry. I…I love you, but—"

"*Lainey?* What's going on?"

After a deep breath, I said, "I can't do this with you."

It was only a few steps, and he reached me in seconds, putting his hands on my shoulders and pulling me closer. "Is *this* why you were crying? Lainey. We can do *anything* together. We've proven that."

I stepped backwards, out from under his touch, until my back hit the door. He didn't try to hold me. "I know," I said. Speaking the next words was equivalent to dragging my heart out through my throat and throwing it at my feet. I wanted to do anything, *anything*, other than say them, except for die. "But I don't want to."

He inhaled audibly and stared at me for a few seconds. Around us the air seemed to tighten, heavy and thick with a kind of anticipation, or disbelief. I was reminded of the first time we met, on the second floor of the bookstore, in the *Rarities and First Editions* section, when I told him I was a Legacy who didn't know who she was and everything changed. It was still my favorite part of the store and I went up there all the time, just to look at the books and remember. After this, I knew I wouldn't really be welcome there anymore.

"What are you saying?" he finally responded. "Are you...are you breaking up with me?"

I stomped on my heart, and his, a few more times when I told him, "Yes. That's what I'm saying."

He shook his head, making his caramel waves catch the lamplight and look something like a halo. "No. This...No, Lainey. I love you. Has...the vision hasn't come back, has it? I thought—"

"No. It's totally gone. I don't even think about it anymore."

"This isn't..." He paused, bewildered. He seemed to waver and then sat on his bed, dragging his fingers through his hair. "This is *cra-zy*," he said. Then tentatively, "Is this about what happened at the range? Did something—I swear—" He touched three fingers to his forehead, pushing hard enough to leave a red mark and I knew he knew. Something was wrong with his memory, but he couldn't remember what. "You've been different ever since."

"No! I mean, it's—" I grabbed on to his reason and let my mouth run, infusing it with some of my real fears to make it ring true. "Yes, sort of. But, it's mostly about me. I could have died, at the range, if your gun had been loaded, or you could have. I've almost died *three times* in the last year. Being with you, it's dangerous." When he started to protest, I cut him off. "N...not just physically. I'm only eighteen. This is too much pressure. You knew...you knew this summer, when you said you'd follow me, you knew I was scared. I should have told you then. I should never have agreed. I love you, but I need to be me, to—to figure out who that even *is*...I *have* to do this. By myself."

He was staring at me, and I could see it. See how he didn't *want* to believe me, but he did. I watched the tears pool in his eyes while his heart began to break, little shards of it stabbing me as they fell and mingled with the broken pieces of mine that already surrounded us.

"Maybe..." I shouldn't have said what I said next, shouldn't have given him any line of hope, but it was for me, too. "Maybe someday. We can be together again." Those five words came out in a rush, because they were dangerous. "But not right now."

His voice cracked and he dropped his head into his hands. "When?"

"I don't know. Just not right now." At the end, I whispered what I feared was true: "Maybe never."

When he looked back up at me, with an expression of pain and desperation I'd never known his features could form, it felt like actually shooting him, or myself, would have been less painful than what I was doing now. "Please. Lainey. Don't do this." The tears in his eyes spilled over and if he said my name one more time, so help me, I would split in two. "Please," he repeated. "I love you."

He held out his hand, reaching to me, pleading, and I did the only thing I could.

I ran.

If I touched him again, I'd never let go. I was wrong. I thought I wasn't willing to die to be with him, but I *was* dying. This was killing me, and Carter too. "I love you, too." My voice broke as I backed out of his bedroom. Out of his life. "But I can't. I'm sorry."

Melinda was in the kitchen, and I rushed past her without stopping. From the tears on her face I knew she'd heard enough to know this was goodbye.

"Lainey!" Carter called once more.

But I was already gone.

Chapter Twenty-Eight

In the morning, up early after a restless, dreamless night, I folded the last of my things while I cried again. On her side of the room, Amy did the same. We were crying for different reasons, though not entirely. She was sad for me, too, and for Carter, who was her friend before I was.

But though she didn't understand, she supported me, and that was all I could ask of her. If it was what I *really* wanted, she said, who was she to tell me I shouldn't be on my own? She *didn't* believe it was what I really wanted and I didn't try too hard to convince her. It didn't matter anyway, whether she believed me or not. I wanted to tell her the real reason, the whole story, but I'd spilled enough secrets to her and Caleb as it was. The danger and burden of keeping the rest would be mine alone.

When the last of our things were finally packed, and before our families came to help take it all away, Amy and I hugged for a really long time.

"I love you, Young."

"You, too."

"Even if you're crazy, and have some scary mind abilities, and I hope you won't make me forget saying that."

"Even though you're too smart for your own good, and a terrible influence, and are bound to get me in trouble someday, I wouldn't dream of it."

After approximately forever, we released each other and I felt bereft all over again. But as not-ready as I was, it was time to go. We both grabbed bags and started our final treks up and down the stairs of Marquise House. Downstairs, Ms. Kim was helping direct chaos and dry tears, so we got goodbye hugs from her, too. It didn't escape my notice the parity between the beginning of my year and the end, and how I'd gone from the one consoling the tearful young creatures to the one being consoled.

Change was scary. I understood, *really* understood, that now, for the first time. Once upon a time change had been my constant, but two years at Northbrook had changed that. Changed *me*. It was time to see how the next years would change me too.

Finally loaded up, Amy and I hugged once more before she climbed in the car with her mom and I made a final trip across the street. Amy rolled down her window before they left. "I'll see you tonight?"

"I'll be the temporarily homeless girl on your doorstep."

"I'll leave out the breadcrumbs."

I waved as she pulled away, and then gave my last hugs to my family. They'd follow me in our caravan to the city. Aunt Tessa had offered to ride with me, as had Amy, but I declined. I'd made a choice to do this alone and I was starting it now. We'd managed to load all of my things into the rental cars, so all I had to do was retrieve my car and lead the way.

But there was one more thing.

WHEN I GOT to the parking area behind Penrose Books, I saw I wasn't the only one with the same idea. Waiting for me on my driver's seat was a book. If the book itself hadn't given it away, the fact that my car had been and was still locked told me who left it.

Modern Poetry, circa the early 1900s. It was pristine and beautiful, looking barely more worn than the first time I'd picked it up—the day I met Cater Penrose. I'd wondered what happened to it; by the time I went back for it, it was already gone. I guess I knew now where it went.

I looked up to the window on the third floor but all I could see was the reflection of the trees behind me. I'd probably never know if he was watching, though I thought probably not. I didn't deserve to hope he would and I didn't raise my hand in goodbye though I desperately wanted to. Instead, I opened his car door, which was never locked, and left the note I'd thought about all night and written in the few moments alone while my roommate was in the shower.

I'd composed a million different versions in my head, crossed it all out and tried to get it right again and again. Finally I decided on a few simple words. He told me himself if I wrote it down he'd never forget. There were so many things I wanted to tell him, but what I wanted him to remember was this:

I will love you always.
—L.

I LOVED CARTER. Sometimes painfully, but in the end, not enough. I didn't love him enough to tell him the truth, to ruin or save his life with it, I didn't know which. I didn't, ultimately, love him more than I loved myself.

Could I live without him? I was going to find out. I got in my car and drove into my future, alone.

No, not alone, I reminded myself.

Free.

Acknowledgments

THANK YOU:

To Tracy, Chris, and the entire Luminis team, for once again making this possible, and also, for making it fun.

To Geri, Susie, Cindy, Rebecca, and Kristine, for their indispensable help in making this story something you actually want to read.

To my agent, April Eberhardt, for the constant support.

To Brit Godish, for the kick-ass cover.

To my daughter, though she can't yet read this, for being so frequently patient even when I'm not.

To my family and friends, whose love and enthusiasm sustain me.

To my husband, for everything, always.

And, of course, to *you*.

About the Author

Cara Bertrand is a former middle school literacy teacher who now lives in the woods outside Boston with: one awesome husband, two large dogs, one small daughter, and lots of words. She is the author of SECOND THOUGHTS and LOST IN THOUGHT, the first novel in the Sententia and one of three finalists for the Amazon/Penguin Breakthrough Novel Award in the Young Adult category.

Visit her online at www.carabertrand.com or on Twitter @carabertrand